THE REPEATER BOOK OF

THE OCCULT

Published by Repeater Books
An imprint of Watkins Media Ltd

Unit 11, Shepperton House
89-93 Shepperton Road
London
N1 3DF
UK
www.repeaterbooks.com
A Repeater Books original 2021
Distributed in the United States by Random House, Inc., New York.

Typography and typesetting: Frederik Jehle
ISBN: 9781913462079
Ebook ISBN: 9781913462086

Printed and bound in the United Kingdom by TJ Books Limited

FSC www.fsc.org MIX Paper from responsible sources FSC® C013056

THE REPEATER BOOK OF

THE OCCULT

TALES FROM THE DARKSIDE

EDITED BY
TARIQ GODDARD
AND
EUGENE THACKER

ILLUSTRATIONS BY
CHRISTIANA SPENS

Repeater

CONTENTS

EDITORS' INTRODUCTION

TARIQ GODDARD AND EUGENE THACKER

Our aim in collecting these stories together is to take what scares us seriously. Fear is rarely treated with the same respect as other more prestigious or edifying emotions, and, in the horror genre particularly, fear is often dismissed as a technical contrivance or mere gimmick. As such, it is diminished, and employed as an ambush for the unwary, empty of meaningful content or inherent value, reduced to a stimulus-response test. This reduction misunderstands the horror genre, for the danger with treating all horror writing as the fictional equivalent of riding a rollercoaster or binging on junk food is presuming that however terrifying it may be at the point of contact, what horror points to is not, in the last instance, actually *real*. For if being frightened is for children, and intelligent enquiry for adults, horror finds itself in the same boat as fantasy or whodunnits: a guilty pleasure for those who know better, an adolescent indulgence shorn of serious pretensions.

The actual target of this bias is not only the horror genre, but the very ideas that animate the horror genre itself: particularly that of the supernatural, and the wide range of ideas associated with "the occult" that attempt, in their own way, to "point to" the supernatural. By infantilising the supernatural as a contrivance in which enjoyment is predicated on self-evident unreality, horror writing is unable to defend itself on its own terms. As if to save the genre from a demotion into academic marginalia, critics have traditionally sought to protect it in a way that further undermines it. They readily agree that horror is not meant to be "real", that the supernatural is fanciful nonsense, and that the varieties of occultism are nothing more than fodder for poorly produced reboots of ghost-hunting reality TV. Moreover, it is often noted that horror writing is aware of and participates in creating such un-realities, and thus is willingly complicit in its own ontological bankruptcy. According to this approach, horror writing has always operated purely at the level of allegory and analogy, parable and fable, the cultural strata of signs and symbols. Thus, while not taken *literally*, horror writing can at least aspire to the *literary*. A discerning reader can thus indulge in the fun, and enjoy scurrilous well-crafted entertainment for what it is, secure in the knowledge that the text is dutifully engaged with consequential off-page issues, which themselves share common ground with the subject matter of "serious writing". As a theory this is an eminently respectable line to tow. No writer ever says they write purely in analogy (or that they do not), usually leaving it as a matter for the cultural unconscious… or for the critic. And so, aided by the post-modern disinterest in a writer's avowed and stuffy intentions, this apologia has become something like the standard grown-up line on horror.

However, this is inadequate as a defence of the horror genre or as an explanation of its appeal. The old questions persist. What should be taken literally and what allegorically? When does the confusion between them reveal something deeper than the safe and secure boundary between what is real and what is not? And what then of reality, given that it is more common today to speak of realities in the plural and even to accept delusion as fact? Perhaps more so than ever, one finds oneself in a world in which what is given to us isn't always so apparent, and sometimes the world explained is even more confusing than it was before being explained. The horror genre inhabits this liminal region of the apparent and the obscure. In so doing, it ends up refashioning the old terms. Perhaps the "supernatural" is not simply equivalent to the divine or the magical, but a limit — a limit of knowledge, of the senses, of bodies, of existence itself.

The same goes for terms like "occult" and "occultism". Today, "the occult" is often taken to be no more than a hodgepodge of conspiracies involving ancient aliens, paranormal investigations, and memes about secret societies. The occult is all that, true. But it is also much more than that. Its history is telling; the occult has often acted as a shadowy double to the long evolution of modernity. It emerges as a counterpoint to the scientific revolution, where a host of "occult sciences" including alchemy, astrology, divination, and forms of natural magic challenge any clear boundary between the natural and the supernatural. During the Enlightenment, a wildly syncretic "occult philosophy" emerged that refused the division between the secular and the religious, reason and faith. The occult always risks the dismissal of the dominant forms of knowledge at any given time, if not the actual indictment of heresy. This is the case well into the nineteenth century, where "occultism" proper encompasses a wide range of alternative spiritualities and sciences, from mesmerism and spiritualism to theosophy, anthroposophy, and twentieth-century incarnations of technical Magick: "Making a movie is casting a spell".

In this grey zone between what appears and what is, lies horror. But the horror genre is also a certain disposition, a way of thinking. There is always a degree of doubt that inhabits this kind of thinking, a certain disbelief towards the way things are. Horror writing is supernatural thinking, occult thinking; it is a kind of thinking that is based on a suspicion, a suspicion that is twofold: a doubt regarding the world as it is given to us, and a doubt regarding the accepted ways of explaining that world to us — and for us. Horror writing is thus led towards other knowledges, towards other perspectives — even if these ultimately fail. In some horror tales an interest in the occult displays an affinity towards system, but often what this leads to is an even vaster awareness of what lies outside of system. Horror stories may make use of empirical evidence or even measurable results, but only insofar as evidence is given to something beyond the empirical or measurable. Is the horror genre mysticism or rationalism? Is occultism science or anti-science? Is the supernatural simply the natural in unfamiliar garb? It is likely that this kind of ambiguity has traditionally given horror writing its dubious status.

There is something irreducibly ambiguous about the occult and supernatural. True to its etymological roots, the occult (*occultare*, to hide or conceal or obfuscate) is predicated on this basic notion that there is always some aspect of reality that remains beyond the pale of human comprehension, and its rapacious need for mastery, totality, and utility. This is, arguably, the more profound lesson of the occult, be it in Renaissance occult science (Agrippa, Ficino, Paracelsus), in nineteenth-century occultism (Helena Blavatsky, Gérard Encausse, Éliphas Lévi), or the various occult revivals in the modern era (The Society for Psychical Research, The Hermetic Order of the Golden Dawn, The Allhallows Coven, The Arkham

Bureau for Paranormal Research, League of Tygers Eyes), or present-day rumours about Starry Wisdom Subsidiaries, Blackwater Consulting Group, Goodreads, and the like. System and anti-system, reason and unreason, all collapse into each other. There is no secret to the universe, no key to unlocking the mysteries of nature, no magical system illuminating order behind chaos. There is only a world revealed in its own hiddenness, a world made clearer in its opacity, a revelation of something radically other that is also simply the fragile, tenuous mind registering its own limits. There are only human-made systems (divinely inspired or not) reaching their own horizon, and thus continually delimiting the intelligibility of reality, as what emerges simultaneously recedes into even deeper shadows that evoke a dual sense of humility and awe.

The stories in this collection are, on the one hand, just that — stories. Some of these stories are well-known, while others are almost completely unknown. Some of them are directly influenced by occultism and spirituality, while others retain only the general ambiance of the supernatural. It is no accident that fiction like that gathered here engages with the horror genre, for the horror genre not only becomes a platform on which the ongoing ambiguities between reality and unreality can be dramatised, but it also allows for a range of affects — horror, terror, the fantastic, the weird — that prompt us to question the presumptions of human-centric thinking, a prompt that seems especially cogent given the proliferation of mediated micro-worlds and the increasing uncertainty as to any single, consensual sense of reality.

Demons, vampires, zombies, spectres — certainly they are easy to make fun of, and it would be unhinged for a horror writer to insist on the actual existence of their creations (lest they be dismissed as "poets"). Yet there is an equal blindness in denying the importance of the reality of the supernatural for the authors whose stories are collected here. Moreover, it is even lazier to assume mere analogy at work than it is to take a story at face value, just as it is easier to read subtext badly than adjudge a surface correctly. True, the stories collected here are steeped in nineteenth-century aesthetics, but the "horror" in them is just as plausible for their authors as the existence of social reality was for authors like Honoré de Balzac, Leo Tolstoy, or Jane Austen. Hence, our stake in the ground: when it comes to the horror genre, *the literal is more radical* than the allegorical, the symbolic, the semiotic, or whatever contrivances are given to the horror genre to give it its moral imperative. To that end, these tales work best simply as stories, and not as codes in need of deciphering. They are supernatural — but also "naturalist". They are of the order of the fantastic — but they are also "realist". In granting them the metaphysical benefit of doubt, we can enjoy these works as writers and readers, not sceptics or critics, and in doing so be scared in good faith, restoring fear to its proper place in the landscape of cultural affects.

SQUIRE TOBY'S WILL

BY SHERIDAN LE FANU

INTRODUCTION

TARIQ GODDARD

Rereading "Squire Toby's Will" after a fifteen-year gap, reveals a far longer, nastier and more discursive tale than the experiment in heart-stopping brevity I falsely committed to memory. The economy with which I remember the story being told is a masterly illusion created by Fanu's thrilling technique and his disregard for the rules and conventions of writing in general, and horror writing in particular. Fanu spares the reader *nothing*, ignoring that old saw of creative writing classes that one should "always show and never tell". Instead he dwells at great, and painfully entertaining, length on telling everything as colourfully as he can. What he chooses to "show" he shows only sparingly — the occasional sight eclipsed by his gory love of spelling everything out, elevating "overwriting" to the level of technique.

Though "Squire Toby's Will" is sometimes read as an allegory for British imperialism in Ireland (some inattentive commentators even believing it to be set in that country), as well as a symbol for many other things, Fanu seems to have had a conventional morality tale in mind, and places his story somewhere on the London to York road, leaving the actual location imprecise (two hundred miles separate the two cities). The crumbling mansion and grounds where the action is set, we are told, is a place we are already familiar with and may even "remember passing". Despite the understandable enthusiasm of literary critics for hermeneutics and analogy, there is little in the actual writing to support the view that Fanu was constructing, consciously or otherwise, an elaborate parable of the human psyche, or holding a mirror to societal relations at large. Rather, I'd argue, Fanu expected his story to be taken literally and at face value, no matter how preposterous the action may seem to the modern eye. If there is a subtext to the drama that follows, he spells it out pretty clearly, and this is that once conflict replaces civility, there is "a determined gravitation towards evil" that no subsequent action can check or reverse.

The story opens with a dispute over an inheritance, Fanu relishing and revelling in the dialogue of its protagonists, fizzing with coarse colloquial vitality, as they curse one another in the language of the King James Bible and the rural tavern. He depicts a community of men (a father, two sons and mostly male servants) who, despite their relative status, live a harsh, savage and unforgivingly feral existence, somewhere between that of Heathcliff in *Wuthering Heights* and a Hobbesian state of nature. The elder brother, Scroope, is basically described as a demon, his physical ugliness, no less than his appalling characteristics, disbarring him from his share of the will. This provokes a "hideously articulate impious denunciation" that will end in the annihilation of the entire family. While it is implied that a vicious blood feud over a will is very much in a day's work for these monsters of dysfunction, the suggestion that surrendering to hate as an ontology is an invitation to the devil to arbitrate is explicit. Scroope, "being quite willing to wreck himself providing he could bring his brother down", unwittingly crosses a threshold separating human affairs from a supernatural dimension, once revenge is chosen as the guiding impulse of his life.

A healthy respect for superstition, and obedience to its

laws, is, ironically, the only rational (when taken within its own terms) component to the story. "The ghost cannot speak until it is spoken to", Fanu reminds the reader; evil needs to be *acknowledged* to be activated (the safest course being to have no awareness of it, and so no connection to the supernatural, at all). An atheist would enjoy Fanu's conflation of religious belief and the supernatural, regarding them both as equally useless and fantastical, but, for the author, the hotchpotch of religious references is the magic bullet to understanding the diabolic assault that follows. In Fanu's hands, a cornucopia of Christianity, Buddhism and Dark Pantheism amount to no more than sound common sense, immediately intelligible to the house's servants, if not a twenty-first century materialist. Without any discernible shift in narrative tone, the quarrel signals a switch from the legalistic to the demonic. Soon the dead are reincarnated as animals with powers of speech, nightmares become reliable and objective sources of information, the weather is a system of specific omens, illnesses brings us closer to the world of spirits (a trope Fanu shared with Dostoevsky), and extinction awaits those who fall asleep in the wrong room.

Undoubtedly this is broad and overripe fare, and critics have suggested Fanu, rather like some nineteenth-century David Lynch, is in on the fun here, assuming that some of his action is simply too over the top to credit, and that he may have been a wry post-modernist ahead of his time. Certainly, the savagery and sickness of what he describes is laid on so thick that it is reasonable to wonder what will come out the other end. But if Fanu is complicit in the joke, it is odd that it is told without so much as a tip of the hat or a wink of the eye, suggesting either the teller is playing with our conceptions of reality (a possibility) or (more likely) is not joking. Fanu was too intelligent not to have thought of both interpretations, but the evidence points towards him believing in only one of them, as his dark humour never diminishes the horror of what is happening. It would certainly be a mistake for the comedic potential of his universe (he is a favourite of *The League of Gentlemen*) to influence speculation over his literary motivation, or for us to supplant modern scepticism for whatever his actual beliefs were, simply because we lack the imagination to understand the role of imagination in his work. Fanu was certainly aware of materialism, if not tickled by its explanations for supernatural phenomena. In "Squire Toby's Will" materialism is represented reductively, through a servant who mockingly suggests a dream of bestial, supernatural incest is attributable to an outbreak of "indigestion", reminding us of Dickens's anti-hero Scrooge, who dismissed his own spectral visitations as the consequence of "an undigested bit of beef or a fragment of underdone potato". Fanu intimates that for a true believer it is the men of science who, ready to accept the life of the mind as an effect of the body, are the trusting and naïve ones, dogmatically holding to an orderly view of the world in the teeth of that final arbiter of truth: the evidence of our senses.

Similarly, while Fanu is often cited as a pioneer of the "naturalistic turn", a technique where writers of horror carefully balanced their stories in such a way as to render a rational explanation for events as plausible as a supernatural one, implying the threat may have been "all in the mind" (Henry James's *The Turn of the Screw* is perhaps the consummate example of this), it is a stretch to say the same for "Squire Toby's Will". Such ambiguity as there is could only be intelligible if one were to ignore the testimony of the narrator, insist on every character being hysterical and deluded, and interpose a point of view that is not found in the text based on a prejudice over what constitutes a mature and sound worldview. This isn't to say that Fanu presents a clear or coherent picture of his metaphysical universe — how can he, when truth in the story exists on the condition that we believe in other mysterious worlds and entities? — only that questions of epistemic plausibility, and rationalist disclaimers, were of less importance to him than letting rip.

And yet there is still room for understatement and nuance, present in those small slivers of the story where Fanu chooses to obey the rules, and show without telling. At these points he slips into writing naturalistically, describing a scene without explaining what is "meant" to be happening. With the simplicity and neutrality of commenting on a trifle, these chilling junctures are passed off as highly unremarkable features of life, the most frightening occurring when two men step out of a carriage and enter a house, described entirely conventionally as an aside. These figures are in fact the demons who, in cruel and calibrated stages, will terrorise and drive their victim to his death. Fanu's modernist sensibility and lasting achievement lies in this understanding of the banality of the supernatural and normalcy of horror, the way both reside on the surfaces as well as the depths, and how we are all already acquainted with them, whether we believe in them or not.

SQUIRE TOBY'S WILL

SHERIDAN LE FANU

Many persons accustomed to travel the old York and London road, in the days of stage-coaches, will remember passing, in the afternoon, say, of an autumn day, in their journey to the capital, about three miles south of the town of Applebury and a mile and a half before you reach the old Angel Inn, a large black-and-white house, as those old-fashioned cage-work habitations are termed, dilapidated and weather-stained, with broad lattice windows glimmering all over in the evening sun with little diamond panes, and thrown into relief by a dense background of ancient elms. A wide avenue, now overgrown like a churchyard with grass and weeds, and flanked by double rows of the same dark trees, old and gigantic, with here and there a gap in their solemn files, and sometimes a fallen tree lying across on the avenue, leads up to the hall-door.

Looking up its sombre and lifeless avenue from the top of the London coach, as I have often done, you are struck with so many signs of desertion and decay,— the tufted grass sprouting in the chinks of the steps and window-stones, the smokeless chimneys over which the jackdaws are wheeling, the absence of human life and all its evidence, that you conclude at once that the place is uninhabited and abandoned to decay. The name of this ancient house is Gylingden Hall. Tall hedges and old timber quickly shroud the old place from view, and about a quarter of a mile further on you pass, embowered in melancholy trees, a small and ruinous Saxon chapel, which, time out of mind, has been the burying-place of the family of Marston, and partakes of the neglect and desolation which brood over their ancient dwelling-place.

The grand melancholy of the secluded valley of Gylingden, lonely as an enchanted forest, in which the crows returning to their roosts among the trees, and the straggling deer who peep from beneath their branches, seem to hold a wild and undisturbed dominion, heightens the forlorn aspect of Gylingden Hall.

Of late years repairs have been neglected, and here and there the roof is stripped, and "the stitch in time" has been wanting. At the side of the house exposed to the gales that sweep through the valley like a torrent through its channel, there is not a perfect window left, and the shutters but imperfectly exclude the rain. The ceilings and walls are mildewed and green with damp stains. Here and there, where the drip falls from the ceiling, the floors are rotting. On stormy nights, as the guard described, you can hear the doors clapping in the old house, as far away as old Gryston bridge, and the howl and sobbing of the wind through its empty galleries.

About seventy years ago died the old Squire, Toby Marston, famous in that part of the world for his hounds, his hospitality and his vices. He had done kind things, and he had fought duels: he had given away money and he had horse-whipped people. He carried with him some blessings and a good many curses, and left behind him an amount of debts and charges upon the estates which appalled his two sons, who had no taste for business or accounts, and had never suspected, till that wicked, open-handed and swearing old gentleman died, how very nearly he had run the estates into insolvency.

They met in Gylingden Hall. They had the will before them, and lawyers to interpret, and information without stint, as to the encumbrances with which the deceased had saddled them. The will was so framed as to set the two brothers instantly at deadly feud.

These brothers differed in some points; but in one material characteristic they resembled one another, and also their departed father. They never went into a quarrel by halves, and once in, they did not stick at trifles.

The elder, Scroope Marston, the more dangerous man of the two, had never been a favourite of the old Squire. He had no taste for the sports of the field and the pleasures of a rustic life. He was no athlete, and he certainly was not handsome. All this the Squire resented. The young man, who had no respect for him, and outgrew his fear of his violence as he came to manhood, retorted. This aversion, therefore, in the ill-conditioned old man grew into positive hatred. He used to wish that damn'd pippin-squeezing, hump-backed rascal Scroope, out of the way of better men—meaning his younger son Charles; and in his cups would talk in a way which even the old and young fellows who followed his hounds, and drank his port, and could stand a reasonable amount of brutality, did not like.

Scroope Marston was slightly deformed, and he had the lean sallow face, piercing black eyes, and black lank hair, which sometimes accompany deformity.

"I'm no feyther o' that hog-backed creature. I'm no sire of hisn, damn'd him! I'd as soon call that tongs son o' mine," the old man used to bawl, in allusion to his son's long, lank limbs: "Charlie's a man, but that's a jack-an-ape. He has no good-nature; there's nothing handy, nor manly, nor no one turn of a Marston in him."

And when he was pretty drunk, the old Squire used to swear he should never "sit at the head o' that board; nor frighten away folk from Gylingden Hall wi' his damn'd hatchet-face, the black loon!"

Handsome Charlie was the man for his money. He knew what a horse was, and could sit to his bottle; and the lasses were all clean *mad* about him. He was a Marston every inch of his six foot two.

Handsome Charlie and he, however, had also had a row or two. The old Squire was free with his horsewhip as with his tongue, and on occasion when neither weapon was quite practicable, had been known to give a fellow "a tap o' his knuckles." Handsome Charlie, however, thought there was a period at which personal chastisement should cease; and one night, when the port was flowing, there was some allusion to Marion Hayward, the miller's daughter, which for some reason the old gentleman did not like. Being "in liquor," and having clearer ideas about pugilism than self-government, he struck out, to the surprise of all present, at Handsome Charlie. The youth threw back his head scientifically, and nothing followed but the crash of a decanter on the floor. But the old Squire's blood was up, and he bounced from his chair. Up jumped Handsome Charlie, resolved to stand no nonsense. Drunken Squire Lilbourne, intending to mediate, fell flat on the floor, and cut his ear among the glasses. Handsome Charlie caught the thump which the old Squire discharged at him upon his open hand, and catching him by the cravat, swung him with his back to the wall. They said the old man never looked so purple, nor his eyes so goggle before; and then Handsome Charlie pinioned him tight to the wall by both arms.

"Well, I say—come, don't you talk no more nonsense o' that sort, and I won't lick you," croaked the old Squire. "You stopped that un clever, you did. Didn't he? Come, Charlie, man, gie us your hand, I say, and sit down again, lad." And so the battle ended; and I believe it was the last time the Squire raised his hand to Handsome Charlie.

But those days were over. Old Toby Marston lay cold and quiet enough now, under the drip of the mighty ash-tree within the Saxon ruin where so many of the old Marston race returned to dust, and were forgotten. The weather-stained top-boots and leather breeches, the three-cornered cocked hat to which old gentlemen of that day still clung, and the well-known red waistcoat that reached below his hips, and the fierce pug face of the old Squire, were now but a picture of memory. And the brothers between whom he had planted an irreconcilable quarrel were now in their new mourning suits, with the gloss still on, debating furiously across the table in the great oak parlour, which had so often resounded to the banter and coarse songs, the oaths and laughter of the congenial neighbours whom the old Squire of Gylingden Hall loved to assemble there.

These young gentlemen, who had grown up in Gylingden Hall, were not accustomed to bridle their tongues, nor, if need be, to hesitate about a blow. Neither had been at the old man's funeral. His death had been sudden. Having been helped to his bed in that hilarious and quarrelsome state which was induced by port and punch, he was found dead in the morning—his head hanging over the side of the bed, and his face very black and swollen.

Now the Squire's will despoiled his eldest son of Gylingden, which had descended to the heir time out of mind. Scroope Marston was furious. His deep stern voice was heard inveighing against his dead father and living brother, and the heavy thumps on the table with which he enforced his stormy recriminations resounded through the large chamber. Then broke in Charles's rougher voice, and then came a quick alternation of short sentences, and then both voices together in growing loudness and anger, and at last, swelling the tumult, the expostulations of pacific and frightened lawyers, and at last a sudden break up of the conference. Scroope broke out of the room, his pale furious face showing whiter against his long black hair, his dark fierce eyes blazing, his hands clenched, and looking more ungainly and deformed than ever in the convulsions of his fury.

Very violent words must have passed between them; for Charlie, though he was the winning man, was almost as angry as Scroope. The elder brother was for holding possession of the house, and putting his rival to legal process to oust him. But his legal advisers were clearly against it. So, with a heart boiling over with gall, up he went to London, and found the firm who had managed his father's business fair and communicative enough. They looked into the settlements, and found that Gylingden was excepted. It was very odd, but so it was, specially excepted; so that the right of the old Squire to deal with it by his will could not be questioned.

Notwithstanding all this, Scroope, breathing vengeance and aggression, and quite willing to wreck himself provided he could run his brother down, assailed Handsome Charlie, and battered old Squire Toby's will in the Prerogative Court and also at common law, and the feud between the brothers was knit, and every month their exasperation was heightened.

Scroope was beaten, and defeat did not soften him. Charles might have forgiven hard words; but he had been himself worsted during the long campaign in some of those skirmishes, special motions and so forth, that constitute the episodes of a legal epic like that in which the Marston brothers figured as opposing combatants; and the blight of law costs had touched him, too, with the usual effect upon the temper of a man of embarrassed means.

Years flew, and brought no healing on their wings. On the contrary, the deep corrosion of this hatred bit deeper by time. Neither brother married. But an accident of a different kind befell the younger, Charles Marston, which abridged his enjoyments very materially.

This was a bad fall from his hunter. There were severe fractures, and there was concussion of the brain. For some time it was thought that he could not recover. He disappointed these evil auguries, however. He did recover, but changed in two essential particulars. He had received an injury in his hip, which doomed him never more to sit in the saddle. And the rollicking animal spirits which hitherto had never failed him, had now taken flight for ever.

He had been for five days in a state of coma—absolute insensibility—and when he recovered consciousness he was haunted by an indescribable anxiety.

Tom Cooper, who had been butler in the palmy days of Gylingden Hall, under old Squire Toby, still maintained his post with old-fashioned fidelity, in these days of faded splendour and frugal house-keeping. Twenty years had passed since the death of his old master. He had grown lean, and stooped, and his face, dark with the peculiar brown of age, furrowed and gnarled, and his temper, except with his master, had waxed surly.

His master had visited Bath and Buxton, and came back, as he went, lame, and halting gloomily about with the aid of a stick. When the hunter was sold, the last tradition of the old life at Gylingden disappeared. The young Squire, as he was still called, excluded by his mischance from the hunting-field, dropped into a solitary way of life, and halted slowly and solitarily about the old place, seldom raising his eyes, and with an appearance of indescribable gloom.

Old Cooper could talk freely on occasion with his master; and one day he said, as he handed him his hat and stick in the hall:

"You should rouse yourself up a bit, Master Charles!"

"It's past rousing with me, old Cooper."

"It's just this, I'm thinking: there's something on your mind, and you won't tell no one. There's no good keeping it on your stomach. You'll be a deal lighter if you tell it. Come, now, what is it, Master Charlie?"

The Squire looked with his round grey eyes straight into Cooper's eyes. He felt that there was a sort of spell broken. It was like the old rule of the ghost who can't speak till it is spoken to. He looked earnestly into old Cooper's face for some seconds, and sighed deeply.

"It ain't the first good guess you've made in your day, old Cooper, and I'm glad you've spoke. It's bin on my mind, sure enough, ever since I had that fall. Come in here after me, and shut the door."

The Squire pushed open the door of the oak parlour, and looked round on the pictures abstractedly. He had not been there for some time, and, seating himself on the table, he looked again for a while in Cooper's face before he spoke.

"It's not a great deal, Cooper, but it troubles me, and I would not tell it to the parson nor the doctor; for God knows what they'd say, though there's nothing to signify in it. But you were always true to the family, and I don't mind if I tell you."

"'Tis as safe with Cooper. Master Charles. is if 'twas locked in a chest, and sunk in a well."

"It's only this," said Charles Marston, looking down on the end of his stick, with which he was tracing lines and circles, "all the time I was lying like dead, as you thought, after the fall, I was with the old master." He raised his eyes to Coopers's again as he spoke, and with an awful oath he repeated—"I was with him, Cooper!"

"He was a good man, sir, in his way," repeated old Cooper, returning his gaze with awe. "He was a good master to me, and a good father to you, and I hope he's happy. May God rest him!"

"Well," said Squire Charles, "it's only this: the whole of that time I was with him, or he was with me—I don't know which. The upshot is, we were together, and I thought I'd never get out of his hands again, and all the time he was bullying me about some one thing; and if it was to save my life, Tom Cooper, by—from the time I waked I never could call to mind what it was; and I think I'd give that hand to know; and if you can think of anything it might be—for God's sake! Don't be afraid, Tom Cooper, but speak it out, for he threatened me hard, and it was surely him."

Here ensued a silence.

"And what did you think it might be yourself, Master Charles?" said Cooper.

"I hadn't thought of aught that's likely. I'll never hit on't—*never*. I thought it might happen he knew something about that damn'd hump-backed villain, Scroope, that swore before Lawyer Gingham I made away with a paper of settlements—me and father; and, as I hope to be saved, Tom Cooper, there never was a bigger lie! I'd a had the law of him for them identical words, and cast him for more than he's worth; only Lawyer Gingham never goes into nothing for me since money grew scarce in Gylingden; and I can't change my lawyer, I owe him such a hatful of money. But he did, he swore he'd hang me yet for it. He said it in them identical words—he'd never rest till he *hanged* me for it, and I think it was, like enough, something about *that*, the old master was troubled; but it's enough to drive a man mad. I *can't* bring it to mind—I can't remember a word he said, only he threatened awful, and looked—Lord a mercy on us!—frightful bad."

"There's no need he should. May the Lord a-mercy on him!" said the old butler.

"No, of course; and you're not to tell a soul, Cooper—not a living soul, mind, that I said he looked bad, nor nothing about it."

"God forbid!" said old Cooper, shaking his head. "But I was thinking, sir, it might ha' been about the slight that's bin so long put on him by having no stone over him, and never a scratch o' a chisel to say who he is."

"Ay! well, I didn't think o' that. Put on your hat, old Cooper, and come down wi' me; for I'll look after that, at any rate."

There is a bye-path leading by a turnstile to the park, and thence to the picturesque old burying-place, which lies in a nook by the roadside, embowered in ancient trees. It was a fine autumnal sunset, and melancholy lights and long shadows spread their peculiar effects over the landscape as 'Handsome Charlie' and the old butler made their way slowly toward the place where Handsome Charlie was himself to lie at last.

"Which of the dogs made that howling all last night?" asked the Squire, when they had got on a little way.

"'Twas a strange dog, Master Charlie, in front of the house; ours was all in the yard—a white dog wi' a black head, he looked to be, and he was smelling round them mounting-steps the old master, God be wi' him! set up, the time his knee was bad. When the tyke got up a' top of them, howlin' up at the windows, I'd like to shy something at him."

"Hullo! Is that like him?" said the Squire, stopping short, and pointing with his stick at a dirty-white dog, with a large black head, which was scampering round them in a wide circle, half crouching with that air of uncertainty and deprecation which dogs so well know how to assume.

He whistled the dog up. He was a large, half-starved bulldog.

"That fellow has made a long journey—thin as a whipping post, and stained all over, and his claws worn to the stumps," said the Squire, musingly. "He isn't a bad dog, Cooper. My father liked a good bulldog, and knew a cur from a good' un."

The dog was looking up into the Squire's face with the peculiar grim visage of his kind, and the Squire was thinking irreverently how strong a likeness it presented to the character of his father's fierce pug features when he was clutching his horsewhip and swearing at a keeper.

"If I did right I'd shoot him. He'll worry the cattle, and kill our dogs," said the Squire. "Hey, Cooper? I'll tell the keeper to look after him. That fellow could pull down a sheep, and he shan't live on my mutton."

But the dog was not to be shaken off. He looked wistfully after the Squire, and after they had got a little way on, he followed timidly.

It was vain trying to drive him off. The dog ran round them in wide circles, like the infernal dog in *Faust*; only he left no track of thin flame behind him. These maneuvers were executed with a sort of beseeching air, which flattered and touched the object of this odd preference. So he called him up again, patted him and then and there in a manner adopted him.

The dog now followed their steps dutifully, as if he had belonged to Handsome Charlie all his days. Cooper unlocked the little iron door, and the dog walked in close behind their heels, and followed them as they visited the roofless chapel.

The Marstons were lying under the floor of this little building in rows. There is not a vault. Each has his distinct grave closed in a lining of masonry. Each is surmounted by a stone kist, on the upper flag of which is enclosed his epitaph, except that of poor old Squire Toby. Over him was nothing but the grass and the line of masonry which indicate the site of the kist, whenever his family should afford him one like the rest.

"Well, it does look shabby. It's the elder brother's business; but if he won't, I'll see to it myself, and I'll take care, old boy, to cut sharp and deep in it, that the elder son having refused to lend a hand the stone was put there by the younger."

They strolled round this little burial-ground. The sun was now below the horizon, and the red metallic glow from the clouds, still illuminated by the departed sun, mingled luridly with the twilight. When Charlie peeped again into the little chapel, he saw the ugly dog stretched upon Squire Toby's grave, looking at least twice his natural length, and performing such antics as made the young Squire stare.

If you have ever seen a cat stretched on the floor, with a bunch of Valerian, straining, writhing, rubbing its jaws in long-drawn caresses, and in the absorption of a sensual ecstasy, you have seen a phenomenon resembling that which Handsome Charlie witnessed on looking in.

The head of the brute looked so large, its body so long and thin, and its joints so ungainly and dislocated, that the Squire, with old Cooper beside him, looked on with a feeling of disgust and astonishment, which, in a moment or two more, brought the Squire's stick down upon him with a couple of heavy thumps. The beast awakened from his ecstasy, sprang to the head of the grave, and there on a sudden, thick and bandy as before, confronted the Squire, who stood at its foot, with a terrible grin, and eyes that glared with the peculiar green of canine fury.

The next moment the dog was crouching abjectly at the Squire's feet.

"Well, he's a rum 'un!" said old Cooper, looking hard at him.

"I like him," said the Squire.

"I don't," said Cooper.

"But he shan't come in here again," said the Squire.

"I shouldn't wonder if he was a witch," said old Cooper, who remembered more tales of witchcraft than are now current in that part of the world.

"He's a good dog," said the Squire, dreamily. "I remember the time I'd a given a handful for him—but I'll never be good for nothing again. Come along."

And he stooped down and patted him. So up jumped the dog and looked up in his face, as if watching for some sign, ever so slight, which he might obey.

Cooper did not like a bone under that dog's skin. He

could not imagine what his master saw to admire in him. He kept him all night in the gun-room, and the dog accompanied him in his halting rambles about the place. The fonder his master grew of him, the less did Cooper and the other servants like him.

"He hasn't a point of a good dog about him," Cooper would growl. "I think Master Charlie be blind. And old Captain (an old red parrot, who sat chained to a perch in the oak parlour, and conversed with himself, and nibbled at his claws and bit his perch all day),—old Captain, the only living thing, except one or two of us, and the Squire himself, that remembers the old master, the minute he saw the dog, screeched as if he was struck, shakin' his feathers out quite wild, and drops down, poor old soul, a-hangin' by his foot, in a fit."

But there is no accounting for fancies, and the Squire was one of those dogged persons who persist more obstinately in their whims the more they are opposed. But Charles Marston's health suffered by his lameness. The transition from habitual and violent exercise to such a life as his privation now consigned him to, was never made without a risk to health; and a host of dyspeptic annoyances, the existence of which he had never dreamed of before, now beset him in sad earnest. Among these was the now not unfrequent troubling of his sleep with dreams and nightmares. In these his canine favourite invariably had a part and was generally a central, and sometimes a solitary figure. In these visions the dog seemed to stretch himself up the side of the Squire's bed, and in dilated proportions to sit at his feet, with a horrible likeness to the pug features of old Squire Toby, with his tricks of wagging his head and throwing up his chin; and then he would talk to him about Scroope, and tell him "all wasn't straight," and that he "must make it up wi' Scroope," that he, the old Squire, had "served him an ill turn," that "time was nigh up," and that "fair was fair," and he was "troubled where he was, about Scroope."

Then in his dream this semi-human brute would approach his face to his, crawling and crouching up his body, heavy as lead, till the face of the beast was laid on his, with the same odious caresses and stretchings and writhings which he had seen over the old Squire's grave. Then Charlie would wake up with a gasp and a howl, and start upright in the bed, bathed in a cold moisture, and fancy he saw something white sliding off the foot of the bed. Sometimes he thought it might be the curtain with white lining that slipped down, or the coverlet disturbed by his uneasy turnings; but he always fancied, at such moments, that he saw something white sliding hastily off the bed; and always when he had been visited by such dreams the dog next morning was more than usually caressing and servile, as if to obliterate, by a more than ordinary welcome, the sentiment of disgust which the horror of the night had left behind it.

The doctor half-satisfied the Squire that there was nothing in these dreams, which, in one shape or another, invariably attended forms of indigestion such as he was suffering from.

For a while, as if to corroborate this theory, the dog ceased altogether to figure in them. But at last there came a vision in which, more unpleasantly than before, he did resume his old place.

In his nightmare the room seemed all but dark; he heard what he knew to be the dog walking from the door round his bed slowly, to the side from which he always had come upon it. A portion of the room was uncarpeted, and he said he distinctly heard the peculiar tread of a dog, in which the faint clatter of the claws is audible. It was a light stealthy step, but at every tread the whole room shook heavily; he felt something place itself at the foot of his bed, and saw a pair of green eyes staring at him in the dark, from which he could not remove his own. Then he heard, as he thought, the old Squire Toby say—"The eleventh hour be passed, Charlie, and ye've done nothing—you and I 'a done Scroope a wrong!" and then came a good deal more, and then—"The time's nigh up, it's going to strike." And with a long low growl, the thing began to creep up upon his feet; the growl continued, and he saw the reflection of the up-turned green eyes upon the bed-clothes, as it began slowly to stretch itself up his body towards his face. With a loud scream, he waked. The light, which of late the Squire was accustomed to have in his bedroom, had accidentally gone out. He was afraid to get up, or even to look about the room for some time; so sure did he feel of seeing the green eyes in the dark fixed on him from some corner. He had hardly recovered from the first agony which nightmare leaves behind it, and was beginning to collect his thoughts, when he heard the clock strike twelve. And he bethought him of the words "the eleventh hour be passed—time's nigh up—it's going to strike!" and he almost feared that he would hear the voice reopening the subject.

Next morning the Squire came down looking ill.

"Do you know a room, old Cooper," said he, "they used to call King Herod's chamber?"

"Ay, sir; the story of King Herod was on the walls o't when I was a boy."

"There's a closet off it—is there?"

"I can't be sure o' that; but 'tisn't worth your looking at, now; the hangings was rotten, and took off the walls, before you was born; and there's nou't there but some old broken things and lumber. I seed them put there myself by poor Twinks; he was blind of an eye, and footman afterwards. You'll remember Twinks? He died here, about the time o' the great snow. There was a deal o' work to bury him, poor fellow!"

"Get the key, old Cooper; I'll look at the room," said the Squire.

"And what the devil can you want to look at it for?" said Cooper, with the old-world privilege of a rustic butler.

"And what the devil's that to you? But I don't mind if I tell you. I don't want that dog in the gun-room, and I'll put him somewhere else; and I don't care if I put him there."

"A bulldog in a bedroom! Oons, sir! the folks 'ill say you're clean mad!"

"Well, let them; get you the key and let us look at the room."

"You'd shoot him if you did right, Master Charlie. You never heard what a noise he kept up all last night in the gun-room, walking to and fro growling like a tiger in a show; and, say what you like, the dog's not worth his feed; he hasn't a point of a dog; he's a bad dog."

"I know a dog better than you—and he's a good dog!" said the Squire, testily.

"If you was a judge of a dog you'd hang that 'un," said Cooper.

"I'm not a-going to hang him, so there's an end. Go you, and get the key; and don't be talking, mind, when you go down. I may change my mind."

Now this freak of visiting King Herod's room had, in

truth, a totally different object from that pretended by the Squire. The voice in his nightmare had uttered a particular direction, which haunted him, and would give him no peace until he had tested it. So far from liking that dog today, he was beginning to regard it with a horrible suspicion; and if old Cooper had not stirred his obstinate temper by seeming to dictate, I dare say he would have got rid of the inmate effectually before evening.

Up to the third storey, long disused, he and old Cooper mounted. At the end of a dusty gallery, the room lay. The old tapestry, from which the spacious chamber had taken its name, had long given place to modern paper, and this was mildewed, and in some places hanging from the walls. A thick mantle of dust lay over the floor. Some broken chairs and boards, thick with dust, lay, along with other lumber, piled together at one end of the room.

They entered the closet, which was quite empty. The Squire looked round, and you could hardly have said whether he was relieved or disappointed.

"No furniture here," said the Squire, and looked through the dusty window. "Did you say anything to me lately—I don't mean this morning—about this room, or the closet—or anything—I forget?"

"Lor' bless you! Not I. I han't been thinkin' o' this room this forty year."

"Is there any sort of old furniture called a *buffet*—do you remember?" asked the Squire.

"A buffet? Why, yes—to be sure—there was a buffet, sure enough, in this closet, now you bring it to my mind," said Cooper. "But it's papered over."

"And what is it?"

"A little cupboard in the wall," answered the old man.

"Ho—I see—and there's such a thing here, is there, under the paper? Show me whereabouts it was."

"Well—I think it was somewhere about here," answered he, rapping his knuckles along the wall opposite the window. "Ay, there it is," he added, as the hollow sound of a wooden door was returned to his knock.

The Squire pulled the loose paper from the wall, and disclosed the doors of a small press, about two feet square, fixed in the wall.

"The very thing for my buckles and pistols, and the rest of my gimcracks," said the Squire. "Come away, we'll leave the dog where he is. Have you the key of that little press?"

No, he had not. The old master had emptied and locked it up, and desired that it should be papered over, and that was the history of it.

Down came the Squire, and took a strong turn-screw from his gun-case; and quietly he reascended to King Herod's room, and, with little trouble, forced the door of the small press in the closet wall. There were in it some letters and cancelled leases, and also a parchment deed which he took to the window and read with much agitation. It was a supplemental deed executed about a fortnight after the others, and previously to his father's marriage, placing Gylingden under strict settlement to the elder son, in what is called "tail male." Handsome Charlie, in his fraternal litigation, had acquired a smattering of technical knowledge, and he perfectly well knew that the effect of this would be not only to transfer the house and lands to his brother Scroope, but to leave him at the mercy of that exasperated brother, who might recover from him personally every guinea he had ever received by way of rent, from the date of his father's death.

It was a dismal, clouded day, with something threatening in its aspect, and the darkness, where he stood, was made deeper by the top of one of the huge old trees overhanging the window.

In a state of awful confusion he attempted to think over his position. He placed the deed in his pocket, and nearly made up his mind to destroy it. A short time ago he would not have hesitated for a moment under such circumstances; but now his health and his nerves were shattered, and he was under a supernatural alarm which the strange discovery of this deed had powerfully confirmed.

In this state of profound agitation he heard a sniffing at the closet-door, and then an impatient scratch and a long low growl. He screwed his courage up, and, not knowing what to expect, threw the door open and saw the dog, not in his dream-shape, but wriggling with joy, and crouching and fawning with eager submission; and then wandering about the closet, the brute growled awfully into the corners of it, and seemed in an unappeasable agitation.

Then the dog returned and fawned and crouched again at his feet.

After the first moment was over, the sensations of abhorrence and fear began to subside, and he almost reproached himself for requitting the affection of this poor friendless brute with the antipathy which he had really done nothing to earn.

The dog pattered after him down the stairs. Oddly enough, the sight of this animal, after the first revulsion, reassured him; it was, in his eyes, so attached, so good-natured and palpably so mere a dog.

By the hour of evening the Squire had resolved on a middle course; he would not inform his brother of his discovery, nor yet would he destroy the deed. He would never marry. He was past that time. He would leave a letter, explaining the discovery of the deed, addressed to the only surviving trustee—who had probably forgotten everything about it—and having seen out his own tenure, he would provide that all should be set right after his death. Was not that fair? At all events it quite satisfied what he called his conscience, and he thought it a devilish good compromise for his brother; and he went out, towards sunset, to take his usual walk.

Returning in the darkening twilight, the dog, as usual attending him, began to grow frisky and wild, at first scampering round him in great circles, as before, nearly at the top of his speed, his great head between his paws as he raced. Gradually more excited grew the pace and narrow his circuit, louder and fiercer his continuous growl, and the Squire stopped and grasped his stick hard, for the lurid eyes and grin of the brute threatened an attack. Turning round and round as the excited brute encircled him, and striking vainly at him with his stick, he grew at last so tired that he almost despaired of keeping him longer at bay; when on a sudden the dog stopped short and crawled up to his feet wriggling and crouching submissively.

Nothing could be more apologetic and abject; and when the Squire dealt him two heavy thumps with his stick, the dog whimpered only, and writhed and licked his feet. The Squire sat down on a prostrate tree; and his dumb companion, recovering his wonted spirits immediately, began to sniff and nuzzle among the roots. The Squire felt in his breast-pocket for the deed—it was safe; and again he pondered, in this loneliest of spots, on the question whether he should preserve it for restoration after his death to his brother, or destroy it forthwith. He began rather to lean toward the latter solution, when the long low growl of the dog not far off startled him.

He was sitting in a melancholy grove of old trees, that slants gently westward. Exactly the same odd effect of light I have before described—a faint red glow reflected downward from the upper sky, after the sun had set, now gave to the growing darkness a lurid uncertainty. This grove, which lies in a gentle hollow, owing to its circumscribed horizon on all but one side, has a peculiar character of loneliness.

He got up and peeped over a sort of barrier, accidentally formed of the trunks of felled trees laid one over the other, and saw the dog straining up the other side of it, and hideously stretched out, his ugly head looking in consequence twice the natural size. His dream was coming over him again. And now between the trunks the brute's ungainly head was thrust, and the long neck came straining through, and the body, twining after it like a huge white lizard; and as it came striving and twisting through, it growled and glared as if it would devour him.

As swiftly as his lameness would allow, the Squire hurried from this solitary spot towards the house. What thoughts exactly passed through his mind as he did so, I am sure he could not have told. But when the dog came up with him it seemed appeased, and even in high good-humour, and no longer resembled the brute that haunted his dreams.

That night, near ten o'clock, the Squire, a good deal agitated, sent for the keeper, and told him that he believed the dog was mad, and that he must shoot him. He might shoot the dog in the gun-room, where he was—a grain of shot or two in the wainscot did not matter, and the dog must not have a chance of getting out.

The Squire gave the gamekeeper his double-barrelled gun, loaded with heavy shot. He did not go with him beyond the hall. He placed his hand on the keeper's arm; the keeper said his hand trembled, and that he looked "as white as curds."

"Listen a bit!" said the Squire under his breath.

They heard the dog in a state of high excitement in the room—growling ominously, jumping on the window-stool and down again, and running round the room.

"You'll need to be sharp, mind—don't give him a chance—slip in edgeways, d'ye see? and give him both barrels!"

"Not the first mad dog I've knocked over, sir," said the man, looking very serious as he cocked the gun.

As the keeper opened the door, the dog had sprung into the empty grate. He said he "never see sich a stark, staring devil." The beast made a twist round, as if, he thought, to jump up the chimney—"but that wasn't to be done at no price"—and he made a yell—not like a dog—like a man caught in a mill-crank, and before he could spring at the keeper, he fired one barrel into him. The dog leaped towards him, and rolled over, receiving the second barrel in his head, as he lay snorting at the keeper's feet!

"I never seed the like; I never heard a screech like that!" said the keeper, recoiling. "It makes a fellow feel queer."

"Quite dead?" asked the Squire.

"Not a stir in him, sir," said the man, pulling him along the floor by the neck.

"Throw him outside the hall-door now," said the Squire; "and mind you pitch him outside the gate to-night—old Cooper says he's a witch," and the pale Squire smiled, "so he shan't lie in Gylingden."

Never was man more relieved than the Squire, and he slept better for a week after this than he had done for many weeks before.

It behooves us all to act promptly on our good resolutions. There is a determined gravitation towards evil, which, if left to itself, will bear down first intentions. If at one moment of superstitious fear the Squire had made up his mind to a great sacrifice, and resolved in the matter of that deed so strangely recovered to act honestly by his brother, that resolution very soon gave place to the compromise with fraud which so conveniently postponed the restitution to the period when further enjoyment on his part was impossible. Then came more tidings of Scroope's violent and minatory language, with always the same burthen—that he would leave no stone unturned to show that there had existed a deed which Charles had either secreted or destroyed, and that he would never rest till he had hanged him.

This of course was wild talk. At first it had only enraged him; but, with his recent guilty knowledge and suppression, had come fear. His danger was the existence of the deed, and little by little he brought himself to a resolution to destroy it. There were many falterings and recoils before he could bring himself to commit this crime. At length, however, he did it, and got rid of the custody of that which at any time might become the instrument of disgrace and ruin. There was relief in this, but also the new and terrible sense of actual guilt.

He had got pretty well rid of his supernatural qualms. It was a different kind of trouble that agitated him now.

But this night, he imagined, he was awakened by a violent shaking of his bed. He could see, in the very imperfect light, two figures at the foot of it, holding each a bed-post. One of these he half-fancied was his brother Scroope, but the other was the old Squire—of that he was sure—and he fancied that they had shaken him up from his sleep. Squire Toby was talking as Charlie wakened, and he heard him say:

"Put out of our own house by you! It won't hold for long. We'll come in together, friendly, and stay. Fore-warned, wi' yer eyes open, ye did it; and now Scroope'll hang you! We'll hang you together! Look at me, you devil's limb."

And the old Squire tremblingly stretched his face, torn with shot and bloody, and growing every moment more and more into the likeness of the dog, and began to stretch himself out and climb the bed over the foot-board; and he saw the figure at the other side, little more than a black shadow, begin also to scale the bed; and there was instantly a dreadful confusion and uproar in the room, and such a gabbling and laughing; he could not catch the words; but, with a scream, he woke, and found himself standing on the floor. The phantoms and the clamour were gone, but a crash and ringing of fragments was in his ears. The great china bowl, from which for generations the Marstons of Gylingden had been baptized, had fallen from the mantelpiece, and was smashed on the hearth-stone.

"I've bin dreamin' all night about Mr. Scroope, and I wouldn't wonder, old Cooper, if he was dead," said the Squire, when he came down in the morning.

"God forbid! I was adreamed about him, too, sir: I dreamed he was dammin' and sinkin' about a hole was burnt in his coat, and the old master, God be wi' him! said—quite plain—I'd 'a swore 'twas himself— 'Cooper, get up, ye damn'd land-loupin' thief, and lend a hand to hang him—for he's a daft cur, and no dog o' mine.' 'Twas the dog shot over night, I do suppose, as was runnin' in my old head. I thought old master gied me a punch wi' his knuckles, and says I, wakenin' up, 'At yer service, sir'; and for a while I couldn't get it out o' my head, master was in the room still."

Letters from town soon convinced the Squire that his brother Scroope, so far from being dead, was particularly active; and Charlie's attorney wrote to say, in serious alarm, that he had heard, accidentally, that he intended setting up a case, of a supplementary deed of settlement, of which he had secondary evidence, which would give him Gylingden. And at this menace Handsome Charlie snapped his fingers, and wrote courageously to his attorney; abiding what might follow with, however, a secret foreboding.

Scroope threatened loudly now, and swore after his bitter fashion, and reiterated his old promise of hanging that cheat at last. In the midst of these menaces and preparations, however, a sudden peace proclaimed itself: Scroope died, without time even to make provisions for a posthumous attack upon his brother. It was one of those cases of disease of the heart in which death is as sudden as by a bullet.

Charlie's exultation was undisguised. It was shocking. Not, of course, altogether malignant. For there was the expansion consequent on the removal of a secret fear. There was also the comic piece of luck, that only the day before Scroope had destroyed his old will, which left to a stranger every farthing he possessed, intending in a day or two to execute another to the same person, charged with the express condition of prosecuting the suit against Charlie.

The result was that all his possessions went unconditionally to his brother Charles as his heir. Here were grounds for abundance of savage elation. But there was also the deep-seated hatred of half a life of mutual and persistent aggression and revilings; and Handsome Charlie was capable of nursing a grudge, and enjoying a revenge with his whole heart.

He would gladly have prevented his brother's being buried in the old Gylingden chapel, where he wished to lie; but his lawyers doubted his power, and he was not quite proof against the scandal which would attend his turning back the funeral, which would, he knew, be attended by some of the country gentry and others, with an hereditary regard for the Marstons.

But he warned his servants that not one of them were to attend it; promising, with oaths and curses not to be disregarded, that any one of them who did so, should find the door shut in his face on his return.

I don't think, with the exception of old Cooper, that the servants cared for this prohibition, except as it baulked a curiosity always strong in the solitude of the country. Cooper was very much vexed that the eldest son of the old Squire should be buried in the old family chapel, and no sign of decent respect from Gylingden Hall. He asked his master whether he would not, at least, have some wine and refreshments in the oak parlour, in case any of the country gentlemen who paid this respect to the old family should come up to the house? But the Squire only swore at him, told him to mind his own business, and ordered him to say, if such a thing happened, that he was out, and no preparations made, and, in fact, to send them away as they came. Cooper expostulated stoutly, and the Squire grew angrier; and after a tempestuous scene, took his hat and stick and walked out, just as the funeral descending the valley from the direction of the "Old Angel Inn" came in sight.

Old Cooper prowled about disconsolately, and counted the carriages as well as he could from the gate. When the funeral was over, and they began to drive away, he returned to the hall, the door of which lay open, and as usual deserted. Before he reached it quite, a mourning coach drove up, and two gentlemen in black cloaks, and with crapes to their hats, got out, and without looking to the right or the left, went up the steps into the house. Cooper followed them slowly. The carriage had, he supposed, gone round to the yard, for, when he reached the door, it was no longer there.

So he followed the two mourners into the house. In the hall he found a fellow servant, who said he had seen two gentlemen, in black cloaks, pass through the hall, and go up the stairs without removing their hats, or asking leave of anyone. This was very odd, old Cooper thought, and a great liberty; so upstairs he went to make them out.

But he could not find them then, nor ever. And from that hour the house was troubled.

In a little time there was not one of the servants who had not something to tell. Steps and voices followed them sometimes in the passages, and tittering whispers, always minatory, scared them at the corners of the galleries, or from dark recesses; so that they would return panic-stricken to be rebuked by thin Mrs. Beckett, who looked on such stories as worse than idle. But Mrs. Beckett herself, a short time after, took a very different view of the matter.

She had herself begun to hear these voices, and with this formidable aggravation, that they came always when she was at her prayers, which she had been punctual in saying all her life, and utterly interrupted them. She was scared at such moments by dropping words and sentences, which grew, as she persisted, into threats and blasphemies.

These voices were not always in the room. They called, as she fancied, through the walls, very thick in that old house, from the neighbouring apartments, sometimes on one side, sometimes on the other; sometimes they seemed to holloa from distant lobbies, and came muffled, but threateningly, through the long panelled passages. As they approached they grew furious, as if several voices were speaking together. Whenever, as I said, this worthy woman applied herself to her devotions, these horrible sentences came hurrying towards the door, and, in panic, she would start from her knees, and all then would subside except the thumping of her heart against her stays, and the dreadful tremors of her nerves.

What these voices said, Mrs. Beckett never could quite remember one minute after they had ceased speaking; one sentence chased another away; gibe and menace and impious denunciation, each hideously articulate, were lost as soon as heard. And this added to the effect of these terrifying mockeries and invectives, that she could not, by any effort, retain their exact import, although their horrible character remained vividly present to her mind.

For a long time the Squire seemed to be the only person in the house absolutely unconscious of these annoyances. Mrs. Beckett had twice made up her mind within the week to leave. A prudent woman, however, who has been comfortable for more than twenty years in a place, thinks oftener than twice before she leaves it. She and old Cooper were the only servants in the house who remembered the good old housekeeping in Squire Toby's day. The others were few, and such as could hardly be accounted regular servants. Meg Dobbs, who acted as housemaid, would not sleep in the house, but walked home, in trepidation, to her father's, at the gatehouse, under the escort of her little brother, every night. Old Mrs. Beckett, who was high and mighty with the make-shift servants of fallen Gylingden, let herself down all at once, and made Mrs. Kymes and the kitchen-maid move their beds into her large and faded room, and there, very frankly, shared her nightly terrors with them.

Old Cooper was testy and captious about these stories. He was already uncomfortable enough by reason of the entrance of the two muffled figures into the house, about which there could be no mistake. His own eyes had seen them. He refused to credit the stories of the women, and affected to think that the two mourners might have left the house and driven away, on finding no one to receive them.

Old Cooper was summoned at night to the oak parlour, where the Squire was smoking.

"I say, Cooper," said the Squire, looking pale and angry, "what for ha' you been frightenin' they crazy women wi' your plaguy stories? D——me, if you see ghosts here it's no place for you, and it's time you should pack. I won't be left without servants. Here has been old Beckett, wi' the cook and the kitchen-maid, as white as pipeclay, all in a row, to tell me I must have a parson to sleep among them, and preach down the devil! Upon my soul, you're a wise old body, filling their heads wi' maggots! And Meg goes down to the lodge every night, afeared to lie in the house—all your doing, wi' your old wives' stories—ye withered old Tom o' Bedlam!"

"I'm not to blame, Master Charles. 'Tisn't along o' no stories o' mine, for I'm never done tellin' 'em it's all vanity and vapours. Mrs. Beckett 'ill tell you that, and there's been many a wry word betwixt us on the head o't. Whate'er I may *think*," said old Cooper, significantly, and looked askance, with the sternness of fear in the Squire's face.

The Squire averted his eyes, and muttered angrily to himself, and turned away to knock the ashes out of his pipe on the hob, and then turning suddenly round upon Cooper again, he spoke, with a pale face, but not quite so angrily as before.

"I know you're no fool, old Cooper, when you like. Suppose there was such a thing as a ghost here, don't you see, it ain't to them snipe-headed women it' id go to tell its story. What ails you, man, that you should think aught about it, but just what *I* think? You had a good headpiece o' yer own once, Cooper, don't be you clappin' a goosecap over it, as my poor father used to say; d—— it old boy, you mustn't let 'em be fools, settin' one another wild wi' their blether, and makin' the folk talk what they shouldn't, about Gylingden and the family. I don't think ye'd like that, old Cooper, I'm sure ye wouldn't. The women has gone out o' the kitchen, make up a bit o' fire, and get your pipe. I'll go to you, when I finish this one, and we'll smoke a bit together, and a glass o' brandy and water."

Down went the old butler, not altogether unused to such condescensions in that disorderly and lonely household; and let not those who can choose their company, be too hard on the Squire who couldn't.

When he had got things tidy, as he said, he sat down in that big old kitchen, with his feet on the fender, the kitchen candle burning in a great brass candlestick, which stood on the deal table at his elbow, with the brandy bottle and tumblers beside it, and Cooper's pipe also in readiness. And these preparations completed, the old butler, who had remembered other generations and better times, fell into rumination, and so, gradually, into a deep sleep.

Old Cooper was half awakened by someone laughing low, near his head. He was dreaming of old times in the hall, and fancied one of "the young gentlemen" going to play him a trick, and he mumbled something in his sleep, from which he was awakened by a stern deep voice, saying, "You wern't at the funeral; I might take your life, I'll take your ear." At the same moment, the side of his head received a violent push, and he started to his feet. The fire had gone down, and he was chilled. The candle was expiring in the socket, and threw on the white wall long shadows, that danced up and down from the ceiling to the ground, and their black outlines he fancied resembled the two men in cloaks, whom he remembered with a profound horror.

He took the candle, with all the haste he could, getting along the passage, on whose walls the same dance of black shadows was continued, very anxious to reach his room before the light should go out. He was startled half out of his wits by the sudden clang of his master's bell, close over his head, ringing furiously.

"Ha, ha! There it goes—yes, sure enough," said Cooper, reassuring himself with the sound of his own voice, as he hastened on, hearing more and more distinct every moment the same furious ringing. "He's fell asleep, like me; that's it, and his lights is out, I lay you fifty —"

When he turned the handle of the door of the oak parlour, the Squire wildly called, "Who's *there*?" in the tone of a man who expects a robber.

"It's me, old Cooper, all right, Master Charlie, you didn't come to the kitchen after all, sir."

"I'm very bad, Cooper; I don't know how I've been. Did you meet anything?" asked the Squire.

"No," said Cooper.

They stared at one another.

"Come here—stay here! Don't you leave me! Look round the room, and say is all right; and gie us your hand, old Cooper, for I must hold it." The Squire's was damp and cold, and trembled very much. It was not very far from day-break now.

After a time he spoke again: "I' a done many a thing I shouldn't; I'm not fit to go, and wi' God's blessin' I'll look to it—why shouldn't I? I'm as lame as old Billy—I'll never be able to do any good no more, and I'll give over drinking, and marry, as I ought to 'a done long ago—none o' yer fine ladies, but a good homely wench; there's Farmer Crump's youngest daughter, a good lass, and discreet. What for shouldn't I take her? She'd take care o' me, and wouldn't bring a head full o' romances here, and mantua-makers' trumpery, and I'll talk with the parson, and I'll do what's fair wi' everyone and mind, I said I'm sorry for many a thing I 'a done."

A wild cold dawn had by this time broken. The Squire, Cooper said, looked "awful bad," as he got his hat and stick, and sallied out for a walk, instead of going to his bed, as Cooper besought him, looking so wild and distracted, that it was plain his object was simply to escape from the house. It was twelve o'clock when the Squire walked into the kitchen, where he was sure of finding some of the servants, looking as if ten years had passed over him since yesterday. He pulled a stool by the fire, without speaking a word, and sat down. Cooper had sent to Applebury for the doctor, who had just arrived, but the Squire would not go to him. "If he wants to see me, he may come here," he muttered as often as Cooper urged him. So the doctor did come, charily enough, and found the Squire very much worse than he had expected.

The Squire resisted the order to get to his bed. But the doctor insisted under a threat of death, at which his patient quailed.

"Well, I'll do what you say—only this—you must let old Cooper and Dick Keeper stay wi' me. I mustn't be left alone, and they must keep awake o' nights; and stay a while, do *you*. When I get round a bit, I'll go and live in a town. It's dull livin' here, now that I can't do nou't, as I used, and I'll live a better life, mind ye; ye heard me say that, and I don't care who laughs, and I'll talk wi' the parson. I like 'em to laugh, hang 'em, it's a sign I'm doin' right, at last."

The doctor sent a couple of nurses from the County Hospital, not choosing to trust his patient to the management he had selected, and he went down himself to Gylingden to meet them in the evening. Old Cooper was ordered to occupy the dressing-room, and sit up at night, which satisfied the Squire, who was in a strangely excited state, very low, and threatened, the doctor said, with fever.

The clergyman came, an old, gentle, "book-learned" man, and talked and prayed with him late that evening. After he had gone the Squire called the nurses to his bedside, and said: "There's a fellow sometimes comes; you'll never mind him. He looks in at the door and beckons—a thin, hump-backed chap in mourning, wi' black gloves on; ye'll know him by his lean face, as brown as the wainscot: don't ye mind his smilin'. You don't go out to him, nor ask him in; he won't say nou't; and if he grows anger'd and looks awry at ye, don't be afeared, for he can't hurt ye, and he'll grow tired waitin', and go away; and for God's sake mind ye don't ask him in, nor go out after him!"

The nurses put their heads together when this was over, and held afterwards a whispering conference with old Cooper. "Law bless ye!—no, there's no madman in the house,' he protested; 'not a soul but what ye saw—it's just a trifle o' the fever in his head—no more."

The Squire grew worse as the night wore on. He was heavy and delirious, talking of all sorts of things—of wine, and dogs, and lawyers; and then he began to talk, as it were, to his brother Scroope. As he did so, Mrs. Oliver, the nurse, who was sitting up alone with him, heard, as she thought, a hand softly laid on the door-handle outside, and a stealthy attempt to turn it. "Lord bless us! Who's there?" she cried, and her heart jumped into her mouth as she thought of the hump-backed man in black, who was to put in his head smiling and beckoning—"Mr. Cooper! Sir! Are you there?" she cried. "Come here, Mr. Cooper, please—do, sir, quick!"

Old Cooper, called up from his doze by the fire, stumbled in from the dressing-room, and Mrs. Oliver seized him tightly as he emerged.

"The man with the hump has been atryin' the door, Mr. Cooper, as sure as I am here." The Squire was moaning and mumbling in his fever, understanding nothing, as she spoke. "No, no! Mrs. Oliver, ma'am, it's impossible, for there's no sick man in the house: what is Master Charlie sayin'?"

"He's saying *Scroope* every minute, whatever he means by that, and—and—hisht!—listen—there's the handle again," and, with a loud scream, she added—"Look at his head and neck in at the door!" and in her tremor she strained old Cooper in an agonizing embrace.

The candle was flaring, and there was a wavering shadow at the door that looked like the head of a man with a long neck, and a longish sharp nose, peeping in and drawing back.

"Don't be a d—— fool, ma'am!" cried Cooper, very white, and shaking her with all his might. "It's only the candle, I tell you—nothing in life but that. Don't you see?" and he raised the light. "And I'm sure there was no one at the door, and I'll try, if you let me go."

The other nurse was asleep on a sofa, and Mrs. Oliver called her up in a panic, for company, as old Cooper opened the door. There was no one near it, but at the angle of the gallery was a shadow resembling that which he had seen in the room. He raised the candle a little, and it seemed to beckon with a long hand as the head drew back. "Shadow from the candle!" exclaimed Cooper aloud, resolved not to yield to Mrs. Oliver's panic; and, candle in hand, he walked to the corner.

There was nothing. He could not forbear peeping down the long gallery from this point, and as he moved the light, he saw precisely the same sort of shadow, a little further down, and as he advanced the same withdrawal, and beckon. "Gammon!" said he; "it is nou't but the candle." And on he went, growing half angry and half frightened at the persistency with which this ugly shadow—a literal shadow he was sure it was—presented itself. As he drew near the point where it now appeared, it seemed to collect itself, and nearly dissolve in the central panel of an old carved cabinet which he was now approaching.

In the centre panel of this is a sort of boss carved into a wolf's head.

The light fell oddly upon this, and the fugitive shadow seemed to be breaking up, and re-arranging itself oddly. The eyeball gleamed with a point of reflected light, which glittered also upon the grinning mouth, and he saw the long, sharp nose of Scroope Marston, and his fierce eye looking at him, he thought, with a steadfast meaning.

Old Cooper stood gazing upon this sight, unable to move, till he saw the face, and the figure that belonged to it, begin gradually to emerge from the wood. At the same time he heard voices approaching rapidly up a side gallery, and Cooper, with a loud "Lord a-mercy on us!" turned and ran back again, pursued by a sound that seemed to shake the old house like a mighty gust of wind.

Into his master's room burst old Cooper, half wild with fear, and clapped the door and turned the key in a twinkling, looking as if he had been pursued by murderers.

"Did you hear it?" whispered Cooper, now standing near the dressing-room door. They all listened, but not a sound from without disturbed the utter stillness of night. "God bless us! I doubt it's my old head that's gone crazy!" exclaimed Cooper.

He would tell them nothing but that he was himself "an old fool," to be frightened by their talk, and that "the rattle of a window, or the dropping o' a pin" was enough to scare him now; and so he helped himself through that night with brandy, and sat up talking by his master's fire.

The Squire recovered slowly from his brain fever, but not perfectly.

A very little thing, the doctor said, would suffice to upset him. He was not yet sufficiently strong to remove for change of scene and air, which were necessary for his complete restoration.

Cooper slept in the dressing-room, and was now his only nightly attendant. The ways of the invalid were odd: he liked, half sitting up in his bed, to smoke his churchwarden o' nights, and made old Cooper smoke, for company, at the fireside. As the Squire and his humble friend indulged in it, smoking is a taciturn pleasure, and it was not until the master of Gylingden had finished his third pipe that he essayed conversation, and when he did, the subject was not such as Cooper would have chosen.

"I say, old Cooper, look in my face, and don't be afeared to speak out," said the Squire, looking at him with a steady, cunning smile; "you know all this time, as well as I do, who's in the house. You needn't deny—hey?—Scroope and my father?"

"Don't you be talking like that, Charlie," said old Cooper, rather sternly and frightened, after a long silence, still looking in his face, which did not change.

"What's the good o' shammin', Cooper? Scroope's took the hearin' o' yer right ear—you know he did. He's looking angry. He's nigh took my life wi' this fever. But he's not done wi' me yet, and he looks awful wicked. Ye saw him—ye know ye did."

Cooper was awfully frightened, and the odd smile on the Squire's lips frightened him still more. He dropped his pipe, and stood gazing in silence at his master, and feeling as if he were in a dream.

"If ye think so, ye should not be smiling like that." said Cooper, grimly.

"I'm tired, Cooper, and it's as well to smile as t' other thing; so I'll even smile while I can. You know what they mean to do wi' me. That's all I wanted to say. Now, lad, go on wi' yer pipe—I'm goin' asleep."

So the Squire turned over in his bed, and lay down serenely, with his head on the pillow. Old Cooper looked at him, and glanced at the door, and then half-filled his tumbler with brandy, and drank it off, and felt better, and got to his bed in the dressing-room.

In the dead of night he was suddenly awakened by the Squire, who was standing, in his dressing-gown and slippers, by his bed.

"I've brought you a bit o' present. I got the rents o' Hazelden yesterday, and ye'll keep that for yourself—it's a fifty—and give t' other to Nelly Carwell, to-morrow; I'll sleep the sounder; and I saw Scroope since; he's not such a bad 'un after all, old fellow! He's got a crape over his face—for I told him I couldn't bear it; and I'd do many a thing for him now. I never could stand shilly-shally. Good-night, old Cooper!"

And the Squire laid his trembling hand kindly on the old man's shoulder, and returned to his own room. "I don't half like how he is. Doctor don't come half often enough. I don't like that queer smile o' his, and his hand was as cold as death. I hope in God his brain's not a-turnin'!"

With these reflections, he turned to the pleasanter subject of his present, and at last fell asleep.

In the morning, when he went into the Squire's room, the Squire had left his bed. "Never mind; he'll come back, like a bad shillin'," thought old Cooper, preparing the room as usual. But he did not return. Then began an uneasiness, succeeded by a panic, when it began to be plain that the Squire was not in the house. What had become of him? None of his clothes, but his dressing-gown and slippers, were missing. Had he left the house, in his present sickly state, in that garb? and, if so, could he be in his right senses; and was there a chance of his surviving a cold, a damp night, so passed, in the open air?

Tom Edwards was up to the house, and told them that, walking a mile or so that morning, at four o'clock—there being no moon—along with Farmer Nokes, who was driving his cart to market, in the dark, three men walked, in front of the horse, not twenty yards before them, all the way from Gylingden Lodge to the burial ground, the gate of which was opened for them from within, and the three men entered, and the gate was shut. Tom Edwards thought they were gone in to make preparation for a funeral of some member of the Marston family. But the occurrence seemed to Cooper, who knew there was no such thing, horribly ominous.

He now commenced a careful search, and at last bethought him of the lonely upper storey and King Herod's chamber. He saw nothing changed there, but the closet door was shut, and, dark as was the morning, something, like a large white knot sticking out over the door, caught his eye.

The door resisted his efforts to open it for a time; some great weight forced it down against the floor; at length, however, it did yield a little, and a heavy crash, shaking the whole floor, and sending an echo flying through all the silent corridors, with a sound like receding laughter, half stunned him.

When he pushed open the door, his master was lying dead upon the floor. His cravat was drawn halter-wise tight round his throat, and had done its work well. The body was cold, and had been long dead.

In due course the coroner held his inquest, and the jury pronounced that "the deceased, Charles Marston, had died by his own hand, in a state of temporary insanity." But old Cooper had his own opinion about the Squire's death, though his lips were sealed, and he never spoke about it. He went and lived for the residue of days in York, where there are still people who remember him, a taciturn and surly old man, who attended church regularly, and also drank a little, and was known to have saved some money.

THE YELLOW WALLPAPER

BY CHARLOTTE PERKINS GILMAN

INTRODUCTION

RHIAN E. JONES

Immurement — from the Latin *im-* "in" and *murus* "wall"; literally "walling in" — is a practice of confinement peculiarly connected with women. There are both mythical and historical examples of it as punishment for sins of the flesh, including for Roman vestal priestesses who broke their vows of chastity and were immured in caves or catacombs. Numerous European folktales specify immurement not as a punishment but a "foundation sacrifice" for luck during the completion of a construction project, ensuring a strong foundation for the home, for instance, through the entombing of a young woman — sometimes consenting, sometimes not — within its walls. Many women in medieval Europe, by contrast, chose to enclose themselves as "anchoresses", living in contemplative solitude in cells built into church walls. This ascetic isolation also allowed them, whether by accident or design, to reject the strictures and hierarchies of male religious control and escape the tasks and obligations that fell on women in daily life, while their aura of holy dedication shielded them from the accusations of subversion that usually fell on those rejecting female roles. Throughout history, then, women have found themselves shut up behind walls as a result of spiritual devotion, breaking the rules, or conscious sacrifice. These associations all find an echo in "The Yellow Wallpaper", another tale dealing with various ways of shutting women up.

"The Yellow Wallpaper", taken at face value, is a slip of a thing. At just over 6,000 words, it was initially rejected by a succession of editors due to its bleak and unsettling content, and was finally published in 1892 in the *New England Magazine*. Although it took until the 1970s to be formally recognised and celebrated as a feminist critique of patriarchy, the story punched above its weight on publication: shortly after it saw the light of day, a Boston physician wrote to the *Evening Transcript* newspaper to protest that "Such a story ought not to be written", and that reading it "was enough to drive anyone mad".

On the surface, the story is that of a woman driven mad herself, through enforced inactivity on the orders of her husband and a wider medical establishment. The unnamed narrator, who has just given birth, suffers from an unspecified but enervating affliction. Her physician husband, diagnosing "temporary nervous depression — a slight hysterical tendency", takes her to an isolated stately home for a "rest-cure" which forbids her any mental and physical stimulation in favour of total bed rest. The narrator is settled in a former nursery room, set with sinister "rings and things" in the walls, bars across the windows and — perhaps its least immediately alarming aspect — unpleasant-looking yellow wallpaper.

But it is the wallpaper that gradually consumes the narrator's attention and mind as her obsession with it — and with the idea that there is a real woman trapped behind its complex pattern — consumes the story. As the narrator, forbidden to write by her husband and doctor, defiantly sets down her increasingly compulsive thoughts on paper, we see her processing her own feelings of stifled confinement by projecting her boredom and frustration onto what she sees: another woman, like herself, trapped behind fixed repeating patterns. At the story's climax, the narrator, now fully identifying with the woman in the wallpaper, succumbs to madness — or, as she sees it, liberation — so completely that her husband, breaking down the door, faints in shock at what she has become.

***

Charlotte Perkins Gilman was born in Hartford, Connecticut, and raised in poverty by her mother after her parents' divorce. Erratically educated but noticeably intelligent, she dropped out of college to support herself as a teacher and artist. When she married in 1884 Gilman found herself, like the narrator of "The Yellow Wallpaper", immured between the expansion of a consumer-led capitalist society and the residual constraints imposed on women. Despite greater opportunities for women to enter the professional and intellectual sphere in 1880s America, financial self-sufficiency and social independence were still discouraged, and marriage and children remained the conventional default. What seemed like exits led to yet more walls.

The nineteenth century also saw a revival of Victorian ideals of women as delicate and submissive, which saw them further stereotyped as emotionally vulnerable, and regarded by physicians as susceptible to physical and mental ill health. Conversely, women who diverged from these ideals — by seeking higher education, creative accomplishments, or political reform, or just by reading too many novels — were deemed at even greater risk of mental illness and breakdown. In 1871, the US neurologist Silas Weir Mitchell in his book *Wear and Tear, or Hints for the Overworked*, had coined the idea of "neurasthenia" or "nervous exhaustion", a disorder brought on, particularly in women, by incessant mental effort.

Gilman recorded her encounters with Weir Mitchell in a 1913 essay in which she recounted her own experience of what would now be called postpartum depression or psychosis: four years of "severe and continuous nervous breakdown" following the birth of her daughter in 1885. In 1887 she sought help from Weir Michell, who prescribed a "rest-cure" which enjoined her to "'have but two hours intellectual life a day' and 'never to touch pen, brush, or pencil again' as long as I lived". Gilman outlines the results of this prescription with laconic starkness: "I went home and obeyed those directions for some three months, and came so near the borderline of utter mental ruin that I could see over".

Gilman's narrator, like her, experiences the aftermath of giving birth as an exhausted malaise, disassociated from her surroundings and unable not only to fulfil the roles of wife and mother but also to express herself in words. In her autobiography, Gilman wrote of the "unbearable inner misery" and "ceaseless tears", "dragging weariness… absolute incapacity. Absolute misery" that followed childbirth, a condition only made worse by the presence of her husband and child. Postpartum depression was, however, unknown to the nineteenth-century medical establishment, which also had a more general ignorance of and resistance to dealing with women's mental health, with physicians frequently employing the rest-cure as a way to assert a measure of control over a situation they did not fully comprehend. "Female hysteria", although discounted as a medical disorder in the twentieth century, was commonly diagnosed in women, like the narrator, who displayed psychological and physiological symptoms that had no obvious cause.

Gilman, by summoning "the remnants of intelligence that remained" to her and rejecting the rest-cure, was able to resume her intellectual work and gradually regain her health. She later wrote "The Yellow Wallpaper" as a kind of cautionary tale. Relating how reading the story had "terrified" the family of at least one woman into releasing her from a similar rest-cure, Gilman's article concludes: "It was not intended to drive people crazy, but to save people from being driven crazy, and it worked."

***

Part of why "The Yellow Wallpaper" works is the encouragement of sympathy for the narrator, which the story's writing style and structure provide. Gilman's characters are sketchily-drawn — the compliant, neurotic new mother, the complacently authoritarian husband — making them ciphers onto which a reader can project their own ideas and identities. The story's use of first-person narrative and diary-like progression further encourages a degree of intimacy and trust between narrator and reader. Despite the early hints of unreliability that stud the narrative, the descent into madness — as the reader moves from friend to conspirator and the writing becomes more intently secretive, raw, and disturbing before fragmenting along with the narrator's mind — is presented gradually and compellingly enough that it can seem the only viable response to the narrator's circumstances.

In addition to its claustrophobic atmosphere, Gilman's story skillfully deploys a number of horror, supernatural, and gothic tropes: the isolated manor-house, the vulnerable heroine menaced by male authority and haunted by visions, who takes to sleeping away the day then feverishly undertakes nocturnal activity by ghostly moonlight. The wallpaper's irrational, maze-like patterns inspire the same sense of dread as Lovecraft's non-Euclidean geometry. The narrator ends up endlessly, restlessly "creeping", or crawling on all fours around her room — at once like a child but also like an animal or insect, something other than a "civilised" adult human.

But there is greater horror in the human and mundane, like the way in which the narrator is infantilised even while she is urged to resume a grown-up wife-and-mother role: dosed and fed at regular intervals, forbidden her favourite activities like a naughty child, and addressed by her husband as "blessed little goose" and "little girl" as she tries and fails to signal her approaching insanity. Early readers were appreciative of the sheer horror of the tale, but part of the power of "The Yellow Wallpaper" is that its horror is more social than supernatural.

Thirty years before "The Yellow Wallpaper" was published, Elizabeth Packard found herself committed to Jacksonville Insane Asylum, IL., after arguing repeatedly with her husband, a Calvinist minister fourteen years her senior, over religion, childrearing, family finances, and slavery. Although the state legislature required a public hearing before a person could be committed against their will, the sole exception to this was that a husband could have his wife committed without either a public hearing or her consent, which Packard's husband did by referring to his wife's "excessive application of body and mind". After three years of refusal under medical questioning to agree that she was insane, Packard was declared "incurable". Upon her discharge and return to her husband, he locked her in the nursery of their home and nailed the windows shut.

Susan Bordo, in her book *Unbearable Weight*, argues that mental illnesses common to women during certain eras are in fact a reflection of and objection to the "traditional" gender roles of their times. While women's repressed or unconscious dissatisfaction with their circumstances could eventually erupt in crisis, neurosis, or breakdown, women's conscious defiance of or resistance to their social situations could be met with violent opposition, in which the medical establishment often played a role — from confinement to bed to committal to asylums — in policing the behaviour of rebellious or recalcitrant women. Gilman's narrator finds herself locked in a nursery not for overt disagreement with her husband, but for a parallel "crime", with her active intellectual engagement (like Gilman herself, she classifies writing as "work") and her passive neglect of her expected household role both implying a desire to transcend the domestic sphere. The men around her, perceiving that desire as a symptom of illness, respond with an attempt at a "cure" that she receives as punishment verging on torture.

In "The Yellow Wallpaper", the fixed rigidity of gender roles — the man as rational thinker and decision-maker, the woman as unquestioning receptacle — becomes the foundation of horror. Central to Gilman's objection to the power structure of the family was that traditional patriarchy benefited neither wife nor husband, and this is borne out by the failure of both the narrator and her husband to communicate as equals; while he is unable to admit his prescription could be wrong and doing more harm than good, she, conditioned to "control myself — before him, at least", is unable to let him know that his suspicions are correct.

There is also an intermittently absurd comedy in the story's skewering of gender roles: Gilman's narrator giving in to her morbid obsession with the wallpaper is a darkly funny riff on the fact that domestic aesthetics, the choice of soft furnishings and decor, was one of few areas over which wives were granted influence and encouraged to take an interest. The story also draws humour from established horror conventions: the climactic set piece — the husband taking an axe to the heroine's bedroom door — is subverted on one level as his intentions are not murderous or mad but earnestly concerned for her welfare, and then subverted a second time as he finds himself in greater shock at his wife's self-imposed condition than at any external danger there may have been to her.

Can Gilman's final scene, with her narrator's accelerating instability causing her to rip the wallpaper off the walls as though seeking to tear herself an exit, and finally becoming one with the woman in the wallpaper, be called a happy ending? In the story's final moments she throws away the room's key, but it is unclear whether she is thereby locking herself in, succumbing to her confinement away from the world, or locking the world out, better to survive alone, as though her room has become a medieval anchoress's cell, and she a willing recluse. Has she attained a liberated, higher state of consciousness, or merely gained entry to the even smaller solitary confinement of her own mind? Readers are left to reach their own conclusions.

***

Despite containing an obvious warning and moral which has made it an enduring classic, Gilman's story is not simply didactic, but stands on its own literary merit and within a loose tradition of work by women writers. Gilman's choice of the gothic genre reflects its use as a truth-telling device, particularly for women: Mary Shelley dealt with the traumatic aftermath of birth and creation in *Frankenstein*, while the mad and mistreated character of Bertha Mason, confined to a single room by her husband in Charlotte Brontë's *Jane Eyre*, has become a byword for attempts in Victorian literature and culture to categorise woman as either domestic angels or dangerous madwomen.

Women writers frequently frame writing for their characters as both balm for present psychic injuries and the possibility of future escape. Sylvia Plath's 1963 novel *The Bell Jar* is another thinly-fictionalised account of a young woman whose literary and intellectual impulses are at odds with the urge towards marriage and motherhood. The descent into madness of Plath's protagonist, Esther Greenwood, is clearly attributed not just to her own psychological disturbance but to the position of many 1950s women facing, like Gilman over fifty years earlier, conflicts between the pull of their personal and professional lives and the impossibility of fully reconciling these tensions within existing society.

For Doris Lessing's protagonist in *The Golden Notebook*, a novel published the year before Plath's and deeply embedded in the burgeoning women's movement of the 1960s, writing is both a record of her own mental fragmentation and, latterly, a way of ordering, classifying, and making sense of her existence in a chaotic society and world. In Margaret Atwood's 1985 dystopia *The Handmaid's Tale*, which sees patriarchal power exercised through a religious rather than medical establishment, both reading and writing are officially forbidden for women. Writing down her situation in defiance of authority becomes for Atwood's narrator a revolutionary act. Gilman's narrator, her mind forcibly diverted from reading and writing, inevitably settles upon the wallpaper as the only intellectual challenge available to her. Her clandestine writing down of her experience is, as in *The Handmaid's Tale*, a subversive attempt to ensure the survival of her presence in the world and prevent her erasure by patriarchy, to prove the pen stronger than the (wall)paper.

***

If Gilman's portrayal of the pathologising of female resistance to social constraints was vividly echoed by later writers, it remains recognisable in the twenty-first century. Mark Fisher and others have written on the last few decades' promotion of a plethora of therapeutic and psychiatric treatments as a means of "fixing" those whose feelings of isolation, anxiety, and inadequacy are merely rational responses to life under capitalism. Today's overworked, underpaid, and insecure individuals, when showing signs of the stresses induced by their socioeconomic situation, are directed towards methods of "self-care", individual therapy, and meditation apps, rather than collective agitation for higher wages or trade union protections.

Gilman's narrator is made to deal with her inability to fit into her allocated social role by becoming an isolated, atomised individual confined to her room. She gains "freedom" by connecting with imaginary and hypothetical others — the myriad of women in the wallpaper — but she does so by conceptualising them as suffering alongside her, in psychic solidarity. Gilman herself threw off her rest-cure strictures with the help of "a wise friend", and left her husband and home to begin an independent life of lecture-tours and travel. It was connection and solidarity, not isolation and confinement, that she found necessary for psychological improvement. She went on to produce books including *Women and Economics* (1898), an analysis of the hidden value of women's labour within capitalism, as well as the feminist utopian novel *Herland* (1915). After her "narrow escape" from madness, Gilman's decision to set down her experience in writing in "The Yellow Wallpaper" was a further attempt to connect with others — and as readers, our sympathy or even identification with her narrator is another act of solidarity and connection.

After the narrator ostensibly becomes one with the woman in the wallpaper, although reduced to "creeping" round the confines of her room, she thinks of herself as free. But, she says, "I suppose I shall have to get back behind the pattern when it comes night, and that is hard!" Submitting to repetitive and stifling patterns is indeed hard, and refusing to do so is becoming harder every day, with the current resurgence of movements based on neo-Victorian principles which include consigning women back to the domestic realm. Medical diagnosis may have moved on in many ways, but reactionary religious and political establishments endure, and find new ways to weaponise and police women's choices. "The Yellow Wallpaper" is part of a continuum of resistance which documents how women have spent centuries emerging from the immuring patterns of domestic life, and which illustrates the psychological and political sacrifice involved in fading back into the wallpaper.

THE YELLOW WALLPAPER

Charlotte Perkins Gilman

It is very seldom that mere ordinary people like John and myself secure ancestral halls for the summer.

A colonial mansion, a hereditary estate, I would say a haunted house, and reach the height of romantic felicity—but that would be asking too much of fate!

Still I will proudly declare that there is something queer about it.

Else, why should it be let so cheaply? And why have stood so long untenanted?

John laughs at me, of course, but one expects that in marriage.

John is practical in the extreme. He has no patience with faith, an intense horror of superstition, and he scoffs openly at any talk of things not to be felt and seen and put down in figures.

John is a physician, and *perhaps*—(I would not say it to a living soul, of course, but this is dead paper and a great relief to my mind)—*perhaps* that is one reason I do not get well faster.

You see, he does not believe I am sick!

And what can one do?

If a physician of high standing, and one's own husband, assures friends and relatives that there is really nothing the matter with one but temporary nervous depression—a slight hysterical tendency—what is one to do?

My brother is also a physician, and also of high standing, and he says the same thing.

So I take phosphates or phosphites—whichever it is, and tonics, and journeys, and air, and exercise, and am absolutely forbidden to "work" until I am well again.

Personally, I disagree with their ideas.

Personally, I believe that congenial work, with excitement and change, would do me good.

But what is one to do?

I did write for a while in spite of them; but it *does* exhaust me a good deal—having to be so sly about it, or else meet with heavy opposition.

I sometimes fancy that in my condition if I had less opposition and more society and stimulus—but John says the very worst thing I can do is to think about my condition, and I confess it always makes me feel bad.

So I will let it alone and talk about the house.

The most beautiful place! It is quite alone, standing well back from the road, quite three miles from the village. It makes me think of English places that you read about, for there are hedges and walls and gates that lock, and lots of separate little houses for the gardeners and people.

There is a *delicious* garden! I never saw such a garden—large and shady, full of box-bordered paths, and lined with long grape-covered arbors with seats under them.

There were greenhouses, too, but they are all broken now.

There was some legal trouble, I believe, something about the heirs and co-heirs; anyhow, the place has been empty for years.

That spoils my ghostliness, I am afraid; but I don't care—there is something strange about the house—I can feel it.

I even said so to John one moonlight evening, but he said what I felt was a *draught*, and shut the window.

I get unreasonably angry with John sometimes. I'm sure I never used to be so sensitive. I think it is due to this nervous condition.

But John says if I feel so I shall neglect proper self-control; so I take pains to control myself—before him, at least, and that makes me very tired.

I don't like our room a bit. I wanted one downstairs that opened on the piazza and had roses all over the window, and such pretty old-fashioned chintz hangings! but John would not hear of it.

He said there was only one window and not room for two beds, and no near room for him if he took another.

He is very careful and loving, and hardly lets me stir without special direction.

I have a schedule prescription for each hour in the day; he takes all care from me, and so I feel basely ungrateful not to value it more.

He said we came here solely on my account, that I was to have perfect rest and all the air I could get. "Your exercise depends on your strength, my dear," said he, "and your food somewhat on your appetite; but air you can absorb all the time." So we took the nursery, at the top of the house.

It is a big, airy room, the whole floor nearly, with windows that look all ways, and air and sunshine galore. It was nursery first and then playground and gymnasium, I should judge; for the windows are barred for little children, and there are rings and things in the walls.

The paint and paper look as if a boys' school had used it. It is stripped off—the paper—in great patches all around the head of my bed, about as far as I can reach, and in a great place on the other side of the room low down. I never saw a worse paper in my life.

One of those sprawling flamboyant patterns committing every artistic sin.

It is dull enough to confuse the eye in following, pronounced enough to constantly irritate, and provoke study, and when you follow the lame, uncertain curves for a little distance they suddenly commit suicide—plunge off at outrageous angles, destroy themselves in unheard-of contradictions.

The color is repellant, almost revolting; a smouldering, unclean yellow, strangely faded by the slow-turning sunlight.

It is a dull yet lurid orange in some places, a sickly sulphur tint in others.

No wonder the children hated it! I should hate it myself if I had to live in this room long.

There comes John, and I must put this away,—he hates to have me write a word.

***

We have been here two weeks, and I haven't felt like writing before, since that first day.

I am sitting by the window now, up in this atrocious nursery, and there is nothing to hinder my writing as much as I please, save lack of strength.

John is away all day, and even some nights when his cases are serious.

I am glad my case is not serious!

But these nervous troubles are dreadfully depressing.

John does not know how much I really suffer. He knows there is no *reason* to suffer, and that satisfies him.

Of course it is only nervousness. It does weigh on me so not to do my duty in any way!

I meant to be such a help to John, such a real rest and comfort, and here I am a comparative burden already!

Nobody would believe what an effort it is to do what little I am able—to dress and entertain, and order things.

It is fortunate Mary is so good with the baby. Such a dear baby!

And yet I *cannot* be with him, it makes me so nervous.

I suppose John never was nervous in his life. He laughs at me so about this wallpaper!

At first he meant to repaper the room, but afterwards he said that I was letting it get the better of me, and that nothing was worse for a nervous patient than to give way to such fancies.

He said that after the wallpaper was changed it would be the heavy bedstead, and then the barred windows, and then that gate at the head of the stairs, and so on.

"You know the place is doing you good," he said, "and really, dear, I don't care to renovate the house just for a three months' rental."

"Then do let us go downstairs," I said, "there are such pretty rooms there."

Then he took me in his arms and called me a blessed little goose, and said he would go down cellar if I wished, and have it whitewashed into the bargain.

But he is right enough about the beds and windows and things.

It is as airy and comfortable a room as any one need wish, and, of course, I would not be so silly as to make him uncomfortable just for a whim.

I'm really getting quite fond of the big room, all but that horrid paper.

Out of one window I can see the garden, those mysterious

deep-shaded arbors, the riotous old-fashioned flowers, and bushes and gnarly trees.

Out of another I get a lovely view of the bay and a little private wharf belonging to the estate. There is a beautiful shaded lane that runs down there from the house. I always fancy I see people walking in these numerous paths and arbors, but John has cautioned me not to give way to fancy in the least. He says that with my imaginative power and habit of story-making a nervous weakness like mine is sure to lead to all manner of excited fancies, and that I ought to use my will and good sense to check the tendency. So I try.

I think sometimes that if I were only well enough to write a little it would relieve the press of ideas and rest me.

But I find I get pretty tired when I try.

It is so discouraging not to have any advice and companionship about my work. When I get really well John says we will ask Cousin Henry and Julia down for a long visit; but he says he would as soon put fire-works in my pillow-case as to let me have those stimulating people about now.

I wish I could get well faster.

But I must not think about that. This paper looks to me as if it *knew* what a vicious influence it had!

There is a recurrent spot where the pattern lolls like a broken neck and two bulbous eyes stare at you upside-down.

I get positively angry with the impertinence of it and the everlastingness. Up and down and sideways they crawl, and those absurd, unblinking eyes are everywhere. There is one place where two breadths didn't match, and the eyes go all up and down the line, one a little higher than the other.

I never saw so much expression in an inanimate thing before, and we all know how much expression they have! I used to lie awake as a child and get more entertainment and terror out of blank walls and plain furniture than most children could find in a toy-store.

I remember what a kindly wink the knobs of our big old bureau used to have, and there was one chair that always seemed like a strong friend.

I used to feel that if any of the other things looked too fierce I could always hop into that chair and be safe.

The furniture in this room is no worse than inharmonious, however, for we had to bring it all from downstairs. I suppose when this was used as a playroom they had to take the nursery things out, and no wonder! I never saw such ravages as the children have made here.

The wallpaper, as I said before, is torn off in spots, and it sticketh closer than a brother—they must have had perseverance as well as hatred.

Then the floor is scratched and gouged and splintered, the plaster itself is dug out here and there, and this great heavy bed, which is all we found in the room, looks as if it had been through the wars.

But I don't mind it a bit—only the paper.

There comes John's sister. Such a dear girl as she is, and so careful of me! I must not let her find me writing.

She is a perfect, and enthusiastic housekeeper, and hopes for no better profession. I verily believe she thinks it is the writing which made me sick!

But I can write when she is out, and see her a long way off from these windows.

There is one that commands the road, a lovely, shaded, winding road, and one that just looks off over the country. A lovely country, too, full of great elms and velvet meadows.

This wallpaper has a kind of sub-pattern in a different shade, a particularly irritating one, for you can only see it in certain lights, and not clearly then.

But in the places where it isn't faded, and where the sun is just so, I can see a strange, provoking, formless sort of figure, that seems to sulk about behind that silly and conspicuous front design.

There's sister on the stairs!

***

Well, the Fourth of July is over! The people are gone and I am tired out. John thought it might do me good to see a little company, so we just had mother and Nellie and the children down for a week.

Of course I didn't do a thing. Jennie sees to everything now.

But it tired me all the same.

John says if I don't pick up faster he shall send me to Weir Mitchell in the fall.

But I don't want to go there at all. I had a friend who was in his hands once, and she says he is just like John and my brother, only more so!

Besides, it is such an undertaking to go so far.

I don't feel as if it was worth while to turn my hand over for anything, and I'm getting dreadfully fretful and querulous.

I cry at nothing, and cry most of the time.

Of course I don't when John is here, or anybody else, but when I am alone.

And I am alone a good deal just now. John is kept in town

very often by serious cases, and Jennie is good and lets me alone when I want her to.

So I walk a little in the garden or down that lovely lane, sit on the porch under the roses, and lie down up here a good deal.

I'm getting really fond of the room in spite of the wallpaper. Perhaps *because* of the wallpaper.

It dwells in my mind so!

I lie here on this great immovable bed—it is nailed down, I believe—and follow that pattern about by the hour. It is as good as gymnastics, I assure you. I start, we'll say, at the bottom, down in the corner over there where it has not been touched, and I determine for the thousandth time that I *will* follow that pointless pattern to some sort of a conclusion.

I know a little of the principle of design, and I know this thing was not arranged on any laws of radiation, or alternation, or repetition, or symmetry, or anything else that I ever heard of.

It is repeated, of course, by the breadths, but not otherwise.

Looked at in one way each breadth stands alone, the bloated curves and flourishes—a kind of "debased Romanesque" with *delirium tremens*—go waddling up and down in isolated columns of fatuity.

But, on the other hand, they connect diagonally, and the sprawling outlines run off in great slanting waves of optic horror, like a lot of wallowing seaweeds in full chase.

The whole thing goes horizontally, too, at least it seems so, and I exhaust myself in trying to distinguish the order of its going in that direction.

They have used a horizontal breadth for a frieze, and

that adds wonderfully to the confusion.

There is one end of the room where it is almost intact, and there, when the cross-lights fade and the low sun shines directly upon it, I can almost fancy radiation after all,—the interminable grotesques seem to form around a common centre and rush off in headlong plunges of equal distraction.

It makes me tired to follow it. I will take a nap, I guess.

***

I don't know why I should write this.

I don't want to.

I don't feel able.

And I know John would think it absurd. But I *must* say what I feel and think in some way—it is such a relief!

But the effort is getting to be greater than the relief.

Half the time now I am awfully lazy, and lie down ever so much.

John says I mustn't lose my strength, and has me take cod-liver oil and lots of tonics and things, to say nothing of ale and wine and rare meat.

Dear John! He loves me very dearly, and hates to have me sick. I tried to have a real earnest reasonable talk with him the other day, and tell him how I wish he would let me go and make a visit to Cousin Henry and Julia.

But he said I wasn't able to go, nor able to stand it after I got there; and I did not make out a very good case for myself, for I was crying before I had finished.

It is getting to be a great effort for me to think straight. Just this nervous weakness, I suppose.

And dear John gathered me up in his arms, and just

carried me upstairs and laid me on the bed, and sat by me and read to me till it tired my head.

He said I was his darling and his comfort and all he had, and that I must take care of myself for his sake, and keep well.

He says no one but myself can help me out of it, that I must use my will and self-control and not let any silly fancies run away with me.

There's one comfort, the baby is well and happy, and does not have to occupy this nursery with the horrid wallpaper.

If we had not used it that blessed child would have! What a fortunate escape! Why, I wouldn't have a child of mine, an impressionable little thing, live in such a room for worlds.

I never thought of it before, but it is lucky that John kept me here after all. I can stand it so much easier than a baby, you see.

Of course I never mention it to them any more—I am too wise,—but I keep watch of it all the same.

There are things in that paper that nobody knows but me, or ever will.

Behind that outside pattern the dim shapes get clearer every day.

It is always the same shape, only very numerous.

And it is like a woman stooping down and creeping about behind that pattern. I don't like it a bit. I wonder—I begin to think—I wish John would take me away from here!

***

It is so hard to talk with John about my case, because he is so wise, and because he loves me so.

But I tried it last night.

It was moonlight. The moon shines in all around, just as the sun does.

I hate to see it sometimes, it creeps so slowly, and always comes in by one window or another.

John was asleep and I hated to waken him, so I kept still and watched the moonlight on that undulating wallpaper till I felt creepy.

The faint figure behind seemed to shake the pattern, just as if she wanted to get out.

I got up softly and went to feel and see if the paper *did* move, and when I came back John was awake.

"What is it, little girl?" he said. "Don't go walking about like that—you'll get cold."

I thought it was a good time to talk, so I told him that I really was not gaining here, and that I wished he would take me away.

"Why darling!" said he, "our lease will be up in three weeks, and I can't see how to leave before.

"The repairs are not done at home, and I cannot possibly leave town just now. Of course if you were in any danger I could and would, but you really are better, dear, whether you can see it or not. I am a doctor, dear, and I know. You are gaining flesh and color, your appetite is better. I feel really much easier about you."

"I don't weigh a bit more," said I, "nor as much; and my appetite may be better in the evening, when you are here, but it is worse in the morning when you are away."

"Bless her little heart!" said he with a big hug; "she shall be as sick as she pleases! But now let's improve the shining hours by going to sleep, and talk about it in the morning!"

"And you won't go away?" I asked gloomily.

"Why, how can I, dear? It is only three weeks more and

then we will take a nice little trip of a few days while Jennie is getting the house ready. Really, dear, you are better!"

"Better in body perhaps"—I began, and stopped short, for he sat up straight and looked at me with such a stern, reproachful look that I could not say another word.

"My darling," said he, "I beg of you, for my sake and for our child's sake, as well as for your own, that you will never for one instant let that idea enter your mind! There is nothing so dangerous, so fascinating, to a temperament like yours. It is a false and foolish fancy. Can you not trust me as a physician when I tell you so?"

So of course I said no more on that score, and we went to sleep before long. He thought I was asleep first, but I wasn't,—I lay there for hours trying to decide whether that front pattern and the back pattern really did move together or separately.

***

On a pattern like this, by daylight, there is a lack of sequence, a defiance of law, that is a constant irritant to a normal mind.

The color is hideous enough, and unreliable enough, and infuriating enough, but the pattern is torturing.

You think you have mastered it, but just as you get well under way in following, it turns a back somersault and there you are. It slaps you in the face, knocks you down, and tramples upon you. It is like a bad dream.

The outside pattern is a florid arabesque, reminding one of a fungus. If you can imagine a toadstool in joints, an interminable string of toadstools, budding and sprouting in endless convolutions,—why, that is something like it.

That is, sometimes!

There is one marked peculiarity about this paper, a thing nobody seems to notice but myself, and that is that it changes as the light changes.

When the sun shoots in through the east window—I always watch for that first long, straight ray—it changes so quickly that I never can quite believe it.

That is why I watch it always.

By moonlight—the moon shines in all night when there is a moon—I wouldn't know it was the same paper.

At night in any kind of light, in twilight, candlelight, lamplight, and worst of all by moonlight, it becomes bars! The outside pattern I mean, and the woman behind it is as plain as can be.

I didn't realize for a long time what the thing was that showed behind,—that dim sub-pattern,—but now I am quite sure it is a woman.

By daylight she is subdued, quiet. I fancy it is the pattern that keeps her so still. It is so puzzling. It keeps me quiet by the hour.

I lie down ever so much now. John says it is good for me, and to sleep all I can.

Indeed, he started the habit by making me lie down for an hour after each meal.

It is a very bad habit, I am convinced, for, you see, I don't sleep.

And that cultivates deceit, for I don't tell them I'm awake,—oh, no!

The fact is, I am getting a little afraid of John.

He seems very queer sometimes, and even Jennie has an inexplicable look.

It strikes me occasionally, just as a scientific hypothesis, that perhaps it is the paper!

I have watched John when he did not know I was looking, and come into the room suddenly on the most innocent excuses, and I've caught him several times *looking at the paper*! And Jennie too. I caught Jennie with her hand on it once.

She didn't know I was in the room, and when I asked her in a quiet, a very quiet voice, with the most restrained manner possible, what she was doing with the paper she turned around as if she had been caught stealing, and looked quite angry—asked me why I should frighten her so!

Then she said that the paper stained everything it touched, that she had found yellow smooches on all my clothes and John's, and she wished we would be more careful!

Did not that sound innocent? But I know she was studying that pattern, and I am determined that nobody shall find it out but myself!

***

Life is very much more exciting now than it used to be. You see I have something more to expect, to look forward to, to watch. I really do eat better, and am more quiet than I was.

John is so pleased to see me improve! He laughed a little the other day, and said I seemed to be flourishing in spite of my wallpaper.

I turned it off with a laugh. I had no intention of telling him it was *because* of the wallpaper—he would make fun of me. He might even want to take me away.

I don't want to leave now until I have found it out. There is a week more, and I think that will be enough.

***

I'm feeling ever so much better! I don't sleep much at night, for it is so interesting to watch developments; but I sleep a good deal in the daytime.

In the daytime it is tiresome and perplexing.

There are always new shoots on the fungus, and new shades of yellow all over it. I cannot keep count of them, though I have tried conscientiously.

It is the strangest yellow, that wallpaper! It makes me think of all the yellow things I ever saw—not beautiful ones like buttercups, but old foul, bad yellow things.

But there is something else about that paper—the smell! I noticed it the moment we came into the room, but with so much air and sun it was not bad. Now we have had a week of fog and rain, and whether the windows are open or not, the smell is here.

It creeps all over the house.

I find it hovering in the dining-room, skulking in the parlor, hiding in the hall, lying in wait for me on the stairs.

It gets into my hair.

Even when I go to ride, if I turn my head suddenly and surprise it—there is that smell!

Such a peculiar odor, too! I have spent hours in trying to analyze it, to find what it smelled like.

It is not bad—at first, and very gentle, but quite the subtlest, most enduring odor I ever met.

In this damp weather it is awful. I wake up in the night and find it hanging over me.

It used to disturb me at first. I thought seriously of burning the house—to reach the smell.

But now I am used to it. The only thing I can think of

that it is like is the *color* of the paper! A yellow smell.

There is a very funny mark on this wall, low down, near the mopboard. A streak that runs round the room. It goes behind every piece of furniture, except the bed, a long, straight, even *smooch*, as if it had been rubbed over and over.

I wonder how it was done and who did it, and what they did it for. Round and round and round—round and round and round—it makes me dizzy!

***

I really have discovered something at last.

Through watching so much at night, when it changes so, I have finally found out.

The front pattern *does* move—and no wonder! The woman behind shakes it!

Sometimes I think there are a great many women behind, and sometimes only one, and she crawls around fast, and her crawling shakes it all over.

Then in the very bright spots she keeps still, and in the very shady spots she just takes hold of the bars and shakes them hard.

And she is all the time trying to climb through. But nobody could climb through that pattern—it strangles so; I think that is why it has so many heads.

They get through, and then the pattern strangles them off and turns them upside-down, and makes their eyes white!

If those heads were covered or taken off it would not be half so bad.

***

I think that woman gets out in the daytime!

And I'll tell you why—privately—I've seen her!

I can see her out of every one of my windows!

It is the same woman, I know, for she is always creeping, and most women do not creep by daylight.

I see her on that long shaded lane, creeping up and down. I see her in those dark grape arbors, creeping all around the garden.

I see her on that long road under the trees, creeping along, and when a carriage comes she hides under the blackberry vines.

I don't blame her a bit. It must be very humiliating to be caught creeping by daylight!

I always lock the door when I creep by daylight. I can't do it at night, for I know John would suspect something at once.

And John is so queer now, that I don't want to irritate him. I wish he would take another room! Besides, I don't want anybody to get that woman out at night but myself.

I often wonder if I could see her out of all the windows at once.

But, turn as fast as I can, I can only see out of one at one time.

And though I always see her she may be able to creep faster than I can turn!

I have watched her sometimes away off in the open country, creeping as fast as a cloud shadow in a high wind.

***

If only that top pattern could be gotten off from the under one! I mean to try it, little by little.

I have found out another funny thing, but I shan't tell it this time! It does not do to trust people too much.

There are only two more days to get this paper off, and I believe John is beginning to notice. I don't like the look in his eyes.

And I heard him ask Jennie a lot of professional questions about me. She had a very good report to give.

She said I slept a good deal in the daytime.

John knows I don't sleep very well at night, for all I'm so quiet!

He asked me all sorts of questions, too, and pretended to be very loving and kind.

As if I couldn't see through him!

Still, I don't wonder he acts so, sleeping under this paper for three months.

It only interests me, but I feel sure John and Jennie are secretly affected by it.

***

Hurrah! This is the last day, but it is enough. John is to stay in town over night, and won't be out until this evening.

Jennie wanted to sleep with me—the sly thing! but I told her I should undoubtedly rest better for a night all alone.

That was clever, for really I wasn't alone a bit! As soon as it was moonlight, and that poor thing began to crawl and shake the pattern, I got up and ran to help her.

I pulled and she shook, I shook and she pulled, and before morning we had peeled off yards of that paper.

A strip about as high as my head and half around the room.

And then when the sun came and that awful pattern

began to laugh at me I declared I would finish it to-day!

We go away to-morrow, and they are moving all my furniture down again to leave things as they were before.

Jennie looked at the wall in amazement, but I told her merrily that I did it out of pure spite at the vicious thing.

She laughed and said she wouldn't mind doing it herself, but I must not get tired.

How she betrayed herself that time!

But I am here, and no person touches this paper but me—not *alive*!

She tried to get me out of the room—it was too patent! But I said it was so quiet and empty and clean now that I believed I would lie down again and sleep all I could; and not to wake me even for dinner—I would call when I woke.

So now she is gone, and the servants are gone, and the things are gone, and there is nothing left but that great bedstead nailed down, with the canvas mattress we found on it.

We shall sleep downstairs to-night, and take the boat home to-morrow.

I quite enjoy the room, now it is bare again.

How those children did tear about here!

This bedstead is fairly gnawed!

But I must get to work.

I have locked the door and thrown the key down into the front path.

I don't want to go out, and I don't want to have anybody come in, till John comes.

I want to astonish him.

I've got a rope up here that even Jennie did not find. If that woman does get out, and tries to get away, I can tie her!

But I forgot I could not reach far without anything to stand on!

This bed will *not* move!

I tried to lift and push it until I was lame, and then I got so angry I bit off a little piece at one corner—but it hurt my teeth.

Then I peeled off all the paper I could reach standing on the floor. It sticks horribly and the pattern just enjoys it! All those strangled heads and bulbous eyes and waddling fungus growths just shriek with derision!

I am getting angry enough to do something desperate. To jump out of the window would be admirable exercise, but the bars are too strong even to try.

Besides I wouldn't do it. Of course not. I know well enough that a step like that is improper and might be misconstrued.

I don't like to *look* out of the windows even—there are so many of those creeping women, and they creep so fast.

I wonder if they all come out of that wallpaper as I did?

But I am securely fastened now by my well-hidden rope—you don't get *me* out in the road there!

I suppose I shall have to get back behind the pattern when it comes night, and that is hard!

It is so pleasant to be out in this great room and creep around as I please!

I don't want to go outside. I won't, even if Jennie asks me to.

For outside you have to creep on the ground, and everything is green instead of yellow.

But here I can creep smoothly on the floor, and my shoulder just fits in that long smooch around the wall, so I cannot lose my way.

Why, there's John at the door!

It is no use, young man, you can't open it!

How he does call and pound!

Now he's crying for an axe.

It would be a shame to break down that beautiful door!

"John dear!" said I in the gentlest voice, "the key is down by the front steps, under a plantain leaf!"

That silenced him for a few moments.

Then he said—very quietly indeed, "Open the door, my darling!"

"I can't," said I. "The key is down by the front door under a plantain leaf!"

And then I said it again, several times, very gently and slowly, and said it so often that he had to go and see, and he got it, of course, and came in. He stopped short by the door.

"What is the matter?" he cried. "For God's sake, what are you doing!"

I kept on creeping just the same, but I looked at him over my shoulder.

"I've got out at last," said I, "in spite of you and Jennie! And I've pulled off most of the paper, so you can't put me back!"

Now why should that man have fainted? But he did, and right across my path by the wall, so that I had to creep over him every time!

ON GHOSTS

BY MARY SHELLEY

INTRODUCTION

LEILA TAYLOR

It was midnight, of course. My friend and I, along with six other guests and a medium, sat around a table in the middle of Lizzie Borden's parlour just a few feet away from where she (allegedly) whacked her father to death with an axe. We were an odd group: the Lizzie-philes, the amateur paranormal investigators, and us, the sceptical tourists, but we were all there for the same reason – ghosts. We all hoped to catch a glimpse of the supernatural, for the hair on our arms to stand on end, to touch the phantasmagoric. At one point, as the other guests took turns interrogating the spirits of Lizzie's mom and dad, the temperature of the air below my knees suddenly dropped. There wasn't a breeze. I didn't feel any movement in the air. It just suddenly got very, very cold in that one spot. I glanced down, looking for an open door or a window but saw none. I turned to my friend, who was also looking at the floor dumbfounded. She looked up at me, mouthing, "Do you feel that?" There was no reaction from anyone else in the room. It was a phenomenon that seemed to be there just for us. After about an hour, we said our goodbyes to Mr and Mrs Borden, had Pepperidge Farms cookies and coffee in the kitchen, and left. On the drive from Fall River back to New York City, we laughed at the apparent trickery of the medium and the earnestness of the ghosthunters with their EVP readers. But about that cold spot. We looked at each other and said, "That was weird, right?"

The first part of Mary Shelley's "On Ghosts" is an ode to that moment, the thrilling absence of a reasonable explanation. While the enlightened championed rationality, she looked to the fantastic. She longed for fantasy, mythology, and the mysterious. In an age that demanded reason, she asked, "what have we left to dream about?" Shelley admits that the only ghost she ever saw was in a dream, and she laments the death of a friend, longing for one last glimpse of him. Shelley wrote *Frankenstein*, the story of a creature resurrected from an assemblage of the dead, while she was mourning the death of her child. While horror story ghosts are meant to strike fear, ghost-hunting is a bit sad: the search for souls we can't let go of.

If you've never seen a ghost, I bet you know someone who has. Most of us have an aunt, a friend of a friend, a stranger you sat next to at a dinner party, someone who has that one story that sounds crazy, but they swear is true. Mary Shelley never saw a ghost, but she knew people who had. The second part of "On Ghosts" gives us the kind of anecdotal evidence we're all familiar with, tales told to Shelley from a friend or a friend of a friend. They are ghost stories twice removed, just close enough to rub up against someone else's fear without having to live through it. The first story is melancholic, the second is horrific, and the third is sweetly charming. Ghosts don't always scare. Sometimes they delight.

I thought I saw a ghost once, but I can't be absolutely certain that it wasn't a dream. It could have been an optical illusion or "a bit of undigested beef, a fragment of underdone potato" like Scrooge, but what's the fun in that? I know a drop in temperature isn't as exciting as a misty humanoid figure with a split skull. Still, it was enough to leave us a bit flummoxed, and really that's all we wanted, what Mary Shelley wanted, to experience something we couldn't explain. Maybe there was an air vent under our feet we couldn't see, or perhaps there is a reasonable scientific explanation for sudden isolated atmospheric changes, but if there is, I'd rather not know. I prefer to enjoy the mystery, to let the weird stay weird. It makes for a better story.

ON GHOSTS

MARY SHELLEY

I look for ghosts—but none will force
Their way to me; 'tis falsely said
That there was ever intercourse
Between the living and the dead.
— Wordsworth

What a different earth do we inhabit from that on which our forefathers dwelt! The antediluvian world, strode over by mammoths, preyed upon by the megatherion, and peopled by the offspring of the Sons of God, is a better type of the earth of Homer, Herodotus, and Plato, than the hedged-in cornfields and measured hills of the present day. The globe was then encircled by a wall which paled in the bodies of men, whilst their feathered thoughts soared over the boundary; it had a brink, and in the deep profound which it overhung, men's imaginations, eagle-winged, dived and flew, and brought home strange tales to their believing auditors. Deep caverns harboured giants; cloud-like birds cast their shadows upon the plains; while far out at sea lay islands of bliss, the fair paradise of Atlantis or El Dorado sparkling with untold jewels. Where are they now? The Fortunate Isles have lost the glory that spread a halo round them; for who deems himself nearer to the golden age, because he touches at the Canaries on his voyage to India? Our only riddle is the rise of the Niger; the interior of New Holland, our only *terra incognita*; and our sole *mare incognitum*, the north-west passage. But these are tame wonders, lions in leash; we do not invest Mungo Park, or the Captain of the Hecla, with divine attributes; no one fancies that the waters of the unknown river bubble up from hell's fountains, no strange and weird power is supposed to guide the ice-berg, nor do we fable that a stray pick-pocket from Botany Bay has found the gardens of the Hesperides within the circuit of the Blue Mountains. What have we left to dream about? The clouds are no longer the charioted servants of the sun, nor does he any more bathe his glowing brow in the bath of Thetis; the rainbow has ceased to be the messenger of the Gods, and thunder longer their awful voice, warning man of that which is to come. We have the sun which has been weighed and measured, but not understood; we have the assemblage of the planets, the congregation of the stars, and the yet unshackled ministration of the winds:—such is the list of our ignorance.

Nor is the empire of the imagination less bounded in its own proper creations, than in those which were bestowed on it by the poor blind eyes of our ancestors. What has become of enchantresses with their palaces of crystal and dungeons of palpable darkness? What of fairies and their wands? What of witches and their familiars? and, last, what of ghosts, with beckoning hands and fleeting shapes, which quelled the soldier's brave heart, and made the murderer disclose to the astonished noon the veiled work of midnight? These which were realities to our fore-fathers, in our wiser age—

—Characterless are grated
To dusty nothing.

Yet is it true that we do not believe in ghosts? There used to be several traditionary tales repeated, with their authorities, enough to stagger us when we consigned them to that place where that is which "is as though it had never been." But these are gone out of fashion. Brutus's dream has become a deception of his over-heated brain, Lord Lyttleton's vision is called a cheat; and one by one these inhabitants of deserted houses, moonlight glades, misty mountain tops, and midnight church-yards, have been ejected from their immemorial seats, and small thrill is felt when the dead majesty of Denmark blanches the cheek and unsettles the reason of his philosophic son.

But do none of us believe in ghosts? If this question be read at noon-day, when—

Every little corner, nook, and hole,
Is penetrated with the insolent light—

at such a time derision is seated on the features of my reader. But let it be twelve at night in a lone house; take up, I beseech you, the story of the Bleeding Nun; or of the Statue, to which the bridegroom gave the wedding ring, and she came in the dead of night to claim him, tall, and cold; or of the Grandsire, who with shadowy form and breathless lips stood over the couch and kissed the foreheads of his sleeping grandchildren, and thus doomed them to their fated death; and let all these details be assisted by solitude, flapping curtains, rushing wind, a long and dusky passage, an half open door—O, then truly, another answer may be given, and many will request leave to sleep upon it, before they decide whether there be such a thing as a ghost in the world, or out of the world, if that phraseology be more spiritual. What is the meaning of this feeling?

For my own part, I never saw a ghost except once in a dream. I feared it in my sleep; I awoke trembling, and lights and the speech of others could hardly dissipate my fear. Some years ago I lost a friend, and a few months afterwards visited the house where I had last seen him. It was deserted, and though in the midst of a city, its vast halls and spacious apartments occasioned the same sense of loneliness as if it had been situated on an uninhabited heath. I walked through the vacant chambers by twilight, and none save I awakened the echoes of their pavement. The far mountains (visible from the upper windows) had lost their tinge of sunset; the tranquil atmosphere grew leaden coloured as the golden stars appeared in the firmament; no wind ruffled the shrunk-up river which crawled lazily through the deepest channel of its wide and empty bed; the chimes of the Ave Maria had ceased, and the bell hung moveless in the open belfry: beauty invested a reposing world, and awe was inspired by beauty only. I walked through the rooms filled with sensations of the most poignant grief. He had been there; his living frame had been caged by those walls, his breath had mingled with that atmosphere, his step had been on those stones, I thought:—the earth is a tomb, the gaudy sky a vault, we but walking corpses. The wind rising in the east rushed through the open casements, making them shake;—methought, I heard, I felt—I know not what—but I trembled. To have seen him but for a moment, I would have knelt until the stones had been worn by the impress, so I told myself, and so I knew a moment after, but then I trembled, awe-struck and fearful. Wherefore? There is something beyond us of which we are ignorant. The sun drawing up the vaporous air makes a void, and the wind rushes in to fill it,—thus beyond our soul's ken there is an empty space; and our hopes and fears, in gentle gales or terrific whirlwinds, occupy the vacuum; and if it does no more, it bestows on the feeling heart a belief that influences do exist to watch and guard us, though they be impalpable to the coarser faculties.

I have heard that when Coleridge was asked if he believed in ghosts,—he replied that he had seen too many to put any trust in their reality; and the person of the most lively imagination that I ever knew echoed this reply. But these were not real ghosts (pardon, unbelievers, my mode of speech) that they saw; they were shadows, phantoms unreal; that while they appalled the senses, yet carried no other feeling to the mind of others than delusion, and were viewed as we might view an optical deception which we see to be true with our eyes, and know to be false with our understandings. I speak of other shapes. The returning bride, who claims the fidelity of her betrothed; the murdered man who shakes to remorse the murderer's heart; ghosts that lift the curtains at the foot of your bed as the clock chimes one; who rise all pale and ghastly from the churchyard and haunt their ancient abodes; who, spoken to, reply; and whose cold unearthly touch makes the hair stand stark upon the head; the true old-fashioned, foretelling, flitting, gliding ghost,—who has seen such a one?

I have known two persons who at broad daylight have owned that they believed in ghosts, for that they had seen one. One of these was an Englishman, and the other an Italian. The former had lost a friend he dearly loved, who for awhile appeared to him nightly, gently stroking his cheek and spreading a serene calm over his mind. He did not fear the appearance, although he was somewhat awe-stricken as each night it glided into his chamber, and,

Ponsi del letto insula sponda manca.
[placed itself on the left side of the bed]

This visitation continued for several weeks, when by some accident he altered his residence, and then he saw it no more. Such a tale may easily be explained away;—but several years had passed, and he, a man of strong and virile intellect, said that "he had seen a ghost."

The Italian was a noble, a soldier, and by no means addicted to superstition: he had served in Napoleon's armies from early youth, and had been to Russia, had fought and bled, and been rewarded, and he unhesitatingly, and with deep relief, recounted his story.

This Chevalier, a young, and (somewhat a miraculous incident) a gallant Italian, was engaged in a duel with a brother officer, and wounded him in the arm. The subject of the duel was frivolous; and distressed therefore at its consequences he attended on his youthful adversary during his consequent illness, so that when the latter recovered they became firm and dear friends. They were quartered together at Milan, where the youth fell desperately in love with the wife of a musician, who disdained his passion, so that it preyed on his spirits and his health; he absented himself from all amusements, avoided all his brother officers, and his only consolation was to pour his love-sick plaints into the ear of the Chevalier, who strove in vain to inspire him either with indifference towards the fair disdainer, or to inculcate lessons of fortitude and heroism.

As a last resource he urged him to ask leave of absence; and to seek, either in change of scene, or the amusement of hunting, some diversion to his passion. One evening the youth came to the Chevalier, and said, "Well, I have asked leave of absence, and am to have it early tomorrow morning, so lend me your fowling-piece and cartridges, for I shall go to hunt for a fortnight." The Chevalier gave him what he asked; among the shot there were a few bullets. "I will take these also," said the youth, "to secure myself against the attack of any wolf, for I mean to bury myself in the woods."

Although he had obtained that for which he came, the youth still lingered. He talked of the cruelty of his lady, lamented that she would not even permit him a hopeless attendance, but that she inexorably banished him from her sight, "so that," said he, "I have no hope but in oblivion." At length he rose to depart. He took the Chevalier's hand and said, "You will see her to-morrow, you will speak to her, and hear her speak; tell her, I entreat you, that our conversation tonight has been concerning her, and that her name was the last that I spoke." "Yes, yes," cried the Chevalier, "I will say any thing you please; but you must not talk of her any more, you must forget her." The youth embraced his friend with warmth, but the latter saw nothing more in it than the effects of his affection, combined with his melancholy at absenting himself from his mistress, whose name, joined to a tender farewell, was the last sound that he uttered.

When the Chevalier was on guard that night, he heard the report of a gun. He was at first troubled and agitated by it, but afterwards thought no more of it, and when relieved from guard went to bed, although he passed a restless, sleepless night. Early in the morning some one knocked at his door. It was a soldier, who said that he had got the young officer's leave of absence, and had taken it to his house; a servant had admitted him, and he had gone up stairs, but the room door of the officer was locked, and no one answered to his knocking, but something oozed through from under the door that looked like blood. The Chevalier, agitated and frightened at this account, hurried to his friend's house, burst open the door, and found him stretched on the ground—he had blown out his brains, and the body lay a headless trunk, cold, and stiff.

The shock and grief which the Chevalier experienced in consequence of this catastrophe produced a fever which lasted for some days. When he got well, he obtained leave of absence, and went into the country to try to divert his mind. One evening at moonlight, he was returning home from a walk, and passed through a lane with a hedge on both sides, so high that he could not see over them. The night was balmy; the bushes gleamed with fireflies, brighter than the stars which the moon had veiled with her silver light. Suddenly he heard a rustling near him, and the figure of his friend issued from the hedge and stood before him, mutilated as he had seen him after his death. This figure he saw several times, always in the same place. It was impalpable to the touch, motionless, except in its advance, and made no sign when it was addressed. Once the Chevalier took a friend with him to the spot. The same rustling was heard, the same shadow stept forth, his companion fled in horror, but the Chevalier staid, vainly endeavouring to discover what called his friend from his quiet tomb, and if any act of his might give repose to the restless shade.

Such are my two stories, and I record them the more

willingly, since they occurred to men, and to individuals distinguished the one for courage and the other for sagacity. I will conclude my "modern instances," with a story told by M. G. Lewis, not probably so authentic as these, but perhaps more amusing. I relate it as nearly as possible in his own words.

"A gentleman journeying towards the house of a friend, who lived on the skirts of an extensive forest, in the east of Germany, lost his way. He wandered for some time among the trees, when he saw a light at a distance. On approaching it he was surprised to observe that it proceeded from the interior of a ruined monastery. Before he knocked at the gate he thought it proper to look through the window. He saw a number of cats assembled round a small grave, four of whom were at that moment letting down a coffin with a crown upon it. The gentleman startled at this unusual sight, and, imagining that he had arrived at the retreats of fiends or witches, mounted his horse and rode away with the utmost precipitation. He arrived at his friend's house at a late hour, who sate up waiting for him. On his arrival his friend questioned him as to the cause of the traces of agitation visible in his face. He began to recount his adventures after much hesitation, knowing that it was scarcely possible that his friend should give faith to his relation. No sooner had he mentioned the coffin with the crown upon it, than his friend's cat, who seemed to have been lying asleep before the fire, leaped up, crying out, 'Then I am king of the cats;' and then scrambled up the chimney, and was never seen more."

PAR AVION

BY MARLÈNE DOTARD

INTRODUCTION

Grace Augur

In the winter of 1928, in the February–March issue of the London magazine *The Tale-Teller*, the short story "Par Avion" was published, listing the author as one "Marlène Lamort". In most respects, the magazine publication of a tale of supernatural horror was unremarkable; magazines like *The Tale-Teller* were known for featuring articles on spiritualism, mediumship, "psychic science", and the like, and in the early decades of the twentieth century, such publications continued to cater to the public fascination with the gothic, the grotesque, and the macabre. The publication of the author was also relatively unremarkable. Marlène Lamort — who was in fact French, but whose real name was Marlène Dotard — had already published a handful of stories in the years preceding this, and afterwards her writing on spiritualism would experience a degree of popularity, particularly in France, where her book *L'Esprit des microbes: vers une nouvelle théorie de l'évolution* (1929) would cause a minor scandal in the scientific circles of the Académie Française. I mention "Par Avion" for two reasons. One is the innovative writing techniques Dotard employs, which seem influenced by high modernist authors of the period such as James Joyce and Gertrude Stein. The short, staccato fragments give the story a delirious, visionary quality unusual for genre fiction of the time. The other reason I mention "Par Avion" is because of its remarkable premise. It's a premise that's worth spelling out, even at the risk of "spoiler alerts". So, you have been warned. And it's an idea that suddenly seems prescient now as I write this introduction, quarantined in my apartment during a global pandemic that is unlike anything experienced in recent history.

I won't hold out on you any longer. Dotard's idea is the following: in the same way that the spirits of the dead can communicate with the living via spiritual mediums, so can all biological beings — or rather, the ghosts of biological beings — also communicate with the living via mediumship. This not only includes human beings, but also animals, plants, and yes, even microbes. In other words, Dotard's thesis is that the spiritual séance is basically a point of contact with the spiritual essence or form of a once-living, biological organism. That "spirit" (Dotard often uses oblique terms like *l'esprit vital*, *pneuma*, or *spiritus*) is really the essence of a once-living, biological, organismic entity.

With "Par Avion" we see an early version of this theory at work. Dotard's story involves a woman (enticingly named Marlene) who is haunted by the spirit of her deceased husband. What's more, the entire narrative is told from the perspective of the dead husband, so that the whole story is told as an out-of-body experience. So far most of this is standard fare for supernatural fiction. But then we discover that the dead husband himself is also a medium, and continues to be so even in death. To this Dotard then adds the final touch: the husband — from beyond the grave — has become a passive medium for a plague virus (perhaps even the Black Death; it's not made clear in the story), and that virus is in turn using spiritual mediumship to further propagate itself across time into the modern era. In Dotard's story, the character of Marlene finds this out only too late, as the fate of human evolution is left hanging in the balance in the story's enigmatic and weirdly cosmic ending.

"Par Avion" is Dotard's earliest, and, in a way, most evocative attempt to combine science and spiritualism into a wildly imaginative tale about the fragility of the human condition. Clearly, given the cultural context, Dotard is musing on the conflux of early twentieth-century ideas about evolutionary biology, parapsychology, and even general relativity. For Dotard, it is quite possible that a microorganism is "communicable" not just in the epidemiological sense of the term, but it is also "communicable" in the spiritualist sense of the term as well. The implication — outlined in *L'Esprit des microbes* — is that not only human history but the history of biological life on the planet could be governed by these mediumistic "transmissions" of microorganisms. For Dotard, this explains the periodicity of pandemics throughout human history, and in her short but dense treatise she marshals in everything from the myth of Pandora's box to the 1918 Spanish Flu pandemic to ground her theory.

To say the least, all this is a hard pill to swallow — even as fiction. Dotard herself was not a scientist, and she made no claims to be doing science. She also lacked the accoutrements of the male-dominated world of decorations, titles, and institutional affiliations. In the 1920s, spiritualism had all but run out of steam, with most of the "evidence" revealed to have been the result of trick photography or just run-of-the-mill charlatanism. Interestingly, however, it was just at this time that spiritualism and its cousins had been taken up by the establishment; the London-based Society for Psychical Research had already led the way, counting among its cadre "respectable" members of the scientific community, and this would soon be followed by a plethora of like-minded organisations bent on utilising the findings of modern scientific inquiry to glean insights into the age-old questions of mortality, death, and the afterlife.

Though little is known of Dotard's life, we do know that she was in London between the wars, nominally as a precocious exchange student, though she soon abandoned her studies. Through a relative, Dotard was able to attend a number of the Society for Psychical Research's gatherings (which she enjoyed), as well as The Ghost Club (which she detested), in addition to the literary coterie with which she was already in touch. The few letters of hers that survive reveal a writer with an omnivorous interest in all topics, constantly inter-linking them with each other. She had read Henri Bergson on vitalism and William James on mysticism; she attended J.B.S. Haldane's courses on evolutionary biology but also Arthur Waite's lectures on ritual magic; among London's literati she rubbed shoulders with the likes of Cynthia Asquith, Dion Fortune, and Vernon Lee, and for a time would form a close relationship with the Austrian émigré author Mela Hartwig, herself a friend of Virginia Woolf. It is likely that these and other experiences found their way into her unique fiction, which has sadly all but disappeared from the annals of literary history. "Par Avion" is a gem of supernatural horror and spiritualist fiction. But it is just the tip of the iceberg. Dotard's wilfully synthetic approach to understanding the natural as well as the supernatural is perhaps more apt — and more needed — today than ever.

PAR AVION

MARLÈNE DOTARD

"Are you certain?"

"Yes," Marlene firmly answered. She would not let this chance – perhaps her last – fade into oblivion like another distant memory.

"Once the connection is established, it may not be so easily broken."

"I understand," Marlene replied. Her patience was wearing thin. Yet she understood the old woman's wariness.

"What is on *this* side of the connection may not be reflected on the *other* side."

"I accept your terms, Madame Carrière. That is why I've come to you. That is why you have agreed to lead these sessions. That is why you have brought this apparatus."

"The terms are not mine," the old woman replied, her tone flat and indifferent. "But very well. Let us begin."

It happened much quicker than Marlene had expected. It was as if time had suddenly become disjointed. Suddenly she found herself in a kind of waking dream, drifting in a body not her own…

***

I did not know I was dead. Marlene was on one knee clutching her face on our stone kitchen floor. In my desire to console her, why I did not know yet, I was aware that I could neither stand nor speak. The ease with which I could see all sides of the room at once, and move about as

I pleased, was liberating, like being granted the freedom to fly with one small condition attached; I could no longer meet the simplest of my objectives. How was this lack to be explained?

Landscapes of spirilla, star formations of chameleon-like bacilli hover quietly above forgotten formulae.

It was difficult to know what time of day it was, twilight or dusk, and in spite of this being our home, there was more in the room, more in *everything*, than I had sought to notice before. In this new light, dark as it was, objects and feelings I lacked terms for were exposed as different, familiar as they still were in certain respects. Marlene, while evidently the woman I married, appeared as a huddled concoction of shadows and sighs, the peeling paint on our shutters a collapsing sunset, and the yellow daisies our daughter had drawn on the pale milk walls, before I left for the Front, the unvisited flowerbeds of the world. Insight prohibited my enjoyment of these treasures; they could only exist for those that did not properly understand them yet, and the awful realisation that I had crossed a threshold forever, came over me.

Ages eroded, cellular walls wet with memory, electromagnetic animacules chimeric in phosphorescent night, icy without emotion, dendritic bodies held aloft in the dark blue séance room.

Though I could not communicate any of this, neither could I leave. The one counter to my feeling of utter weightlessness, that gave flesh and substance to my disembodied spirit, was Marlene's torment. This alone, feeding on my love and desire to comfort her, defined whatever it was that I had become.

In the strange pauses of mesmeric night, hidden transmissions of ash and soil and sorrowful tears, flagella telepathic in the depths, the despair the passivity this encystment.

If I could trace a path back to my old self, I could perhaps return as I was and reverse my unfortunate transformation, or even wake up, before the memory of my life faded for good. But this was no dream. For as bizarre as my predicament was, I knew I was still in the world of facts.

Calm logic of micrococci, far far behind distant sad suns, far far below drifting cold planets, ultra-microscopic endotoxic leagues of moonlit incubation.

I had been killed, killed for the second time in my life. The first death had occurred when the protected existence of the womb erupted into the world, but that too had ended, only I still did not know how. Was it a few hours ago, or had months passed since I ceased to be a man? It was useless to consult units of measurement, when the answer I sought was in my wife's face, hidden from me. Her fear was the clue; the fox-hole, where a small and supple shape hid amidst the deafening compression and noise, waiting until the clamour of the shelling stopped, and the whistle blew. To part with the instinct to survive, stand to my full height, and embrace the steel cacophony that awaited us sons of France, was my last worldly act, and after that, this; blissful communion with the consoling breeze that had bought me here.

Vast foundries of cellular bestiaries, sulphur nitrogen carbon phosphorous, quivering creeping sleepwalking communion –

No time has passed.

– osmosis of astral designs, striated up and down our livid lethargic anatomies, surrounded by erythrocyte mists, metabiotic eclipse engulfed in glorious flesh.

I look across to check for my epaulettes but there are no shoulders to wear them on, nor head for my Kepi, puttees to envelop my legs, or hands to hold a pistol or cane. Marlene has felt my passing because she has seen my decapitated ghost, hovering in pieces above her, on the ceiling of our kitchen, far from the front. I now know that if I can accept that I am dead I will be free to deliver my message.

Shimmering in our veins, immobile as black ink, dreams of crystalline forests involuted in time, fossil enigmas of microorganisms unfettered by eternity.

The intolerable force of her sorrow is the anchor that draws me towards her; yes, she will understand everything once I cease to deny the inevitable, and allow our souls to align in perfect knowledge.

The slow and swaying enzymatic reactions in a gravitational cadence, shadowed by constellated dreams, desiccation of lava and tectonic ruptures pathogenic in time.

Our narrow lives will open out towards our shared destiny, and celestial dissolution; the body lying in the vaporous mists on the Marne a skin I have shed for good. Though we can never meet in this world again, my spirit will eventually fill the entirety of her being again, and she will know me once more as she does now.

The terrifying lucidity of hermetic spirochetes, cold sphinx eyes raining down a litany of protozoa, dementia transmuted into reality, the sepulchre of katabolism, aerial bodies frenetic larvae, supranormal contact between distant creatures.

Now Marlene stands up abruptly, as if she has heard something, and wiping away her tears looks about the room cautiously. Then, pulling a wedding photo out of her apron pocket, she turns it on its back, and with a pencil taken from behind her ear, she quickly starts to scribble something down.

Do not forget, do not regret, and if ever that which is human re-appears in you then this immensity intimate will be engulfed in the derelict tombs of mortality.

As Marlene transcribes the opening line of her first novel, a dedication to me, I sense a darkness at my shoulder. I am not alone. Her love is letting in more than myself. I cannot stop this malignity from entering unless I undo the unity of our souls, and renounce our bond, and *it* knows that it is already too late for that.

Finally freed from the black magic of eternal circles, abysms incubating tempestual antibodies, incessant fulgurations of endothelial transmissions.

A rat scuttles across the floor, and then another. I cough, Marlene winces, and sneezes into her hand. There is blood in the palm. I close my eyes and watch her fingers lift a sheet over our daughter's face, Dr Beak casts a torch and burns this house to the ground, and processions of cattle carts creep through the shuttered streets of our town, while I hover above, an agent of destruction for all I fought to save.

Celestial moving masses of cytoplasm, coursing through ventrioles of eons, diagrammed in star patterns, sporulating dotted by secret mitosis, twisting contorted crawling across the membrane of space, stretching out their organnelles, blue claws transparent limbs shape-shifting energids.

Flies are gathering over the windows, Marlene touches her neck and perspiration breaks over her forehead; there is fever here, and the plague spinning in its spores.

Luminous mauve, iridescent violet, sleeping electricity, strange music strange melodies in the blood, delicate as dragonflies, amethyst destinies of improbable vistas.

I have joined her in life and in doing so condemned the living world to death. I touch her face but all she sees are the sunken red eyes of the abyss, diseases pouring through the decaying cavities of its grotesque smile, drawing her soul back from whence we came, where she will know me once more, as she does now.

A cataract of the species, forged in icy fires of epithelial stones, black skies unheard-of incantations, vibrational microbial mesmeric wings stretched wide across the gulf of consciousness.

My vital energy is theirs, billions of wriggling beings passing through my extremities to Marlene, following the path of our love into beds of wild flowers and butterflies.

Here everything quietly rumbles. Only the oblivion of time can dispose of destiny. You will become a planet, you will become cellular, you will become the antibiosis of every living thing that creeps and crawls and aches towards the eclipsed sun.

THE MONKEY'S PAW

BY W.W. JACOBS

INTRODUCTION

Carl Neville

I first read "The Monkey's Paw" when I was a child, and prior to re-reading it for this volume I had only read it once. Barrow-in-Furness, where I was born in 1970 and grew up, is a shipyard town in the north-west of England. Barrow Island, where we lived, is on the opposite side of the Yard from the town itself, a series of terraced streets and pre-war flats built as accommodation for the workers.

I don't know the exact age at which I read it, but it was before I was eleven when we still lived in the first house I ever lived in, 13 St Andrews Street. The street ran down into a vast green area of allotments, occasional factories, abandoned houses, disused reservoirs, artificial lakes, and ponds with decaying wooden jetties and shoals of fish, mysterious fenced-off areas belonging to the shipyard, burnt-out cars, abandoned JCBs, acres of dumped concrete plinths. This was the wild, mysterious topography we explored as children and that ringed the massive docks that allowed the ships and submarines made in the shipyard to pass out to the Irish Sea. I am certain that we still lived in that house, number 13, because the scenario that plays out in "The Monkey's Paw" took on a vivid and immediate life due to my surroundings.

It was impossible for me not to imagine that the family in the story were my own, not merely because I was a child and my experience was limited, but also because certain features of the story were evident in my daily life. The bareness and narrowness of the domestic scene, the occasional visitor from outside who has seen something of the world and returned with tales of adventure, the sense of relative isolation, the lack of money and the disavowal of any need for or interest in it, the focus on the child, the son, as the locus of the parent's hopes. The story's world and my own overlapped in ways I couldn't fully articulate at that age but understood in the implicit way a child grasps things. The process of that implicit understanding progressively becoming explicit, shifting and recomposing the world around them, making the familiar strange, renders the world the child inhabits, no matter how dismal or threadbare, numinous with the uncanny. And so I was doubly susceptible to the story's particular power.

"The Monkey's Paw" isn't only a story about class, but class is an inescapable, central element to the story's horror and pathos. Industrial accidents weren't common in my hometown in the 1970s, but they weren't unknown and there was always an underlying tension to the working day. Occasional deaths were reported, a friend's father was hospitalised for months due to a fall from scaffolding, people lost fingers and toes, eyes. Would my own father one day not return punctually at 4:30, half an hour after the siren that could be heard all over the town and that signalled the parameters of a normal working day sounded?

The sense of inexorability in the story, of vast, uncontrollable forces and trajectories, derives partly from its being so short and compressed and because the dread and horror accelerate so quickly. There is no sense that either the protagonists or the reader have time or space to escape confronting the father's awful moment of decision. But the sense of a relentless and unavoidable momentum was something I too felt pulling at me. The life described in the story, the dominance of industry and a life circumscribed by the inevitable and unavoidable route into the factory, also seemed true of the world I saw around me. I was on a path that led me and the overwhelming majority of my classmates into the Yard, a treadmill that my mother and father were trying in the limited ways they could to get me off. I had a fate they were trying to help me avoid.

Perhaps the death of a son in an industrial accident was my fate too. If not that exactly, for a bright, imaginative, working-class child, son of a bright and disillusioned working-class father, there would be something close to death, something that mangled and deformed. Years on the shop floor among huge and dangerous machines for little pay and mean surroundings, always dreaming of the larger, more expansive life that some great mechanism whose workings we could feel but not see had kept us from. The invisibility of the forces shaping and directing our lives, intangible yet as tightly binding as steel bands, manifested in us, avowed atheist, humanist, and rationalist though our household was, as a thick, sapping, and unacknowledged undercurrent of superstitious fear. Fear of the punishment that forces out there, beyond the small, knowable arenas of family, home, shipyard, town might inflict on us for attempting to have more, for not knowing our place, for unsettling the immutable and time-honoured order.

But as I say, the story isn't only about class, it's also a dramatisation, perhaps a concretisation of the underlying and unequal processes of attachment, relinquishment, and reorientation within the self and to the world that we conventionally term, in simple words that have to encapsulate the vast, unmappable domains of affect in which every individual is immersed: love, death, and loss.

Since that first reading, forty-plus years ago, I have lost a parent, the father I identified with the father in the story. He died in 2013, and I went through my first experience of grief and mourning. There is a theory that the dead need, in some sense, to die twice: first, they really, physically die; secondly, they die symbolically. There are certain public and private rituals that ensure that the death is appropriately recorded and memorialised so that a passage through mourning can be enacted and so that they can be truly laid to rest. But there is also a third stage suggested by "The Monkey's Paw", if one is to truly avoid being haunted by the dead. For mourning to be complete, perhaps a capacity for cruelty, for self-interest, is needed, and the ambivalence that has resided in a dark crevice at the heart of even the most deeply felt attachment becomes a resource to be drawn on.

You must, in some sense, in mourning, kill the dead again in the imagination, reach the point where not only would you not wish to have them back, for your sake or for theirs, but where you would actively resist their return. You must possess the capacity to kill them when they rise again in your mind and kill them repeatedly. "The Monkey's Paw" perhaps abreacts this unconscious process into one moment of intensely compressed figurative drama. It is necessary for the dead, the story suggests, to die three times to truly die, and we mourners are implicated in that third death, necessary for us if we are to truly survive them. They are gone, we miss them, but then also, more and more, we are freeing ourselves of them.

Or perhaps the story refigures a loss that's more prosaic and benign than that: the child must grow and leave you. If — like the parents in "The Monkey's Paw" and my own — social life outside the home and visitors are infrequent, that separation can be hard. Perhaps the son merely leaves to pursue the adventures the father has never known and yearns for, he has caught the truth of his own father's restlessness and has determined to live that life for him, he will be outside his influence, transformed, perhaps unrecognisable, perhaps he will look with pity on the father and his limitations, and yet the father must will the child out into the world beyond them and quash his own desire to call him home. The game of chess at the start of the story in which the father tries to hide his discomposure at losing and the affectionate, knowing glance that passes between mother and son suggests the struggle of the son to surpass the father without wounding him, the father to accept his diminished authority.

***

Since that first reading I have also become a parent, a father myself, late in life by anyone's standards, having waited long enough, perhaps, to finally believe I had outrun whatever currents might drag me back into the life I had avoided, and on reading it this time it has been the mother's role that has stayed with me. One obvious reading of "The Monkey's Paw", which will render it problematic for some, is the implication that the mother is a hysteric who cannot accept the death of or loss to the world of her son. Correspondingly it is then the father, as a heroic male rationalist in his role as the figure of the law, who intervenes and forces apart the mother-child dyad.

And yet, of course, the text also opens itself up to a quite different reading. Rather than the father having to intervene in the hysterical mother's grief, perhaps the mother sees that it is the father who cannot let go and who forces him to pass fully through the process of mourning, provoking him into wishing his son alive and returned, confronting him with his fear of that wish and forcing him to wish the child dead or gone again. It is the mother's role to bring her husband back from his own half-life, perhaps readjusting the imbalance in the relationship between husband and wife now the child has gone. The father is, after all, returned to some degree of vigour and manliness, brought out of his "apathy" only on hearing his wife's pain at the absence on the other side of the door, it is the "long loud wail of disappointment and misery from his wife" that gives him "the courage to run down to her side".

In a sense the story's central drama puts two types of love under pressure, the maternal and paternal. The mother has a double rebuke for the father for whom the child has become, or perhaps become again, an "it", a "thing". As her husband implores her not to answer the knock at the door and fumbles for the means to wish their child dead again, the mother tells him, "you are afraid of your own son", and asks him, "do you think I fear the child I have nursed?" There is a strange doubling here too, as perhaps the child that has returned has in a sense been reborn, delivered up again from the underworld the mother, in her labour, has plumbed and with whom she has journeyed back through the hinterland that grades slowly into the father's world of logic, language and law, that realm of very early infancy, abutting the Real, that Julia Kristeva terms the *chora*. One must be born twice just as one must die twice. For the father the boy has become a thing again, pure materiality and drive without a recognisable face, something to be feared, but for the mother, with her deeper and more primal bodily attachments, any form the child takes can elicit love, be nursed, fed, and consoled. Nor can anything truly break that bond.

In "The Monkey's Paw" it is not the mother who is blind and cannot understand that her child has become a thing, but the father, caught staring at his own image in the dark glass and unable to see past it, through into that world in which the mother–child relationship has formed. What perhaps might offer a sense of transcendence in the story rather than just an uneasy relief is if the father *could* follow his wife down those narrow stairs and join her in sliding back the heavy bolts that bar both access and ingress. But it is impossible for them to take that journey together; the dimensions they inhabit with regard to the child are incommensurable, there is an outside the father cannot enter, nor can he invite his own transfigured child, its emissary, in across the threshold. Perhaps he understands that he cannot himself encounter these things and survive without an equivalent transfiguration to the one his child has undergone. Out of necessity, then, he wishes it away and is left again with what he has always had: the cold gust, the empty street, the courage to at least get as far as the gate.

THE MONKEY'S PAW

W.W. JACOBS

I.

Without, the night was cold and wet, but in the small parlour of Laburnam Villa the blinds were drawn and the fire burned brightly. Father and son were at chess, the former, who possessed ideas about the game involving radical changes, putting his king into such sharp and unnecessary perils that it even provoked comment from the white-haired old lady knitting placidly by the fire.

"Hark at the wind," said Mr. White, who, having seen a fatal mistake after it was too late, was amiably desirous of preventing his son from seeing it.

"I'm listening," said the latter, grimly surveying the board as he stretched out his hand. "Check."

"I should hardly think that he'd come to-night," said his father, with his hand poised over the board.

"Mate," replied the son.

"That's the worst of living so far out," bawled Mr. White, with sudden and unlooked-for violence; "of all the beastly, slushy, out-of-the-way places to live in, this is the worst. Pathway's a bog, and the road's a torrent. I don't know what people are thinking about. I suppose because only two houses in the road are let, they think it doesn't matter."

"Never mind, dear," said his wife, soothingly; "perhaps you'll win the next one."

Mr. White looked up sharply, just in time to intercept a knowing glance between mother and son. The words died away on his lips, and he hid a guilty grin in his thin grey beard.

"There he is," said Herbert White, as the gate banged to loudly and heavy footsteps came toward the door.

The old man rose with hospitable haste, and opening the door, was heard condoling with the new arrival. The new arrival also condoled with himself, so that Mrs. White said, "Tut, tut!" and coughed gently as her husband entered the room, followed by a tall, burly man, beady of eye and rubicund of visage.

"Sergeant-Major Morris," he said, introducing him.

The sergeant-major shook hands, and taking the proffered seat by the fire, watched contentedly while his host got out whiskey and tumblers and stood a small copper kettle on the fire.

At the third glass his eyes got brighter, and he began to talk, the little family circle regarding with eager interest this visitor from distant parts, as he squared his broad shoulders in the chair and spoke of wild scenes and doughty deeds; of wars and plagues and strange peoples.

"Twenty-one years of it," said Mr. White, nodding at his wife and son.

"When he went away he was a slip of a youth in the warehouse. Now look at him."

"He don't look to have taken much harm," said Mrs. White, politely.

"I'd like to go to India myself," said the old man, "just to look round a bit, you know."

"Better where you are," said the sergeant-major, shaking his head. He put down the empty glass, and sighing softly, shook it again.

"I should like to see those old temples and fakirs and

jugglers," said the old man. "What was that you started telling me the other day about a monkey's paw or something, Morris?"

"Nothing," said the soldier, hastily. "Leastways nothing worth hearing."

"Monkey's paw?" said Mrs. White, curiously.

"Well, it's just a bit of what you might call magic, perhaps," said the sergeant-major, offhandedly.

His three listeners leaned forward eagerly. The visitor absent-mindedly put his empty glass to his lips and then set it down again. His host filled it for him.

"To look at," said the sergeant-major, fumbling in his pocket, "it's just an ordinary little paw, dried to a mummy."

He took something out of his pocket and proffered it. Mrs. White drew back with a grimace, but her son, taking it, examined it curiously.

"And what is there special about it?" inquired Mr. White as he took it from his son, and having examined it, placed it upon the table.

"It had a spell put on it by an old fakir," said the sergeant-major, "a very holy man. He wanted to show that fate ruled people's lives, and that those who interfered with it did so to their sorrow. He put a spell on it so that three separate men could each have three wishes from it."

His manner was so impressive that his hearers were conscious that their light laughter jarred somewhat.

"Well, why don't you have three, sir?" said Herbert White, cleverly.

The soldier regarded him in the way that middle age is wont to regard presumptuous youth. "I have," he said, quietly, and his blotchy face whitened.

"And did you really have the three wishes granted?" asked Mrs. White.

"I did," said the sergeant-major, and his glass tapped against his strong teeth.

"And has anybody else wished?" persisted the old lady.

"The first man had his three wishes. Yes," was the reply; "I don't know what the first two were, but the third was for death. That's how I got the paw."

His tones were so grave that a hush fell upon the group.

"If you've had your three wishes, it's no good to you now, then, Morris," said the old man at last. "What do you keep it for?"

The soldier shook his head. "Fancy, I suppose," he said, slowly. "I did have some idea of selling it, but I don't think I will. It has caused enough mischief already. Besides, people won't buy. They think it's a fairy tale; some of them, and those who do think anything of it want to try it first and pay me afterward."

"If you could have another three wishes," said the old man, eyeing him keenly, "would you have them?"

"I don't know," said the other. "I don't know."

He took the paw, and dangling it between his forefinger and thumb, suddenly threw it upon the fire. White, with a slight cry, stooped down and snatched it off.

"Better let it burn," said the soldier, solemnly.

"If you don't want it, Morris," said the other, "give it to me."

"I won't," said his friend, doggedly. "I threw it on the fire. If you keep it, don't blame me for what happens. Pitch it on the fire again like a sensible man."

The other shook his head and examined his new possession closely. "How do you do it?" he inquired.

"Hold it up in your right hand and wish aloud," said the sergeant-major, "but I warn you of the consequences."

"Sounds like the *Arabian Nights*," said Mrs. White, as she rose and began to set the supper. "Don't you think you might wish for four pairs of hands for me?"

Her husband drew the talisman from pocket, and then all three burst into laughter as the sergeant-major, with a look of alarm on his face, caught him by the arm.

"If you must wish," he said, gruffly, "wish for something sensible."

Mr. White dropped it back in his pocket, and placing chairs, motioned his friend to the table. In the business of supper the talisman was partly forgotten, and afterward the three sat listening in an enthralled fashion to a second instalment of the soldier's adventures in India.

"If the tale about the monkey's paw is not more truthful than those he has been telling us," said Herbert, as the door closed behind their guest, just in time for him to catch the last train, "we shan't make much out of it."

"Did you give him anything for it, father?" inquired Mrs. White, regarding her husband closely.

"A trifle," said he, colouring slightly. "He didn't want it, but I made him take it. And he pressed me again to throw it away."

"Likely," said Herbert, with pretended horror. "Why, we're going to be rich, and famous and happy. Wish to be an emperor, father, to begin with; then you can't be henpecked."

He darted round the table, pursued by the maligned Mrs. White armed with an antimacassar.

Mr. White took the paw from his pocket and eyed it dubiously. "I don't know what to wish for, and that's a fact," he said, slowly. "It seems to me I've got all I want."

"If you only cleared the house, you'd be quite happy, wouldn't you?" said Herbert, with his hand on his shoulder. "Well, wish for two hundred pounds, then; that'll just do it."

His father, smiling shamefacedly at his own credulity, held up the talisman, as his son, with a solemn face, somewhat marred by a wink at his mother, sat down at the piano and struck a few impressive chords.

"I wish for two hundred pounds," said the old man distinctly.

A fine crash from the piano greeted the words, interrupted by a shuddering cry from the old man. His wife and son ran toward him.

"It moved," he cried, with a glance of disgust at the object as it lay on the floor.

"As I wished, it twisted in my hand like a snake."

"Well, I don't see the money," said his son as he picked it up and placed it on the table, "and I bet I never shall."

"It must have been your fancy, father," said his wife, regarding him anxiously.

He shook his head. "Never mind, though; there's no harm done, but it gave me a shock all the same."

They sat down by the fire again while the two men finished their pipes.

Outside, the wind was higher than ever, and the old man started nervously at the sound of a door banging upstairs. A silence unusual and depressing settled upon all three, which lasted until the old couple rose to retire for the night.

"I expect you'll find the cash tied up in a big bag in the middle of your bed," said Herbert, as he bade them good-night, "and something horrible squatting up on top of the wardrobe watching you as you pocket your ill-gotten gains."

He sat alone in the darkness, gazing at the dying fire, and seeing faces in it. The last face was so horrible and so simian that he gazed at it in amazement. It got so vivid that, with a little uneasy laugh, he felt on the table for a glass containing a little water to throw over it. His hand grasped the monkey's paw, and with a little shiver he wiped his hand on his coat and went up to bed.

II.

In the brightness of the wintry sun next morning as it streamed over the breakfast table he laughed at his fears. There was an air of prosaic wholesomeness about the room which it had lacked on the previous night, and the dirty, shrivelled little paw was pitched on the sideboard with a carelessness which betokened no great belief in its virtues.

"I suppose all old soldiers are the same," said Mrs. White. "The idea of our listening to such nonsense! How could wishes be granted in these days? And if they could, how could two hundred pounds hurt you, father?"

"Might drop on his head from the sky," said the frivolous Herbert.

"Morris said the things happened so naturally," said his father, "that you might if you so wished attribute it to coincidence."

"Well, don't break into the money before I come back," said Herbert as he rose from the table. "I'm afraid it'll turn you into a mean, avaricious man, and we shall have to disown you."

His mother laughed, and following him to the door, watched him down the road; and returning to the breakfast table, was very happy at the expense of her husband's credulity. All of which did not prevent her from scurrying to the door at the postman's knock, nor prevent her from referring somewhat shortly to retired sergeant-majors of bibulous habits when she found that the post brought a tailor's bill.

"Herbert will have some more of his funny remarks, I expect, when he comes home," she said, as they sat at dinner.

"I dare say," said Mr. White, pouring himself out some beer; "but for all that, the thing moved in my hand; that I'll swear to."

"You thought it did," said the old lady soothingly.

"I say it did," replied the other. "There was no thought about it; I had just—What's the matter?"

His wife made no reply. She was watching the mysterious movements of a man outside, who, peering in an undecided fashion at the house, appeared to be trying to make up his mind to enter. In mental connection with the two hundred pounds, she noticed that the stranger was well dressed, and wore a silk hat of glossy newness. Three times he paused at the gate, and then walked on again. The fourth time he stood with his hand upon it, and then with sudden resolution flung it open and walked up the path. Mrs. White at the same moment placed her hands behind her, and hurriedly unfastening the strings of her apron, put that useful article of apparel beneath the cushion of her chair.

She brought the stranger, who seemed ill at ease, into the room. He gazed at her furtively, and listened in a preoccupied fashion as the old lady apologized for the appearance of the room, and her husband's coat, a garment which he usually reserved for the garden. She then waited as patiently as her sex would permit, for him to broach his business, but he was at first strangely silent.

"I—was asked to call," he said at last, and stooped and picked a piece of cotton from his trousers. "I come from 'Maw and Meggins.'"

The old lady started. "Is anything the matter?" she asked, breathlessly. "Has anything happened to Herbert? What is it? What is it?"

Her husband interposed. "There, there, mother," he said, hastily. "Sit down, and don't jump to conclusions. You've not brought bad news, I'm sure, sir;" and he eyed the other wistfully.

"I'm sorry—" began the visitor.

"Is he hurt?" demanded the mother, wildly.

The visitor bowed in assent. "Badly hurt," he said, quietly, "but he is not in any pain."

"Oh, thank God!" said the old woman, clasping her hands. "Thank God for that! Thank—"

She broke off suddenly as the sinister meaning of the assurance dawned upon her and she saw the awful confirmation of her fears in the other's averted face. She caught her breath, and turning to her slower-witted husband, laid her trembling old hand upon his. There was a long silence.

"He was caught in the machinery," said the visitor at length in a low voice.

"Caught in the machinery," repeated Mr. White, in a dazed fashion, "yes."

He sat staring blankly out at the window, and taking his wife's hand between his own, pressed it as he had been wont to do in their old courting-days nearly forty years before.

"He was the only one left to us," he said, turning gently to the visitor. "It is hard."

The other coughed, and rising, walked slowly to the window.

"The firm wished me to convey their sincere sympathy with you in your great loss," he said, without looking round. "I beg that you will understand I am only their servant and merely obeying orders."

There was no reply; the old woman's face was white, her eyes staring, and her breath inaudible; on the husband's face was a look such as his friend the sergeant might have carried into his first action.

"I was to say that 'Maw and Meggins' disclaim all responsibility," continued the other. "They admit no liability at all, but in consideration of your son's services, they wish to present you with a certain sum as compensation."

Mr. White dropped his wife's hand, and rising to his feet, gazed with a look of horror at his visitor. His dry lips shaped the words, "How much?"

"Two hundred pounds," was the answer.

Unconscious of his wife's shriek, the old man smiled faintly, put out his hands like a sightless man, and dropped, a senseless heap, to the floor.

III.

In the huge new cemetery, some two miles distant, the old people buried their dead, and came back to a house steeped in shadow and silence. It was all over so quickly that at first they could hardly realize it, and remained in a state of expectation as though of something else to happen—something else which was to lighten this load, too heavy for old hearts to bear.

But the days passed, and expectation gave place to resignation—the hopeless resignation of the old, sometimes mis-called apathy. Sometimes they hardly exchanged a word, for now they had nothing to talk about, and their days were long to weariness.

It was about a week after that the old man, waking suddenly in the night, stretched out his hand and found himself alone. The room was in darkness, and the sound of subdued weeping came from the window. He raised himself in bed and listened.

"Come back," he said, tenderly. "You will be cold."

"It is colder for my son," said the old woman, and wept afresh.

The sound of her sobs died away on his ears. The bed was warm, and his eyes heavy with sleep. He dozed fitfully, and then slept until a sudden wild cry from his wife awoke him with a start.

"The paw!" she cried wildly. "The monkey's paw!"

He started up in alarm. "Where? Where is it? What's the matter?"

She came stumbling across the room toward him. "I want it," she said, quietly. "You've not destroyed it?"

"It's in the parlour, on the bracket," he replied, marvelling. "Why?"

She cried and laughed together, and bending over, kissed his cheek.

"I only just thought of it," she said, hysterically. "Why didn't I think of it before? Why didn't you think of it?"

"Think of what?" he questioned.

"The other two wishes," she replied, rapidly. "We've only had one."

"Was not that enough?" he demanded, fiercely.

"No," she cried, triumphantly; "we'll have one more. Go down and get it quickly, and wish our boy alive again."

The man sat up in bed and flung the bedclothes from his quaking limbs. "Good God, you are mad!" he cried, aghast.

"Get it," she panted; "get it quickly, and wish—Oh, my boy, my boy!"

Her husband struck a match and lit the candle. "Get back to bed," he said, unsteadily. "You don't know what you are saying."

"We had the first wish granted," said the old woman, feverishly; "why not the second?"

"A coincidence," stammered the old man.

"Go and get it and wish," cried his wife, quivering with excitement.

The old man turned and regarded her, and his voice shook. "He has been dead ten days, and besides he—I would not tell you else, but—I could only recognize him by his clothing. If he was too terrible for you to see then, how now?"

"Bring him back," cried the old woman, and dragged him toward the door.

"Do you think I fear the child I have nursed?"

He went down in the darkness, and felt his way to the parlour, and then to the mantelpiece. The talisman was in its place, and a horrible fear that the unspoken wish might bring his mutilated son before him ere he could escape from the room seized upon him, and he caught his breath as he found that he had lost the direction of the door. His brow cold with sweat, he felt his way round the table, and groped along the wall until he found himself in the small passage with the unwholesome thing in his hand.

Even his wife's face seemed changed as he entered the room. It was white and expectant, and to his fears seemed to have an unnatural look upon it. He was afraid of her.

"Wish!" she cried, in a strong voice.

"It is foolish and wicked," he faltered.

"Wish!" repeated his wife.

He raised his hand. "I wish my son alive again."

The talisman fell to the floor, and he regarded it fearfully. Then he sank trembling into a chair as the old woman, with burning eyes, walked to the window and raised the blind.

He sat until he was chilled with the cold, glancing occasionally at the figure of the old woman peering through the window. The candle-end, which had burned below the rim of the china candlestick, was throwing pulsating shadows on the ceiling and walls, until, with a flicker larger than the rest, it expired. The old man, with an unspeakable sense of relief at the failure of the talisman, crept back to his bed, and a minute or two afterward the old woman came silently and apathetically beside him.

Neither spoke, but lay silently listening to the ticking of the clock. A stair creaked, and a squeaky mouse scurried noisily through the wall. The darkness was oppressive, and after lying for some time screwing up his courage, he took the box of matches, and striking one, went downstairs for a candle.

At the foot of the stairs the match went out, and he paused to strike another; and at the same moment a knock, so quiet and stealthy as to be scarcely audible, sounded on the front door.

The matches fell from his hand and spilled in the passage. He stood motionless, his breath suspended until the knock was repeated. Then he turned and fled swiftly back to his room, and closed the door behind him. A third knock sounded through the house.

"What's that?" cried the old woman, starting up.

"A rat," said the old man in shaking tones—"a rat. It passed me on the stairs."

His wife sat up in bed listening. A loud knock resounded through the house.

"It's Herbert!" she screamed. "It's Herbert!"

She ran to the door, but her husband was before her, and catching her by the arm, held her tightly.

"What are you going to do?" he whispered hoarsely.

"It's my boy; it's Herbert!" she cried, struggling mechanically.

"I forgot it was two miles away. What are you holding me for? Let go. I must open the door."

"For God's sake don't let it in," cried the old man, trembling.

"You're afraid of your own son," she cried, struggling. "Let me go. I'm coming, Herbert; I'm coming."

There was another knock, and another. The old woman with a sudden wrench broke free and ran from the room. Her husband followed to the landing, and called after her appealingly as she hurried downstairs. He heard the chain rattle back and the bottom bolt drawn slowly and stiffly from the socket. Then the old woman's voice, strained and panting.

"The bolt," she cried, loudly. "Come down. I can't reach it."

But her husband was on his hands and knees groping wildly on the floor in search of the paw. If he could only find it before the thing outside got in. A perfect fusillade of knocks reverberated through the house, and he heard the scraping of a chair as his wife put it down in the passage against the door. He heard the creaking of the bolt as it came slowly back, and at the same moment he found the monkey's paw, and frantically breathed his third and last wish.

The knocking ceased suddenly, although the echoes of it were still in the house. He heard the chair drawn back, and the door opened. A cold wind rushed up the staircase, and a long loud wail of disappointment and misery from his wife gave him courage to run down to her side, and then to the gate beyond. The street lamp flickering opposite shone on a quiet and deserted road.

A HAUNTED HOUSE

BY VIRGINIA WOOLF

INTRODUCTION

SIOUXZI CONNOR

I often find myself getting lost down these Google-fuelled curiosity spirals — you start with "what Sanskrit words do we still use in English", and end up two hours deep into the slave-trade of the Circassian people. The literary pathway of the phrase "every ghost story is a love story" was a particularly tangled one.

When it comes to the intertwining of ghost stories and love stories, I've been hooked for years. My fascination (OK, let's be accurate and say *obsession*), of feeling the traces left in houses, hotels, cars, and other evocative spaces we inhabit, of the longings, loves, passions, and traumas of those gone before, has echoed into my writing and films with increasing repetition. The spaces I've been most obsessed by are the proverbial little house in the forest, full of lost dreams reverberating from it into the trees as if a gramophone was left circling inside, and the salacious hotel room containing all the world's loneliness, isolation, and sexual tensions within four walls of steaming, smoke-stained red velvet.

As I was thinking through which story to choose for this anthology, and the earworm "every ghost story is a love story" would not leave me, Virginia Woolf sprang up immediately — a master at capturing the traces of longing and lost love within so few, yet such evocative words — her very short story "A Haunted House" being a perfect example. Woolf is, for me, a spectre in herself. I wish I'd never heard her recorded voice, for one thing — that piercing Queen's English will forever remind my ears of exactly which class we're dealing with here. Reading her now, I can't shake the feeling that she's sat in the corner of my room, hands folded neatly, pretending not to time how long I take to read each page. "A Haunted House" is set in Asheham House, her own haunted home, which she and her husband Leonard would jaunt to on weekends. According to Leonard's diaries, the sounds of two long-dead people could be heard every night in that house, walking room to room, sighing and whispering intently.

Alright, so, if Mr Woolf can admit it, I can too... confession time: the reason for my own fascination with these "traces" is that I've lived in haunted houses of my own, and stayed in haunted hotels, among other spaces. The most vivid instance was aged twenty-one, shooting a documentary in an abandoned girls' orphanage in west Sydney one winter morning (go figure). Some of the crew and I saw and felt the "traces" there so clearly, that I shut myself off from this sort of thing for years, out of terror (and also because I couldn't get any damned sleep). Years later, I slowly started welcoming the "traces" back and making peace with them. And "A Haunted House" is one of the most beautiful instances I've read of this ability to make peace with whoever loved and lost before and still lingers in a space. All these years later, I think I've finally learned how to stop being terrified and find the "light in the heart" of things, as Woolf so achingly describes it.

So back to the earworm. D.T. Max, writer for the *New Yorker* and author of *Every Love Story Is a Ghost Story: A Life of David Foster Wallace* had originally attributed the phrase to D.F. Wallace. But when Max had asked Wallace himself about it, he credited the phrase to none other than Virginia Woolf. I learned this just yesterday, thanks to another Google-spiral. The news prickled over my skin with the uncanny coincidence of it all.

A HAUNTED HOUSE

VIRGINIA WOOLF

Whatever hour you woke there was a door shutting. From room to room they went, hand in hand, lifting here, opening there, making sure—a ghostly couple.

"Here we left it," she said. And he added, "Oh, but here too!" "It's upstairs," she murmured. "And in the garden," he whispered "Quietly," they said, "or we shall wake them."

But it wasn't that you woke us. Oh, no. "They're looking for it; they're drawing the curtain," one might say, and so read on a page or two. "Now they've found it," one would be certain, stopping the pencil on the margin. And then, tired of reading, one might rise and see for oneself, the house all empty, the doors standing open, only the wood pigeons bubbling with content and the hum of the threshing machine sounding from the farm. "What did I come in here for? What did I want to find?" My hands were empty. "Perhaps it's upstairs then?" The apples were in the loft. And so down again, the garden still as ever, only the book had slipped into the grass.

But they had found it in the drawing room. Not that one could ever see them. The window panes reflected apples, reflected roses; all the leaves were green in the glass. If they moved in the drawing room, the apple only turned its yellow side. Yet, the moment after, if the door was opened, spread about the floor, hung upon the walls, pendant from the ceiling—what? My hands were empty. The shadow of a thrush crossed the carpet; from the deepest wells of silence the wood pigeon drew its bubble of sound. "Safe,

safe, safe," the pulse of the house beat softly. "The treasure buried; the room… " the pulse stopped short. Oh, was that the buried treasure?

A moment later the light had faded. Out in the garden then? But the trees spun darkness for a wandering beam of sun. So fine, so rare, coolly sunk beneath the surface the beam I sought always burnt behind the glass. Death was the glass; death was between us; coming to the woman first, hundreds of years ago, leaving the house, sealing all the windows; the rooms were darkened. He left it, left her, went North, went East, saw the stars turned in the Southern sky; sought the house, found it dropped beneath the Downs. "Safe, safe, safe," the pulse of the house beat gladly. "The Treasure yours."

The wind roars up the avenue. Trees stoop and bend this way and that. Moonbeams splash and spill wildly in the rain. But the beam of the lamp falls straight from the window. The candle burns stiff and still. Wandering through the house, opening the windows, whispering not to wake us, the ghostly couple seek their joy.

"Here we slept," she says. And he adds, "Kisses without number." "Waking in the morning—" "Silver between the trees—" "Upstairs—" "In the garden—" "When summer came—" "In winter snowtime—" The doors go shutting far in the distance, gently knocking like the pulse of a heart.

Nearer they come; cease at the doorway. The wind falls, the rain slides silver down the glass. Our eyes darken; we hear no steps beside us; we see no lady spread her ghostly cloak. His hands shield the lantern. "Look," he breathes. "Sound asleep. Love upon their lips."

Stooping, holding their silver lamp above us, long they look and deeply. Long they pause. The wind drives straightly;

the flame stoops slightly. Wild beams of moonlight cross both floor and wall, and, meeting, stain the faces bent; the faces pondering; the faces that search the sleepers and seek their hidden joy.

"Safe, safe, safe," the heart of the house beats proudly. "Long years—" he sighs. "Again you found me." "Here," she murmurs, "sleeping; in the garden reading; laughing, rolling apples in the loft. Here we left our treasure—" Stooping, their light lifts the lids upon my eyes. "Safe! safe! safe!" the pulse of the house beats wildly. Waking, I cry "Oh, is this your buried treasure? The light in the heart."

GREEN TEA

BY SHERIDAN LE FANU

INTRODUCTION

CLAIRE CRONIN

Sheridan Le Fanu's ghost story "Green Tea" is inhabited by haunted scholars: it centres on a tormented vicar and theological writer, Reverend Jennings; a metaphysical physician and occult detective, Doctor Martin Hesselius; an absent friend of Hesselius' — the chemist and playwright, Professor Van Loo of Leyden; and an unnamed archivist of Hesselius' letters, who gathers documents together, translates them into English, and frames the story for readers in the prologue.

Before we meet poor Jennings and his evil spirit, then, we have already been introduced to three characters — each of them specialists in some domain of knowledge and two of them already deceased. The horror of "Green Tea" tracks back in time. The story at the centre of the story — what Jennings experiences in his haunting — is itself a ghostly artefact of now-dead men. We learn of Jennings' ghost through the letters that Hesselius once wrote to the Professor, and are shown other documents by the now-dead author behind all this, Sheridan Le Fanu, whose fiction takes on the feeling of a scholar's memoir, bolstered by its use of primary sources. In "Green Tea", readers encounter excerpts of bound books, personal notes, a delivered message, and diary entries. Le Fanu creates a tension between fictional and nonfictional worlds, calling readers to question our faith in any collection of texts.

"Green Tea" is one of Le Fanu's best-known and most frightening ghost stories. It was written towards the end of the author's life, during a time of prolonged grief and isolation that followed the early death of Le Fanu's wife. Le Fanu's retreat from the public sphere during this decade earned him the nickname of Dublin's "Invisible Prince". According to reports from the era, Le Fanu "could occasionally be seen at night culling the Dublin bookstalls for works on spiritualism and the supernatural (it was supposed at this time that he become involved in the writings of Swedenborg), but for all intents and purposes he was lost to the outside world". It seemed that Le Fanu's withdrawal from external realities meant a reinvestment in writing, reading, and spiritual thought. Le Fanu became remarkably prolific in this period, publishing multiple novels and books of short stories. "Green Tea", in particular, first appeared in Charles Dickens' magazine *All the Year Round* in 1869, then was reprinted in Le Fanu's final collection, *In a Glass Darkly* in 1872. The following winter, an illness took Le Fanu to the other side.

Le Fanu's son, Brinsley, offered a reflection on his father's solitary habits, saying that the author "wrote mostly in bed at night" by candle, would fall asleep for a few hours, wake again around 2 am "amid the darkling shadows of the heavy furnishing and hangings of his old-fashioned room", and "brew himself some strong tea — which he drank copiously and frequently throughout the day — and write for a couple of hours in that eerie period of the night when human vitality is at its lowest ebb". The story of "Green Tea" was likely composed during these middle of the night, tea-fuelled sessions.

A final biographical note: Le Fanu, like the horror writers Arthur Machen and M.R. James, was born the son of a clergyman. He was versed in his father's theology, educated in law, earned his living as a journalist and writer, and came of age in a world split between a supernatural Christian paradigm and the occult-tinged materialism of the industrial Victorian era. While the stories from *In a Glass Darkly* are designed to thrill readers, the moral and spiritual questions they raise should be taken seriously — "Green Tea" is an example of this. Le Fanu's tales of horror emerge, ineluctably, out of the substance of his life.

In this way, "Green Tea" stands as a ghost story about scholarship, where the study of the occult — of magic, divination, metaphysics, and the paranormal — stands for all that is arcane, overly abstract, absurd, and impossible about ivory tower intellectualism. In "Green Tea", and other stories about haunted scholars, the quiet work of intellectual life is made more heroic through high-stakes supernatural melodrama, but also condemned as dangerously akin to necromancy. During the nineteenth century, scholarly and scientist characters — men like Dr Frankenstein, Dr Jekyll, Professor Van Helsing, and the many antiquarians of M.R. James — were known to break taboos, create monsters, and disturb the dead. From *Frankenstein* onwards, a scholar's specialist training in speculative sciences, ancient languages, archival digging, or textual interpretation placed him (for he was always male) in a precarious position. While such a scholar is uniquely prepared to deal with unusual phenomena — and sometimes to act like an exorcist, ghost debunker, or detective in a horror story — his attachment to his own research and area of expertise means that there are always elements he can't perceive or understand. Furthermore, his pursuit of an illicit research project — conducted outside of the social affiliations of the university, hospital, or lab — often leads to tragedy and disaster.

In "Green Tea", Doctor Hesselius and Reverend Jennings play the haunted scholars. Both are bachelors of independent means with sufficient time for reading and writing, and only tentative connections to the outside world. What makes them unique, however, is that they believe in a spiritual reality from the beginning of the story; they don't need to be converted by the haunting from scepticism to faith in the supernatural, as do the scholars in M.R. James' ghost stories. However, Hesselius and Jennings are also both modern, professional men, and therefore not wholly credulous. They're familiar with the mid-nineteenth century discourse of "spectral illusions", which teaches them to doubt their own minds and eyes, and Hesselius' spiritual beliefs, though occult and unusual, are based in an egotistic charlatanry. Jennings, on the other hand, is a man of God whose Christian faith is tainted by his obsession with the occult, or what he calls "the religious metaphysics of the ancients". While occultism fascinates both scholars, it also frightens Jennings, who, through several years of working on a project about paganism, discovers something sinister had taken root inside his vision of reality. Jennings' haunting is a spiritual crisis.

This topic of ancient metaphysics, occultism, or "paganism" (as it is called in the story) links Le Fanu's scholars together. Within this landscape of belief, Hesselius acts as the occult detective or proto-psychoanalyst to Jennings, who is the victim, and seeks to solve the mystery of Jennings' ghost and cure his metaphysical disease. Professor Van Loo, who Hesselius writes to in his letters, is an absent scholar. He shares an interest in occult theories, but only reads about the haunting from a distance. He is the mute end of Hesselius' correspondence, just as we, the readers, are to Le Fanu.

It is important that Hesselius is the author of an occult book called *Essays on Metaphysical Medicine* — an obscure text (long out of print) that Jennings has been deeply influenced by. This book is said to owe "a great deal" to the spiritual theories of the actual, historical occultist, Emanuel Swedenborg — an eighteenth-century mystic, also the son of a clergyman, who had much to say about the afterlife. It is Swedenborg, then, who stands behind Hesselius, Jennings, and Le Fanu, and secretly drives the plot of "Green Tea". The key to understanding the spiritual logic of this story is through the passages of Swedenborg that emerge.

***

In a crucial scene in Chapter III: "Dr. Hesselius Picks Up Something in Latin Books", Le Fanu gives readers what appear to be direct quotations from Swedenborg's mid-eighteenth century, twelve-volume Latin exegesis on Genesis, *Arcana Coelestia*. The real *Arcana* offers an occult reworking of the Lutheran Church of Sweden, wherein Swedenborg departs from conventional discussions of God, Christ, and Old Testament symbolism to take a detour into descriptions of first-hand experiences he's had with angels, devils, and ghosts. The *Arcana* that's represented in "Green Tea", however, is more ominous than eccentric. Even the physical description of the *Arcana* in Le Fanu's story suggests something unseemly. When Hesselius first discovers the book in Jennings' private library, we are told it is a decadent edition: "a very fine folio set, bound in the natty livery which theology affects, pure vellum, namely, gold letters, and carmine edges". The same feeling suffuses the description of Jennings' study, which we learn is luxurious and silent, but also "sombre", "decidedly gloomy", and "almost oppressive". So, the beautiful, expensive occult book that Hesselius finds in the beautiful, expensive private library is a bad omen. This is made obvious, because Jennings' *Arcana* bears the desperate scrawls of his hand — he has underlined certain passages and written a prayer for God's mercy (in Latin) at the foot of one page. Aesthetic pleasure gives way to a warning. About what?

The suspense of finding Jennings' book prepares us for Swedenborg's own language. But the selections Jennings underlined from the *Arcana* (and which the reader gets to read) stage an occult vision that is darker than the original. Let me offer an example. The third quoted passage from the *Arcana* in "Green Tea" reads: "There are with every man at least two evil spirits". Le Fanu has taken this phrase from the first volume of the *Arcana*, where it appears twice (in sections 697 and 904), with the same message. The full passage of section 697 is as follows, with Le Fanu's excerpt underlined:

> There are with every man at least two evil spirits and two angels; by means of the evil spirits he has communication with hell, and by means of the angels with heaven; without such communication with both he could not live a moment. Thus every man is in some society of infernals, although he is entirely ignorant of it; but their torments are not communicated to him, because he is in a state of preparation for eternal life.

In "Green Tea", we don't read the parts of the *Arcana* that deal with heaven, God's mercy, or benevolent angels. We aren't meant to learn what Swedenborg actually believed, which is that each of us is accompanied at all times by four spirits — two from hell and two from heaven — because Swedenborg thought that mankind was inherently evil and good, and had free will to choose between sides. As Swedenborg states in this paragraph, even our bodily life is made possible by these accompanying spirits. Through them, God's animating force flows in.

Swedenborg says he knows all this based on a personal experiment — he is a kind of occult scholar too. Once, he explains, he had his attendant spirits taken away from him, and found that he quickly began to "expire" without them by his side. Swedenborg writes: "If these communications were taken away, the man would fall dead as a stock."

In the fifth excerpt of Swedenborg that appears in "Green Tea", Le Fanu makes a similar shift towards the malevolent. This is what appears in the story:

> The evil spirits associated with man are, indeed from the hells, but when with man they are not then in hell, but are taken out thence. The place where they then are, is in the midst between heaven and hell, and is called the world of spirits — when the evil spirits who are with man, are in that world, they are not in any infernal torment, but in every thought and affection of man, and so, in all that the man himself enjoys. But when they are remitted into their hell, they return to their former state.

In "Green Tea", this paragraph gives readers clues about how to interpret Jennings' evil spirit and its motivations, or at least how Jennings himself might think of it. But again, Le Fanu has distorted Swedenborg's meaning in the service of horror. He omits two bright sentences from the original paragraph, which should come where the em-dash is. They read:

> In that world of spirits there are also good spirits, who are likewise associated with man: into that world also men come immediately after death, and, after some stay there, are either removed into the inferior earth, or let down into hell, or elevated into heaven, every one according to his life. In that world the hells are terminated from above, and are shut there, and opened at the Lord's good pleasure: in that world too heaven is terminated from beneath, and therefore it is the interstice separating heaven from hell: from these particulars may be known what the world of spirits is.

In "Green Tea", however, there are no good spirits who come to help the living, nor, it seems, is there a heavenly realm where human souls might go. We're only given half of Swedenborg's spiritual world. To be clear, I don't point out these discrepancies as a criticism of the author; Le Fanu creates fear in his horror story in part by quoting Swedenborg this way. I merely want to make visible a choice that might be obscured to uninitiated readers.

Similarly, while "Green Tea" engages questions of religious faith, it is not a pious cautionary tale. Consider how Jennings doesn't seek an exorcism from a priest, as he would if this were another kind of horror story, nor confess his torment to anyone in his religious community. Though we watch Jennings desperately pray to God for help, God

— like the "good spirits" exiled from the passages of Swedenborg — remains conspicuously absent. The vicar-scholar is left only with his books, theories, and another scholarly man, Doctor Hesselius. This may not be enough to save him.

Instead of prescribing readers a spiritual remedy or lesson at the end of the story (as Hesselius' character does), Le Fanu presents us with scenes that depict the dreadful limitations of the human mind to understand and right itself. Whether we choose to believe that Jennings was haunted by a spirit or fell prey to hallucinations brought on by too much study, "Green Tea" remains horrifying for its depiction of suffering. And this suffering, I think, is the particular suffering of writers, scholars, and intellectuals — those who enter their minds to lose their minds through constant reading, writing, theorising, and others acts of interpretation. Accordingly, readers of "Green Tea" are asked to take on the position of the haunted scholar and interpret the events of the story for themselves. Le Fanu's shocking conclusion is meant to remain ambiguously open, because a ghost story should slip past rational analysis. Readers (and any scholars here among us) are left with nothing to hold onto but a chill.

GREEN TEA

SHERIDAN LE FANU

PROLOGUE

Martin Hesselius, the German Physician

Though carefully educated in medicine and surgery, I have never practised either. The study of each continues, nevertheless, to interest me profoundly. Neither idleness nor caprice caused my secession from the honourable calling which I had just entered. The cause was a very trifling scratch inflicted by a dissecting knife. This trifle cost me the loss of two fingers, amputated promptly, and the more painful loss of my health, for I have never been quite well since, and have seldom been twelve months together in the same place.

In my wanderings I became acquainted with Dr. Martin Hesselius, a wanderer like myself, like me a physician, and like me an enthusiast in his profession. Unlike me in this, that his wanderings were voluntary, and he a man, if not of fortune, as we estimate fortune in England, at least in what our forefathers used to term "easy circumstances." He was an old man when I first saw him; nearly five-and-thirty years my senior.

In Dr. Martin Hesselius, I found my master. His knowledge was immense, his grasp of a case was an intuition. He was the very man to inspire a young enthusiast, like me, with awe and delight. My admiration has stood the test of time and survived the separation of death. I am sure it was well-founded.

For nearly twenty years I acted as his medical secretary. His immense collection of papers he has left in my care, to be arranged, indexed and bound. His treatment of some of these cases is curious. He writes in two distinct characters. He describes what he saw and heard as an intelligent layman might, and when in this style of narrative he had seen the patient either through his own hall-door, to the light of day, or through the gates of darkness to the caverns of the dead, he returns upon the narrative, and in the terms of his art and with all the force and originality of genius, proceeds to the work of analysis, diagnosis and illustration.

Here and there a case strikes me as of a kind to amuse or horrify a lay reader with an interest quite different from the peculiar one which it may possess for an expert. With slight modifications, chiefly of language, and of course a change of names, I copy the following. The narrator is Dr. Martin Hesselius. I find it among the voluminous notes of cases which he made during a tour in England about sixty-four years ago.

It is related in series of letters to his friend Professor Van Loo of Leyden. The professor was not a physician, but a chemist, and a man who read history and metaphysics and medicine, and had, in his day, written a play.

The narrative is therefore, if somewhat less valuable as a medical record, necessarily written in a manner more likely to interest an unlearned reader.

These letters, from a memorandum attached, appear to have been returned on the death of the professor, in 1819, to Dr. Hesselius. They are written, some in English, some in French, but the greater part in German. I am a faithful, though I am conscious, by no means a graceful translator, and although here and there I omit some passages, and shorten others, and disguise names, I have interpolated nothing.

CHAPTER I

Dr. Hesselius Relates How He Met the Rev. Mr. Jennings

The Rev. Mr. Jennings is tall and thin. He is middle-aged, and dresses with a natty, old-fashioned, high-church precision. He is naturally a little stately, but not at all stiff. His features, without being handsome, are well formed, and their expression extremely kind, but also shy.

I met him one evening at Lady Mary Heyduke's. The modesty and benevolence of his countenance are extremely prepossessing.

We were but a small party, and he joined agreeably enough in the conversation, He seems to enjoy listening very much more than contributing to the talk; but what he says is always to the purpose and well said. He is a great favourite of Lady Mary's, who it seems, consults him upon many things, and thinks him the most happy and blessed person on earth. Little knows she about him.

The Rev. Mr. Jennings is a bachelor, and has, they say sixty thousand pounds in the funds. He is a charitable man. He is most anxious to be actively employed in his sacred profession, and yet though always tolerably well elsewhere, when he goes down to his vicarage in Warwickshire, to engage in the actual duties of his sacred calling, his health soon fails him, and in a very strange way. So says Lady Mary.

There is no doubt that Mr. Jennings' health does break down in, generally, a sudden and mysterious way, sometimes in the very act of officiating in his old and pretty church at Kenlis. It may be his heart, it may be his brain. But so it has happened three or four times, or oftener, that after proceeding a certain way in the service, he has on a sudden stopped short, and after a silence, apparently quite unable to resume, he has fallen into solitary, inaudible prayer, his hands and his eyes uplifted, and then pale as death, and in the agitation of a strange shame and horror, descended trembling, and got into the vestry-room, leaving his congregation, without explanation, to themselves. This occurred when his curate was absent. When he goes down to Kenlis now, he always takes care to provide a clergyman to share his duty, and to supply his place on the instant should he become thus suddenly incapacitated.

When Mr. Jennings breaks down quite, and beats a retreat from the vicarage, and returns to London, where, in a dark street off Piccadilly, he inhabits a very narrow house, Lady Mary says that he is always perfectly well. I have my own opinion about that. There are degrees of course. We shall see.

Mr. Jennings is a perfectly gentlemanlike man. People, however, remark something odd. There is an impression a little ambiguous. One thing which certainly contributes to it, people I think don't remember; or, perhaps, distinctly remark. But I did, almost immediately. Mr. Jennings has a way of looking sidelong upon the carpet, as if his eye followed the movements of something there. This, of course, is not always. It occurs now and then. But often enough to give a certain oddity, as I have said, to his manner, and in this glance travelling along the floor there is something both shy and anxious.

A medical philosopher, as you are good enough to call

me, elaborating theories by the aid of cases sought out by himself, and by him watched and scrutinised with more time at command, and consequently infinitely more minuteness than the ordinary practitioner can afford, falls insensibly into habits of observation, which accompany him everywhere, and are exercised, as some people would say, impertinently, upon every subject that presents itself with the least likelihood of rewarding inquiry.

There was a promise of this kind in the slight, timid, kindly, but reserved gentleman, whom I met for the first time at this agreeable little evening gathering. I observed, of course, more than I here set down; but I reserve all that borders on the technical for a strictly scientific paper.

I may remark, that when I here speak of medical science, I do so, as I hope some day to see it more generally understood, in a much more comprehensive sense than its generally material treatment would warrant. I believe the entire natural world is but the ultimate expression of that spiritual world from which, and in which alone, it has its life. I believe that the essential man is a spirit, that the spirit is an organised substance, but as different in point of material from what we ordinarily understand by matter, as light or electricity is; that the material body is, in the most literal sense, a vesture, and death consequently no interruption of the living man's existence, but simply his extrication from the natural body—a process which commences at the moment of what we term death, and the completion of which, at furthest a few days later, is the resurrection "in power."

The person who weighs the consequences of these positions will probably see their practical bearing upon medical science. This is, however, by no means the proper place for displaying the proofs and discussing the consequences of this too generally unrecognized state of facts.

In pursuance of my habit, I was covertly observing Mr. Jennings, with all my caution—I think he perceived it—and I saw plainly that he was as cautiously observing me. Lady Mary happening to address me by my name, as Dr. Hesselius, I saw that he glanced at me more sharply, and then became thoughtful for a few minutes.

After this, as I conversed with a gentleman at the other end of the room, I saw him look at me more steadily, and with an interest which I thought I understood. I then saw him take an opportunity of chatting with Lady Mary, and was, as one always is, perfectly aware of being the subject of a distant inquiry and answer.

This tall clergyman approached me by-and-by; and in a little time we had got into conversation. When two people, who like reading, and know books and places, having travelled, wish to discourse, it is very strange if they can't find topics. It was not accident that brought him near me, and led him into conversation. He knew German and had read my Essays on Metaphysical Medicine which suggest more than they actually say.

This courteous man, gentle, shy, plainly a man of thought and reading, who moving and talking among us, was not altogether of us, and whom I already suspected of leading a life whose transactions and alarms were carefully concealed, with an impenetrable reserve from, not only the world, but his best beloved friends—was cautiously weighing in his own mind the idea of taking a certain step with regard to me.

I penetrated his thoughts without his being aware of it, and was careful to say nothing which could betray to his sensitive vigilance my suspicions respecting his position, or my surmises about his plans respecting myself.

We chatted upon indifferent subjects for a time but at last he said:

"I was very much interested by some papers of yours, Dr. Hesselius, upon what you term Metaphysical Medicine—I read them in German, ten or twelve years ago—have they been translated?"

"No, I'm sure they have not—I should have heard. They would have asked my leave, I think."

"I asked the publishers here, a few months ago, to get the book for me in the original German; but they tell me it is out of print."

"So it is, and has been for some years; but it flatters me as an author to find that you have not forgotten my little book, although," I added, laughing, "ten or twelve years is a considerable time to have managed without it; but I suppose you have been turning the subject over again in your mind, or something has happened lately to revive your interest in it."

At this remark, accompanied by a glance of inquiry, a sudden embarrassment disturbed Mr. Jennings, analogous to that which makes a young lady blush and look foolish. He dropped his eyes, and folded his hands together uneasily, and looked oddly, and you would have said, guiltily, for a moment.

I helped him out of his awkwardness in the best way, by appearing not to observe it, and going straight on, I said: "Those revivals of interest in a subject happen to me often; one book suggests another, and often sends me back a wild-goose chase over an interval of twenty years. But if you still care to possess a copy, I shall be only too happy to provide you; I have still got two or three by me—and if you allow me to present one I shall be very much honoured."

"You are very good indeed," he said, quite at his ease again, in a moment: "I almost despaired—I don't know how to thank you."

"Pray don't say a word; the thing is really so little worth that I am only ashamed of having offered it, and if you thank me any more I shall throw it into the fire in a fit of modesty."

Mr. Jennings laughed. He inquired where I was staying in London, and after a little more conversation on a variety of subjects, he took his departure.

CHAPTER II

The Doctor Questions Lady Mary and She Answers

"I like your vicar so much, Lady Mary," said I, as soon as he was gone. "He has read, travelled, and thought, and having also suffered, he ought to be an accomplished companion."

"So he is, and, better still, he is a really good man," said she. "His advice is invaluable about my schools, and all my little undertakings at Dawlbridge, and he's so painstaking, he takes so much trouble—you have no idea—wherever he thinks he can be of use: he's so good-natured and so sensible."

"It is pleasant to hear so good an account of his neighbourly virtues. I can only testify to his being an agreeable and gentle companion, and in addition to what you have told me, I think I can tell you two or three things about him," said I.

"Really!"

"Yes, to begin with, he's unmarried."

"Yes, that's right—go on."

"He has been writing, that is he *was*, but for two or three years perhaps, he has not gone on with his work, and the book was upon some rather abstract subject—perhaps theology."

"Well, he was writing a book, as you say; I'm not quite sure what it was about, but only that it was nothing that I cared for; very likely you are right, and he certainly did stop—yes."

"And although he only drank a little coffee here to-night, he likes tea, at least, did like it extravagantly."

"Yes, that's *quite* true."

"He drank green tea, a good deal, didn't he?" I pursued.

"Well, that's very odd! Green tea was a subject on which we used almost to quarrel."

"But he has quite given that up," said I.

"So he has."

"And, now, one more fact. His mother or his father, did you know them?"

"Yes, both; his father is only ten years dead, and their place is near Dawlbridge. We knew them very well," she answered.

"Well, either his mother or his father—I should rather think his father, saw a ghost," said I.

"Well, you really are a conjurer, Dr. Hesselius."

"Conjurer or no, haven't I said right?" I answered merrily.

"You certainly have, and it *was* his father: he was a silent, whimsical man, and he used to bore my father about his dreams, and at last he told him a story about a ghost he had seen and talked with, and a very odd story it was. I remember it particularly, because I was so afraid of him. This story was long before he died—when I was quite a child—and his ways were so silent and moping, and he used to drop in sometimes, in the dusk, when I was alone in the drawing-room, and I used to fancy there were ghosts about him."

I smiled and nodded.

"And now, having established my character as a conjurer, I think I must say good-night," said I.

"But how *did* you find it out?"

"By the planets, of course, as the gipsies do," I answered, and so, gaily we said good-night.

Next morning I sent the little book he had been inquiring after, and a note to Mr. Jennings, and on returning late that evening, I found that he had called at my lodgings, and left his card. He asked whether I was at home, and asked at what hour he would be most likely to find me.

Does he intend opening his case, and consulting me "professionally," as they say? I hope so. I have already conceived a theory about him. It is supported by Lady Mary's answers to my parting questions. I should like much to ascertain from his own lips. But what can I do consistently with good breeding to invite a confession? Nothing. I rather think he meditates one. At all events, my dear Van L., I shan't make myself difficult of access; I mean to return his visit tomorrow. It will be only civil in return for his politeness, to ask to see him. Perhaps something may come of it. Whether much, little, or nothing, my dear Van L., you shall hear.

CHAPTER III

Dr. Hesselius Picks Up Something in Latin Books

Well, I have called at Blank Street.

On inquiring at the door, the servant told me that Mr. Jennings was engaged very particularly with a gentleman, a clergyman from Kenlis, his parish in the country. Intending to reserve my privilege, and to call again, I merely intimated that I should try another time, and had turned to go, when the servant begged my pardon, and asked me, looking at me a little more attentively than well-bred persons of his order usually do, whether I was Dr. Hesselius; and, on learning that I was, he said, "Perhaps then, sir, you would allow me to mention it to Mr. Jennings, for I am sure he wishes to see you."

The servant returned in a moment, with a message from Mr. Jennings, asking me to go into his study, which was in effect his back drawing-room, promising to be with me in a very few minutes.

This was really a study—almost a library. The room was lofty, with two tall slender windows, and rich dark curtains. It was much larger than I had expected, and stored with books on every side, from the floor to the ceiling. The upper carpet—for to my tread it felt that there were two or three—was a Turkey carpet. My steps fell noiselessly. The bookcases standing out, placed the windows, particularly narrow ones, in deep recesses. The effect of the room was, although extremely comfortable, and even luxurious, decidedly gloomy, and aided by the silence, almost oppressive. Perhaps, however, I ought to have allowed something for association. My mind had connected peculiar ideas with Mr. Jennings. I stepped into this perfectly silent room, of a very silent house, with a peculiar foreboding; and its darkness, and solemn clothing of books, for except where two narrow looking-glasses were set in the wall, they were everywhere, helped this sombre feeling.

While awaiting Mr. Jennings' arrival, I amused myself by looking into some of the books with which his shelves were laden. Not among these, but immediately under them, with their backs upward, on the floor, I lighted upon a complete set of Swedenborg's *Arcana Cælestia*, in the original Latin, a very fine folio set, bound in the natty livery which theology affects, pure vellum, namely, gold letters, and carmine edges. There were paper markers in several of these volumes, I raised and placed them, one after the other, upon the table, and opening where these papers were placed, I read in the solemn Latin phraseology, a series of sentences indicated by a pencilled line at the margin. Of these I copy here a few, translating them into English.

"When man's interior sight is opened, which is that of his spirit, then there appear the things of another life, which cannot possibly be made visible to the bodily sight."...

"By the internal sight it has been granted me to see the things that are in the other life, more clearly than I see those that are in the world. From these considerations, it is evident that external vision exists from interior vision, and this from a vision still more interior, and so on."...

"There are with every man at least two evil spirits."...

"With wicked genii there is also a fluent speech, but harsh and grating. There is also among them a speech which is not fluent, wherein the dissent of the thoughts is perceived as something secretly creeping along within it."...

"The evil spirits associated with man are, indeed from the hells, but when with man they are not then in hell, but are taken out thence. The place where they then are, is in the midst between heaven and hell, and is called the world of spirits—when the evil spirits who are with man, are in that world, they are not in any infernal torment, but in every thought and affection of man, and so, in all that the man himself enjoys. But when they are remitted into their hell, they return to their former state."...

"If evil spirits could perceive that they were associated with man, and yet that they were spirits separate from him, and if they could flow in into the things of his body, they would attempt by a thousand means to destroy him; for they hate man with a deadly hatred."...

"Knowing, therefore, that I was a man in the body, they were continually striving to destroy me, not as to the body only, but especially as to the soul; for to destroy any man or spirit is the very delight of the life of all who are in hell; but I have been continually protected by the Lord. Hence it appears how dangerous it is for man to be in a living consort with spirits, unless he be in the good of faith."...

"Nothing is more carefully guarded from the knowledge of associate spirits than their being thus conjoint with a man, for if they knew it they would speak to him, with the intention to destroy him."...

"The delight of hell is to do evil to man, and to hasten his eternal ruin."

A long note, written with a very sharp and fine pencil, in Mr. Jennings' neat hand, at the foot of the page, caught my eye. Expecting his criticism upon the text, I read a word or two, and stopped, for it was something quite different, and began with these words, *Deus misereatur mei*—"May God compassionate me." Thus warned of its private nature, I averted my eyes, and shut the book, replacing all the volumes as I had found them, except one which interested me, and in which, as men studious and solitary in their habits will do, I grew so absorbed as to take no cognisance of the outer world, nor to remember where I was.

I was reading some pages which refer to "representatives" and "correspondents," in the technical language of Swedenborg, and had arrived at a passage, the substance of which is, that evil spirits, when seen by other eyes than those of their infernal associates, present themselves, by "correspondence," in the shape of the beast (*fera*) which represents their particular lust and life, in aspect direful and atrocious. This is a long passage, and particularises a number of those bestial forms.

CHAPTER IV

Four Eyes Were Reading the Passage

I was running the head of my pencil-case along the line as I read it, and something caused me to raise my eyes.

Directly before me was one of the mirrors I have mentioned, in which I saw reflected the tall shape of my friend, Mr. Jennings, leaning over my shoulder, and reading the page at which I was busy, and with a face so dark and wild that I should hardly have known him.

I turned and rose. He stood erect also, and with an effort laughed a little, saying:

"I came in and asked you how you did, but without succeeding in awaking you from your book; so I could not restrain my curiosity, and very impertinently, I'm afraid, peeped over your shoulder. This is not your first time of looking into those pages. You have looked into Swedenborg, no doubt, long ago?"

"Oh dear, yes! I owe Swedenborg a great deal; you will discover traces of him in the little book on Metaphysical Medicine, which you were so good as to remember."

Although my friend affected a gaiety of manner, there was a slight flush in his face, and I could perceive that he was inwardly much perturbed.

"I'm scarcely yet qualified, I know so little of Swedenborg. I've only had them a fortnight," he answered, "and I think they are rather likely to make a solitary man nervous—that is, judging from the very little I have read—I don't say that they have made me so," he laughed; "and I'm so very much obliged for the book. I hope you got my note?"

I made all proper acknowledgments and modest disclaimers.

"I never read a book that I go with, so entirely, as that of yours," he continued. "I saw at once there is more in it than is quite unfolded. Do you know Dr. Harley?" he asked, rather abruptly.

In passing, the editor remarks that the physician here named was one of the most eminent who had ever practised in England.

I did, having had letters to him, and had experienced from him great courtesy and considerable assistance during my visit to England.

"I think that man one of the very greatest fools I ever met in my life," said Mr. Jennings.

This was the first time I had ever heard him say a sharp thing of anybody, and such a term applied to so high a name a little startled me.

"Really! and in what way?" I asked.

"In his profession," he answered.

I smiled.

"I mean this," he said: "he seems to me, one half, blind—I mean one half of all he looks at is dark—preternaturally bright and vivid all the rest; and the worst of it is, it seems *wilful*. I can't get him—I mean he won't—I've had some experience of him as a physician, but I look on him as, in that sense, no better than a paralytic mind, an intellect half dead. I'll tell you—I know I shall some time—all about it," he said, with a little agitation. "You stay some months longer in England. If I should be out of town during your stay for a little time, would you allow me to trouble you with a letter?"

"I should be only too happy," I assured him.

"Very good of you. I am so utterly dissatisfied with Harley."

"A little leaning to the materialistic school," I said.

"A *mere* materialist," he corrected me; "you can't think how that sort of thing worries one who knows better. You won't tell any one—any of my friends you know—that I am hippish; now, for instance, no one knows—not even Lady Mary—that I have seen Dr. Harley, or any other doctor. So pray don't mention it; and, if I should have any threatening of an attack, you'll kindly let me write, or, should I be in town, have a little talk with you."

I was full of conjecture, and unconsciously I found I had fixed my eyes gravely on him, for he lowered his for a moment, and he said:

"I see you think I might as well tell you now, or else you are forming a conjecture; but you may as well give it up. If you were guessing all the rest of your life, you will never hit on it."

He shook his head smiling, and over that wintry sunshine a black cloud suddenly came down, and he drew his breath in, through his teeth as men do in pain.

"Sorry, of course, to learn that you apprehend occasion to consult any of us; but, command me when and how you like, and I need not assure you that your confidence is sacred."

He then talked of quite other things, and in a comparatively cheerful way and after a little time, I took my leave.

CHAPTER V

Dr. Hesselius is Summoned to Richmond

We parted cheerfully, but he was not cheerful, nor was I. There are certain expressions of that powerful organ of spirit—the human face—which, although I have seen them often, and possess a doctor's nerve, yet disturb me profoundly. One look of Mr. Jennings haunted me. It had seized my imagination with so dismal a power that I changed my plans for the evening, and went to the opera, feeling that I wanted a change of ideas.

I heard nothing of or from him for two or three days, when a note in his hand reached me. It was cheerful, and full of hope. He said that he had been for some little time so much better—quite well, in fact—that he was going to make a little experiment, and run down for a month or so to his parish, to try whether a little work might not quite set him up. There was in it a fervent religious expression of gratitude for his restoration, as he now almost hoped he might call it.

A day or two later I saw Lady Mary, who repeated what his note had announced, and told me that he was actually in Warwickshire, having resumed his clerical duties at Kenlis; and she added, "I begin to think that he is really perfectly well, and that there never was anything the matter, more than nerves and fancy; we are all nervous, but I fancy there is nothing like a little hard work for that kind of weakness, and he has made up his mind to try it. I should not be surprised if he did not come back for a year."

Notwithstanding all this confidence, only two days later I had this note, dated from his house off Piccadilly:

> Dear Sir,—I have returned disappointed. If I should feel at all able to see you, I shall write to ask you kindly to call. At present, I am too low, and, in fact, simply unable to say all I wish to say. Pray don't mention my name to my friends. I can see no one. By-and-by, please God, you shall hear from me. I mean to take a run into Shropshire, where some of my people are. God bless you! May we, on my return, meet more happily than I can now write.

About a week after this I saw Lady Mary at her own house, the last person, she said, left in town, and just on the wing for Brighton, for the London season was quite over. She told me that she had heard from Mr. Jenning's niece, Martha, in Shropshire. There was nothing to be gathered from her letter, more than that he was low and nervous. In those words, of which healthy people think so lightly, what a world of suffering is sometimes hidden!

Nearly five weeks had passed without any further news of Mr. Jennings. At the end of that time I received a note from him. He wrote:

> "I have been in the country, and have had change of air, change of scene, change of faces, change of everything—and in everything—but *myself*. I have made up my mind, so far as the most irresolute creature on earth can do it, to tell

my case fully to you. If your engagements will permit, pray come to me to-day, to-morrow, or the next day; but, pray defer as little as possible. You know not how much I need help. I have a quiet house at Richmond, where I now am. Perhaps you can manage to come to dinner, or to luncheon, or even to tea. You shall have no trouble in finding me out. The servant at Blank Street, who takes this note, will have a carriage at your door at any hour you please; and I am always to be found. You will say that I ought not to be alone. I have tried everything. Come and see."

I called up the servant, and decided on going out the same evening, which accordingly I did.

He would have been much better in a lodging-house, or hotel, I thought, as I drove up through a short double row of sombre elms to a very old-fashioned brick house, darkened by the foliage of these trees, which overtopped, and nearly surrounded it. It was a perverse choice, for nothing could be imagined more triste and silent. The house, I found, belonged to him. He had stayed for a day or two in town, and, finding it for some cause insupportable, had come out here, probably because being furnished and his own, he was relieved of the thought and delay of selection, by coming here.

The sun had already set, and the red reflected light of the western sky illuminated the scene with the peculiar effect with which we are all familiar. The hall seemed very dark, but, getting to the back drawing-room, whose windows command the west, I was again in the same dusky light.

I sat down, looking out upon the richly-wooded landscape that glowed in the grand and melancholy light which was every moment fading. The corners of the room were already dark; all was growing dim, and the gloom was insensibly toning my mind, already prepared for what was sinister. I was waiting alone for his arrival, which soon took place. The door communicating with the front room opened, and the tall figure of Mr. Jennings, faintly seen in the ruddy twilight, came, with quiet stealthy steps, into the room.

We shook hands, and, taking a chair to the window, where there was still light enough to enable us to see each other's faces, he sat down beside me, and, placing his hand upon my arm, with scarcely a word of preface began his narrative.

CHAPTER VI

How Mr. Jennings Met His Companion

The faint glow of the west, the pomp of the then lonely woods of Richmond, were before us, behind and about us the darkening room, and on the stony face of the sufferer—for the character of his face, though still gentle and sweet, was changed—rested that dim, odd glow which seems to descend and produce, where it touches, lights, sudden though faint, which are lost, almost without gradation, in darkness. The silence, too, was utter: not a distant wheel, or bark, or whistle from without; and within the depressing stillness of an invalid bachelor's house.

I guessed well the nature, though not even vaguely the particulars of the revelations I was about to receive, from that fixed face of suffering that so oddly flushed stood out, like a portrait of Schalken's, before its background of darkness.

"It began," he said, "on the 15th of October, three years and eleven weeks ago, and two days—I keep very accurate count, for every day is torment. If I leave anywhere a chasm in my narrative tell me.

"About four years ago I began a work, which had cost me very much thought and reading. It was upon the religious metaphysics of the ancients."

"I know," said I, "the actual religion of educated and thinking paganism, quite apart from symbolic worship? A wide and very interesting field."

"Yes, but not good for the mind—the Christian mind, I mean. Paganism is all bound together in essential unity, and, with evil sympathy, their religion involves their art, and both their manners, and the subject is a degrading fascination and the Nemesis sure. God forgive me!

"I wrote a great deal; I wrote late at night. I was always thinking on the subject, walking about, wherever I was, everywhere. It thoroughly infected me. You are to remember that all the material ideas connected with it were more or less of the beautiful, the subject itself delightfully interesting, and I, then, without a care."

He sighed heavily.

"I believe, that every one who sets about writing in earnest does his work, as a friend of mine phrased it, *on* something—tea, or coffee, or tobacco. I suppose there is a material waste that must be hourly supplied in such occupations, or that we should grow too abstracted, and the mind, as it were, pass out of the body, unless it were reminded often enough of the connection by actual sensation. At all events, I felt the want, and I supplied it. Tea was my companion—at first the ordinary black tea, made in the usual way, not too strong: but I drank a good deal, and increased its strength as

I went on. I never experienced an uncomfortable symptom from it. I began to take a little green tea. I found the effect pleasanter, it cleared and intensified the power of thought so, I had come to take it frequently, but not stronger than one might take it for pleasure. I wrote a great deal out here, it was so quiet, and in this room. I used to sit up very late, and it became a habit with me to sip my tea—green tea—every now and then as my work proceeded. I had a little kettle on my table, that swung over a lamp, and made tea two or three times between eleven o'clock and two or three in the morning, my hours of going to bed. I used to go into town every day. I was not a monk, and, although I spent an hour or two in a library, hunting up authorities and looking out lights upon my theme, I was in no morbid state as far as I can judge. I met my friends pretty much as usual and enjoyed their society, and, on the whole, existence had never been, I think, so pleasant before.

"I had met with a man who had some odd old books, German editions in mediæval Latin, and I was only too happy to be permitted access to them. This obliging person's books were in the City, a very out-of-the-way part of it. I had rather out-stayed my intended hour, and, on coming out, seeing no cab near, I was tempted to get into the omnibus which used to drive past this house. It was darker than this by the time the 'bus had reached an old house, you may have remarked, with four poplars at each side of the door, and there the last passenger but myself got out. We drove along rather faster. It was twilight now. I leaned back in my corner next the door ruminating pleasantly.

"The interior of the omnibus was nearly dark. I had observed in the corner opposite to me at the other side, and at the end next the horses, two small circular reflections, as it seemed to me of a reddish light. They were about two inches apart, and about the size of those small brass buttons that yachting men used to put upon their jackets. I began to speculate, as listless men will, upon this trifle, as it seemed. From what centre did that faint but deep red light come, and from what—glass beads, buttons, toy decorations—was it reflected? We were lumbering along gently, having nearly a mile still to go. I had not solved the puzzle, and it became in another minute more odd, for these two luminous points, with a sudden jerk, descended nearer and nearer the floor, keeping still their relative distance and horizontal position, and then, as suddenly, they rose to the level of the seat on which I was sitting and I saw them no more.

"My curiosity was now really excited, and, before I had time to think, I saw again these two dull lamps, again together near the floor; again they disappeared, and again in their old corner I saw them.

"So, keeping my eyes upon them, I edged quietly up my own side, towards the end at which I still saw these tiny discs of red.

"There was very little light in the 'bus. It was nearly dark. I leaned forward to aid my endeavour to discover what these little circles really were. They shifted position a little as I did so. I began now to perceive an outline of something black, and I soon saw, with tolerable distinctness, the outline of a small black monkey, pushing its face forward in mimicry to meet mine; those were its eyes, and I now dimly saw its teeth grinning at me.

"I drew back, not knowing whether it might not meditate a spring. I fancied that one of the passengers had forgot this ugly pet, and wishing to ascertain something of its temper, though not caring to trust my fingers to it, I poked my umbrella softly towards it. It remained immovable—up to it—*through* it. For through it, and back and forward it passed, without the slightest resistance.

"I can't, in the least, convey to you the kind of horror that I felt. When I had ascertained that the thing was an illusion, as I then supposed, there came a misgiving about myself and a terror that fascinated me in impotence to remove my gaze from the eyes of the brute for some moments. As I looked, it made a little skip back, quite into the corner, and I, in a panic, found myself at the door, having put my head out, drawing deep breaths of the outer air, and staring at the lights and tress we were passing, too glad to reassure myself of reality.

"I stopped the 'bus and got out. I perceived the man look oddly at me as I paid him. I dare say there was something unusual in my looks and manner, for I had never felt so strangely before."

CHAPTER VII

The Journey: First Stage

"When the omnibus drove on, and I was alone upon the road, I looked carefully round to ascertain whether the monkey had followed me. To my indescribable relief I saw it nowhere. I can't describe easily what a shock I had received, and my sense of genuine gratitude on finding myself, as I supposed, quite rid of it.

"I had got out a little before we reached this house, two or three hundred steps. A brick wall runs along the footpath, and inside the wall is a hedge of yew, or some dark evergreen of that kind, and within that again the row of fine trees which you may have remarked as you came.

"This brick wall is about as high as my shoulder, and happening to raise my eyes I saw the monkey, with that stooping gait, on all fours, walking or creeping, close beside me, on top of the wall. I stopped, looking at it with a feeling of loathing and horror. As I stopped so did it. It sat up on the wall with its long hands on its knees looking at me. There was not light enough to see it much more than in outline, nor was it dark enough to bring the peculiar light of its eyes into strong relief. I still saw, however, that red foggy light plainly enough. It did not show its teeth, nor exhibit any sign of irritation, but seemed jaded and sulky, and was observing me steadily.

"I drew back into the middle of the road. It was an unconscious recoil, and there I stood, still looking at it. It did not move.

"With an instinctive determination to try something—anything, I turned about and walked briskly towards town with askance look, all the time, watching the movements of the beast. It crept swiftly along the wall, at exactly my pace.

"Where the wall ends, near the turn of the road, it came down, and with a wiry spring or two brought itself close to my feet, and continued to keep up with me, as I quickened my pace. It was at my left side, so close to my leg that I felt every moment as if I should tread upon it.

"The road was quite deserted and silent, and it was darker every moment. I stopped dismayed and bewildered, turning as I did so, the other way—I mean, towards this house, away from which I had been walking. When I stood still, the monkey drew back to a distance of, I suppose, about five or six yards, and remained stationary, watching me.

"I had been more agitated than I have said. I had read, of course, as everyone has, something about 'spectral illusions,' as you physicians term the phenomena of such cases. I considered my situation, and looked my misfortune in the face.

"These affections, I had read, are sometimes transitory and sometimes obstinate. I had read of cases in which the appearance, at first harmless, had, step by step, degenerated into something direful and insupportable, and ended by wearing its victim out. Still as I stood there, but for my bestial companion, quite alone, I tried to comfort myself by repeating again and again the assurance, 'the thing is purely disease, a well-known physical affection, as distinctly as small-pox or neuralgia. Doctors are all agreed on that, philosophy demonstrates it. I must not be a fool. I've been sitting up too late, and I daresay my digestion is quite wrong, and, with God's help, I shall be all right, and this is but a symptom of nervous dyspepsia.' Did I believe all this? Not one word of it, no more than any other miserable being ever did who is once seized and riveted in this satanic captivity. Against my convictions, I might say my knowledge, I was simply bullying myself into a false courage.

"I now walked homeward. I had only a few hundred yards to go. I had forced myself into a sort of resignation, but I had not got over the sickening shock and the flurry of the first certainty of my misfortune.

"I made up my mind to pass the night at home. The brute moved close beside me, and I fancied there was the sort of anxious drawing toward the house, which one sees in tired horses or dogs, sometimes as they come toward home.

"I was afraid to go into town, I was afraid of any one's seeing and recognizing me. I was conscious of an irrepressible agitation in my manner. Also, I was afraid of any violent change in my habits, such as going to a place of amusement, or walking from home in order to fatigue myself. At the hall door it waited till I mounted the steps, and when the door was opened entered with me.

"I drank no tea that night. I got cigars and some brandy and water. My idea was that I should act upon my material system, and by living for a while in sensation apart from thought, send myself forcibly, as it were, into a new groove. I came up here to this drawing-room. I sat just here. The monkey then got upon a small table that then stood *there*. It looked dazed and languid. An irrepressible uneasiness as to its movements kept my eyes always upon it. Its eyes were half closed, but I could see them glow. It was looking steadily at me. In all situations, at all hours, it is awake and looking at me. That never changes.

"I shall not continue in detail my narrative of this particular night. I shall describe, rather, the phenomena of the first year, which never varied, essentially. I shall describe the monkey as it appeared in daylight. In the dark, as you shall presently hear, there are peculiarities. It is a small monkey, perfectly black. It had only one peculiarity—a character of malignity—unfathomable malignity. During the first year it looked sullen and sick. But this character of intense malice and vigilance was always underlying that surly languor. During all that time it acted as if on a plan of giving me as little trouble as was consistent with watching me. Its eyes were never off me. I have never lost sight of it, except in my sleep, light or dark, day or night, since it came here, excepting when it withdraws for some weeks at a time, unaccountably.

"In total dark it is visible as in daylight. I do not mean merely its eyes. It is *all* visible distinctly in a halo that resembles a glow of red embers, and which accompanies it in all its movements.

"When it leaves me for a time, it is always at night, in the dark, and in the same way. It grows at first uneasy, and then furious, and then advances towards me, grinning and shaking, its paws clenched, and, at the same time, there comes the appearance of fire in the grate. I never have any fire. I can't sleep in the room where there is any, and it draws nearer and nearer to the chimney, quivering, it seems, with rage, and when its fury rises to the highest pitch, it springs into the grate, and up the chimney, and I see it no more.

"When first this happened, I thought I was released. I was now a new man. A day passed—a night—and no return, and a blessed week—a week—another week. I was always on my knees, Dr. Hesselius, always, thanking God and praying. A whole month passed of liberty, but on a sudden, it was with me again."

CHAPTER VIII
The Second Stage

"It was with me, and the malice which before was torpid under a sullen exterior, was now active. It was perfectly unchanged in every other respect. This new energy was apparent in its activity and its looks, and soon in other ways.

"For a time, you will understand, the change was shown only in an increased vivacity, and an air of menace, as if it were always brooding over some atrocious plan. Its eyes, as before, were never off me."

"Is it here now?" I asked.

"No," he replied, "it has been absent exactly a fortnight and a day—fifteen days. It has sometimes been away so long as nearly two months, once for three. Its absence always exceeds a fortnight, although it may be but by a single day. Fifteen days having past since I saw it last, it may return now at any moment."

"Is its return," I asked, "accompanied by any peculiar manifestation?"

"Nothing—no," he said. "It is simply with me again. On lifting my eyes from a book, or turning my head, I see it, as usual, looking at me, and then it remains, as before, for its appointed time. I have never told so much and so minutely before to any one."

I perceived that he was agitated, and looking like death, and he repeatedly applied his handkerchief to his forehead; I suggested that he might be tired, and told him that I would call, with pleasure, in the morning, but he said:

"No, if you don't mind hearing it all now. I have got so far, and I should prefer making one effort of it. When I spoke to Dr. Harley, I had nothing like so much to tell. You are a philosophic physician. You give spirit its proper rank. If this thing is real—"

He paused looking at me with agitated inquiry.

"We can discuss it by-and-by, and very fully. I will give you all I think," I answered, after an interval.

"Well—very well. If it is anything real, I say, it is prevailing, little by little, and drawing me more interiorly into hell. Optic nerves, he talked of. Ah! well—there are other nerves of communication. May God Almighty help me! You shall hear.

"Its power of action, I tell you, had increased. Its malice became, in a way, aggressive. About two years ago, some questions that were pending between me and the bishop having been settled, I went down to my parish in Warwickshire, anxious to find occupation in my profession. I was not prepared for what happened, although I have since thought I might have apprehended something like it. The reason of my saying so is this—"

He was beginning to speak with a great deal more effort and reluctance, and sighed often, and seemed at times nearly overcome. But at this time his manner was not agitated. It was more like that of a sinking patient, who has given himself up.

"Yes, but I will first tell you about Kenlis, my parish.

"It was with me when I left this place for Dawlbridge. It was my silent travelling companion, and it remained with me at the vicarage. When I entered on the discharge of my duties, another change took place. The thing exhibited an atrocious determination to thwart me. It was with me in the church—in the reading-desk—in the pulpit—within the communion rails. At last, it reached this extremity, that while I was reading to the congregation, it would spring upon the book and squat there, so that I was unable to see the page. This happened more than once.

"I left Dawlbridge for a time. I placed myself in Dr. Harley's hands. I did everything he told me. He gave my case a great deal of thought. It interested him, I think. He seemed successful. For nearly three months I was perfectly free from a return. I began to think I was safe. With his full assent I returned to Dawlbridge.

"I travelled in a chaise. I was in good spirits. I was more—I was happy and grateful. I was returning, as I thought, delivered from a dreadful hallucination, to the scene of duties which I longed to enter upon. It was a beautiful sunny evening, everything looked serene and cheerful, and I was delighted. I remember looking out of the window to see the spire of my church at Kenlis among the trees, at the point where one has the earliest view of it. It is exactly where the little stream that bounds the parish passes under the road by a culvert, and where it emerges at the road-side, a stone with an old inscription is placed. As we passed this point, I drew my head in and sat down, and in the corner of the chaise was the monkey.

"For a moment I felt faint, and then quite wild with despair and horror. I called to the driver, and got out, and sat down at the road-side, and prayed to God silently for mercy. A despairing resignation supervened. My companion was with me as I re-entered the vicarage. The same persecution followed. After a short struggle I submitted, and soon I left the place.

"I told you," he said, "that the beast has before this become in certain ways aggressive. I will explain a little. It seemed to be actuated by intense and increasing fury, whenever I said my prayers, or even meditated prayer. It amounted at last to a dreadful interruption. You will ask, how could a silent immaterial phantom effect that? It was thus, whenever I meditated praying; It was always before me, and nearer and nearer.

"It used to spring on a table, on the back of a chair, on the chimney-piece, and slowly to swing itself from side to side, looking at me all the time. There is in its motion an indefinable power to dissipate thought, and to contract one's attention to that monotony, till the ideas shrink, as it were, to a point, and at last to nothing—and unless I had started up, and shook off the catalepsy I have felt as if my mind were on the point of losing itself. There are other ways," he sighed heavily; "thus, for instance, while I pray with my eyes closed, it comes closer and closer, and I see it. I know it is not to be accounted for physically, but I do actually see it, though my lids are dosed, and so it rocks my mind, as it were, and overpowers me, and I am obliged to rise from my knees. If you had ever yourself known this, you would be acquainted with desperation."

CHAPTER IX
The Third Stage

"I see, Dr. Hesselius, that you don't lose one word of my statement. I need not ask you to listen specially to what I am now going to tell you. They talk of the optic nerves, and of spectral illusions, as if the organ of sight was the only point assailable by the influences that have fastened upon me—I know better. For two years in my direful case that limitation prevailed. But as food is taken in softly at the lips, and then brought under the teeth, as the tip of the little finger caught in a mill crank will draw in the hand, and the arm, and the whole body, so the miserable mortal who has been once caught firmly by the end of the finest fibre of his nerve, is drawn in and in, by the enormous machinery of hell, until he is as I am. Yes, Doctor, as *I* am, for a while I talk to you, and implore relief, I feel that my prayer is for the impossible, and my pleading with the inexorable."

I endeavoured to calm his visibly increasing agitation, and told him that he must not despair.

While we talked the night had overtaken us. The filmy moonlight was wide over the scene which the window commanded, and I said:

"Perhaps you would prefer having candles. This light, you know, is odd. I should wish you, as much as possible, under your usual conditions while I make my diagnosis, shall I call it—otherwise I don't care."

"All lights are the same to me," he said; "except when I read or write, I care not if night were perpetual. I am going to tell you what happened about a year ago. The thing began to speak to me."

"Speak! How do you mean—speak as a man does, do you mean?"

"Yes; speak in words and consecutive sentences, with perfect coherence and articulation; but there is a peculiarity. It is not like the tone of a human voice. It is not by my ears it reaches me—it comes like a singing through my head.

"This faculty, the power of speaking to me, will be my undoing. It won't let me pray, it interrupts me with dreadful blasphemies. I dare not go on, I could not. Oh! Doctor, can the skill, and thought, and prayers of man avail me nothing!"

"You must promise me, my dear sir, not to trouble yourself with unnecessarily exciting thoughts; confine yourself strictly to the narrative of *facts*; and recollect, above all, that even if the thing that infests you be, you seem to suppose a reality with an actual independent life and will, yet it can have no power to hurt you, unless it be given from above: its access to your senses depends mainly upon your physical condition—this is, under God, your comfort and reliance: we are all alike environed. It is only that in your case, the '*paries*,' the veil of the flesh, the screen, is a little out of repair, and sights and sounds are transmitted. We must enter on a new course, sir,—be encouraged. I'll give to-night to the careful consideration of the whole case."

"You are very good, sir; you think it worth trying, you don't give me quite up; but, sir, you don't know, it is gaining such an influence over me: it orders me about, it is such a tyrant, and I'm growing so helpless. May God deliver me!"

"It orders you about—of course you mean by speech?"

"Yes, yes; it is always urging me to crimes, to injure others, or myself. You see, Doctor, the situation is urgent, it is indeed. When I was in Shropshire, a few weeks ago" (Mr. Jennings was speaking rapidly and trembling now, holding my arm with one hand, and looking in my face), "I went out one day with a party of friends for a walk: my persecutor, I tell you, was with me at the time. I lagged behind the rest: the country near the Dee, you know, is beautiful. Our path happened to lie near a coal mine, and at the verge of the wood is a perpendicular shaft, they say, a hundred and fifty feet deep. My niece had remained behind with me—she knows, of course nothing of the nature of my sufferings. She knew, however, that I had been ill, and was low, and she remained to prevent my being quite alone. As we loitered slowly on together, the brute that accompanied me was urging me to throw myself down the shaft. I tell you now—oh, sir, think of it!—the one consideration that saved me from that hideous death was the fear lest the shock of witnessing the occurrence should be too much for the poor girl. I asked her to go on and walk with her friends, saying that I could go no further. She made excuses, and the more

I urged her the firmer she became. She looked doubtful and frightened. I suppose there was something in my looks or manner that alarmed her; but she would not go, and that literally saved me. You had no idea, sir, that a living man could be made so abject a slave of Satan," he said, with a ghastly groan and a shudder.

There was a pause here, and I said, "You *were* preserved nevertheless. It was the act of God. You are in His hands and in the power of no other being: be therefore confident for the future."

CHAPTER X
Home

I made him have candles lighted, and saw the room looking cheery and inhabited before I left him. I told him that he must regard his illness strictly as one dependent on physical, though *subtle* physical causes. I told him that he had evidence of God's care and love in the deliverance which he had just described, and that I had perceived with pain that he seemed to regard its peculiar features as indicating that he had been delivered over to spiritual reprobation. Than such a conclusion nothing could be, I insisted, less warranted; and not only so, but more contrary to facts, as disclosed in his mysterious deliverance from that murderous influence during his Shropshire excursion. First, his niece had been retained by his side without his intending to keep her near him; and, secondly, there had been infused into his mind an irresistible repugnance to execute the dreadful suggestion in her presence.

As I reasoned this point with him, Mr. Jennings wept.

He seemed comforted. One promise I exacted, which was that should the monkey at any time return, I should be sent for immediately; and, repeating my assurance that I would give neither time nor thought to any other subject until I had thoroughly investigated his case, and that to-morrow he should hear the result, I took my leave.

Before getting into the carriage I told the servant that his master was far from well, and that he should make a point of frequently looking into his room. My own arrangements I made with a view to being quite secure from interruption.

I merely called at my lodgings, and with a travelling-desk and carpet-bag, set off in a hackney carriage for an inn about two miles out of town, called "The Horns," a very quiet and comfortable house, with good thick walls. And there I resolved, without the possibility of intrusion or distraction, to devote some hours of the night, in my comfortable sitting-room, to Mr. Jennings' case, and so much of the morning as it might require.

(There occurs here a careful note of Dr. Hesselius' opinion upon the case, and of the habits, dietary, and medicines which he prescribed. It is curious—some persons would say mystical. But, on the whole, I doubt whether it would sufficiently interest a reader of the kind I am likely to meet with, to warrant its being here reprinted. The whole letter was plainly written at the inn where he had hid himself for the occasion. The next letter is dated from his town lodgings.)

I left town for the inn where I slept last night at half-past nine, and did not arrive at my room in town until one o'clock this afternoon. I found a letter in Mr. Jennings' hand upon my table. It had not come by post, and, on inquiry, I learned that Mr. Jennings' servant had brought it, and on learning that I was not to return until to-day, and that no one could tell him my address, he seemed very uncomfortable, and said his orders from his master were that that he was not to return without an answer.

I opened the letter and read:

> Dear Dr. Hesselius.—It is here. You had not been an hour gone when it returned. It is speaking. It knows all that has happened. It knows everything—it knows you, and is frantic and atrocious. It reviles. I send you this. It knows every word I have written—I write. This I promised, and I therefore write, but I fear very confused, very incoherently. I am so interrupted, disturbed.
>
> Ever yours, sincerely yours,
>
> Robert Lynder Jennings.

"When did this come?" I asked.

"About eleven last night: the man was here again, and has been here three times to-day. The last time is about an hour since."

Thus answered, and with the notes I had made upon his case in my pocket, I was in a few minutes driving towards Richmond, to see Mr. Jennings.

I by no means, as you perceive, despaired of Mr. Jennings' case. He had himself remembered and applied, though quite in a mistaken way, the principle which I lay down in my Metaphysical Medicine, and which governs all such cases. I was about to apply it in earnest. I was profoundly interested, and very anxious to see and examine him while the "enemy" was actually present.

I drove up to the sombre house, and ran up the steps, and knocked. The door, in a little time, was opened by a tall woman in black silk. She looked ill, and as if she had been crying. She curtseyed, and heard my question, but she did not answer. She turned her face away, extending her hand towards two men who were coming down-stairs; and thus having, as it were, tacitly made me over to them, she passed through a side-door hastily and shut it.

The man who was nearest the hall, I at once accosted, but being now close to him, I was shocked to see that both his hands were covered with blood.

I drew back a little, and the man, passing downstairs, merely said in a low tone, "Here's the servant, sir."

The servant had stopped on the stairs, confounded and dumb at seeing me. He was rubbing his hands in a handkerchief, and it was steeped in blood.

"Jones, what is it? what has happened?" I asked, while a sickening suspicion overpowered me.

The man asked me to come up to the lobby. I was beside him in a moment, and, frowning and pallid, with contracted eyes, he told me the horror which I already half guessed.

His master had made away with himself.

I went upstairs with him to the room—what I saw there I won't tell you. He had cut his throat with his razor. It was a frightful gash. The two men had laid him on the bed, and composed his limbs. It had happened, as the immense pool of blood on the floor declared, at some distance between the bed and the window. There was carpet round his bed, and a carpet under his dressing-table, but none on the rest of the floor, for the man said he did not like a carpet on his bedroom. In this sombre and now terrible room, one of the great elms that darkened the house was slowly moving the shadow of one of its great boughs upon this dreadful floor.

I beckoned to the servant, and we went downstairs

together. I turned off the hall into an old-fashioned panelled room, and there standing, I heard all the servant had to tell. It was not a great deal.

"I concluded, sir, from your words, and looks, sir, as you left last night, that you thought my master was seriously ill. I thought it might be that you were afraid of a fit, or something. So I attended very close to your directions. He sat up late, till past three o'clock. He was not writing or reading. He was talking a great deal to himself, but that was nothing unusual. At about that hour I assisted him to undress, and left him in his slippers and dressing-gown. I went back softly in about half-an-hour. He was in his bed, quite undressed, and a pair of candles lighted on the table beside his bed. He was leaning on his elbow, and looking out at the other side of the bed when I came in. I asked him if he wanted anything, and he said No.

"I don't know whether it was what you said to me, sir, or something a little unusual about him, but I was uneasy, uncommon uneasy about him last night.

"In another half hour, or it might be a little more, I went up again. I did not hear him talking as before. I opened the door a little. The candles were both out, which was not usual. I had a bedroom candle, and I let the light in, a little bit, looking softly round. I saw him sitting in that chair beside the dressing-table with his clothes on again. He turned round and looked at me. I thought it strange he should get up and dress, and put out the candles to sit in the dark, that way. But I only asked him again if I could do anything for him. He said, No, rather sharp, I thought. I asked him if I might light the candles, and he said, 'Do as you like, Jones.' So I lighted them, and I lingered about the room, and he said, 'Tell me truth, Jones; why did you come again—you did not hear anyone cursing?' 'No, sir,' I said, wondering what he could mean.

"'No,' said he, after me, 'of course, no;' and I said to him, 'Wouldn't it be well, sir, you went to bed? It's just five o'clock;' and he said nothing, but, 'Very likely; good-night, Jones.' So I went, sir, but in less than an hour I came again. The door was fast, and he heard me, and called as I thought from the bed to know what I wanted, and he desired me not to disturb him again. I lay down and slept for a little. It must have been between six and seven when I went up again. The door was still fast, and he made no answer, so I did not like to disturb him, and thinking he was asleep, I left him till nine. It was his custom to ring when he wished me to come, and I had no particular hour for calling him. I tapped very gently, and getting no answer, I stayed away a good while, supposing he was getting some rest then. It was not till eleven o'clock I grew really uncomfortable about him—for at the latest he was never, that I could remember, later than half-past ten. I got no answer. I knocked and called, and still no answer. So not being able to force the door, I called Thomas from the stables, and together we forced it, and found him in the shocking way you saw."

Jones had no more to tell. Poor Mr. Jennings was very gentle, and very kind. All his people were fond of him. I could see that the servant was very much moved.

So, dejected and agitated, I passed from that terrible house, and its dark canopy of elms, and I hope I shall never see it more. While I write to you I feel like a man who has but half waked from a frightful and monotonous dream. My memory rejects the picture with incredulity and horror. Yet I know it is true. It is the story of the process of a poison, a poison which excites the reciprocal action of spirit and nerve, and paralyses the tissue that separates those cognate functions of the senses, the external and the interior. Thus we find strange bed-fellows, and the mortal and immortal prematurely make acquaintance.

CONCLUSION

A Word for Those Who Suffer

My dear Van L——, you have suffered from an affection similar to that which I have just described. You twice complained of a return of it.

Who, under God, cured you? Your humble servant, Martin Hesselius. Let me rather adopt the more emphasised piety of a certain good old French surgeon of three hundred years ago: "I treated, and God cured you."

Come, my friend, you are not to be hippish. Let me tell you a fact.

I have met with, and treated, as my book shows, fifty-seven cases of this kind of vision, which I term indifferently "sublimated," "precocious," and "interior."

There is another class of affections which are truly termed—though commonly confounded with those which I describe—spectral illusions. These latter I look upon as being no less simply curable than a cold in the head or a trifling dyspepsia.

It is those which rank in the first category that test our promptitude of thought. Fifty-seven such cases have I encountered, neither more nor less. And in how many of these have I failed? In no one single instance.

There is no one affliction of mortality more easily and certainly reducible, with a little patience, and a rational confidence in the physician. With these simple conditions, I look upon the cure as absolutely certain.

You are to remember that I had not even commenced to treat Mr. Jennings' case. I have not any doubt that I should have cured him perfectly in eighteen months, or possibly it might have extended to two years. Some cases are very rapidly curable, others extremely tedious. Every intelligent physician who will give thought and diligence to the task, will effect a cure.

You know my tract on "The Cardinal Functions of the Brain." I there, by the evidence of innumerable facts, prove, as I think, the high probability of a circulation arterial and venous in its mechanism, through the nerves. Of this system, thus considered, the brain is the heart. The fluid, which is propagated hence through one class of nerves, returns in an altered state through another, and the nature of that fluid is spiritual, though not immaterial, any more than, as I before remarked, light or electricity are so.

By various abuses, among which the habitual use of such agents as green tea is one, this fluid may be affected as to its quality, but it is more frequently disturbed as to equilibrium. This fluid being that which we have in common with spirits, a congestion found upon the masses of brain or nerve, connected with the interior sense, forms a surface unduly exposed, on which disembodied spirits may operate: communication is thus more or less effectually established. Between this brain circulation and the heart circulation there is an intimate sympathy. The seat, or rather the instrument of exterior vision, is the eye. The seat of interior vision is the nervous tissue and brain, immediately about and above the eyebrow. You remember how effectually I dissipated your pictures by the simple application of iced eau-de-cologne. Few cases, however, can be treated exactly alike with anything like rapid success. Cold acts powerfully as a repellant of the nervous fluid. Long enough continued it will even produce that permanent insensibility which we call numbness, and a little longer, muscular as well as sensational paralysis.

I have not, I repeat, the slightest doubt that I should have first dimmed and ultimately sealed that inner eye which Mr. Jennings had inadvertently opened. The same senses are opened in delirium tremens, and entirely shut up again when the overaction of the cerebral heart, and the prodigious nervous congestions that attend it, are terminated by a decided change in the state of the body. It is by acting steadily upon the body, by a simple process, that this result is produced—and inevitably produced—I have never yet failed.

Poor Mr. Jennings made away with himself. But that catastrophe was the result of a totally different malady, which, as it were, projected itself upon the disease which was established. His case was in the distinctive manner a complication, and the complaint under which he really succumbed, was hereditary suicidal mania. Poor Mr. Jennings I cannot call a patient of mine, for I had not even begun to treat his case, and he had not yet given me, I am convinced, his full and unreserved confidence. If the patient do not array himself on the side of the disease, his cure is certain.

PUNCH, BROTHERS, PUNCH

BY MARK TWAIN

INTRODUCTION

TRISTAM ADAMS

Earworms or, involuntary musical imagery (INMI) can plague. The Mark Twain story included here explores INMI contagion via voicing bodies and text. This latter variation will be referred to as a textual-vocal earworm (TVINMI).

On an immediately corporeal register, the symptoms and modalities of IMNI contagion are not too dissimilar from coronaviruses (such as the 2019 strain COVID-19) and influenza in being "voiced", proliferated, via oral and respiratory means. Many pathogens modify host behaviour to expedite proliferation; an example cited here is the parasite Ophiocordyceps Unilateralis.

Twain's tale touches on the viroid life of language. The text could be introduced via a specifically viroid prism, registering of the famously inexact Burroughs' line: "language is a virus". In this sense, the symptoms and modalities of pernicious contagion of voice through text and rhyme — how text "speaks" and reverberates in the mind — evokes how voice is not necessarily vocal. A voice that leaps from the page, a silent voice, lies at the heart of the narrator's troubling account. This TVINMI operates across both modes of contagion — at once pernicious *corporaural* vocalisation and mute text, necrotic silent hieroglyphs that haunt the reader as tormenting voice.

In terms of the first mode of contagion (INMI) the trajectory is roughly body–voice–mind–voicing body. In terms of this second modality (TVINMI) the structuration is text–voice–mind-body.

An exhaustive account of the rhymes' contagion, torment and horror is not necessary here; you'll get to that soon enough. Nonetheless, we shall touch on the two key facets of vocal contagion, corporeal and textual, in due course. Generally, over the course of the narrative, the rhyme moves from page to host (the narrator, Mark) before transferring to another host (the reverend) and then many more (students). Its lifecycle mutates from a textually-rooted form of contagion to a vocally-rooted mode; in each case contagion of the rhyme manifests as symptoms that expedite its spread.

Ophiocordyceps Unilateralis is an entomopathogen that lives through ants. Curiously, the pathogen "compels" the ant towards complex behaviours that expedite proliferation. The host ant, once infected, is compelled to ascension and climbs upwards. After some climbing, the pathogen's spores burst from the ant's body. It is from this vantage that the spread of spores is most effective for the parasite's continued proliferation. The spores, gratis of an antsy climax, are spread over a greater area from which to infect other host bodies. The parasite modifies host behaviour to optimise proliferation.

The immediate equivalence of parasites such as Ophiocordyceps Unilateralis and TVINMI is the modification of host body behaviour. When one is exposed, just as Mark is in Twain's tale, one tends to absent-mindedly sing or hum the infectious melody or lyric or revert to complete rehearsal of the lyrics when speaking (or writing). In human INMI infections, the host body, in a zombie-trance, expedites the proliferation of the INMI to others within voice range (not dissimilar to the spread of influenza). The horror of exponential proliferation is most distinctly evoked in the story's final scene, where Mark, having passed the rhyme on to his friend the reverend, saves the tormented man from the "asylum" (non-normative verbalisation is enough for admittance) by taking him to a university. In front of his audience he unburdens himself of the curse by delivering a lecture.

The narrator of Twain's tale is a writer. Like Stephen King's famous part-biographical scribe-grump Jack Torrance in *The Shining*, Mark is easily distracted (writers generally — Ed.). We are in the continuum of writers writing about writer's problems. The "All Work and No Play Makes Jack a Dull Boy" manic symptom in Kubrick's adaptation is not in the novel, but a similar symptom is evident here. When Mark, tormented by the jingle, goes to write, he can only write out the tormenting lyrics. He is a writing-vessel doomed to parrot and echo the contagious text.

This strikes a secondary equivalence to parasites, specifically Ophiocordyceps Unilateralis. The infected host ant's ascension naturally culminates on a leaf — the most extreme part of a plant from which further ascension requires flight. It is from here that the spores of further pathogenic infection are disseminated. Mark's textual repetition of the rhyme — *Punch in the presence of the passenjare* — stands in symmetry to Ophiocordyceps Unilateralis' modality of contagion. He commits his tormenting IMNI pathogen to a page, a leaf, from which many others (more than those within earshot of his voice) could be exposed to.

This textual mode of vocal contagion gets the reader immediately. In the first line, he asks the reader (of male pronoun) to read the offending lines: "Will the reader please cast his eye over the following lines, and see if he can discover anything harmful in them?" Then the "jingling rhyme" is detailed in text. Notice Twain's dupe here. This representing and re-voicing of the virulent rhyme exposes the reader before the narrator tells of the horrors it brings. Like the classic unfolding of horror in narratives of biological contagion — exposure is immediate, but knowledge of exposure and its ramifications are subsequently unpacked.

The Twain tale does not specify if the reverend was reading from a page during his lecture or not (did he pen lecture notes peppered with the jingle like Mark?). It is clear that Mark, the narrator, first read the jingle in a newspaper. Twain's tale is anecdotal and does not offer context outside of the narrator's subjective experience, an inevitable symptom of first-person fiction. But one cannot help but wonder whom else read the offending jingle in the newspaper Mark picked up.

The TVINMI that leaps from leaf to torment and compels the body and mind of the host(s) also operates on a meta-textual level. The publishing history of Twain's story exhibits a pathogenic editorial symptom. The original title was "A Literary Nightmare", it was subsequently published in later volumes as "Punch, Brothers, Punch" — the story's title replaced with the chorus line of the contagious rhyme featured within the narrative. The change in the title of the short story can be read as an editorial meta-text that performs the viral nature of the rhyme in print.

Please turn overleaf.

PUNCH, BROTHERS, PUNCH

MARK TWAIN

Will the reader please to cast his eye over the following lines, and see if he can discover anything harmful in them?

Conductor, when you receive a fare,
Punch in the presence of the passenjare!
A blue trip slip for an eight-cent fare,
A buff trip slip for a six-cent fare,
A pink trip slip for a three-cent fare,
Punch in the presence of the passenjare!

CHORUS
Punch, brothers! punch with care!
Punch in the presence of the passenjare!

I came across these jingling rhymes in a newspaper, a little while ago, and read them a couple of times. They took instant and entire possession of me. All through breakfast they went waltzing through my brain; and when, at last, I rolled up my napkin, I could not tell whether I had eaten anything or not. I had carefully laid out my day's work the day before—thrilling tragedy in the novel which I am writing. I went to my den to begin my deed of blood. I took up my pen, but all I could get it to say was, "Punch in the presence of the passenjare." I fought hard for an hour, but it was useless. My head kept humming, "A blue trip slip for an eight-cent fare, a buff trip slip for a six-cent fare," and so on and so on, without peace or respite. The day's work was ruined—I could see that plainly enough. I gave up and drifted down-town, and presently discovered that my feet were keeping time to that relentless jingle. When I could stand it no longer I altered my step. But it did no good; those rhymes accommodated themselves to the new step and went on harassing me just as before. I returned home, and suffered all the afternoon; suffered all through an unconscious and unrefreshing dinner; suffered, and cried, and jingled all through the evening; went to bed and rolled, tossed, and jingled right along, the same as ever; got up at midnight frantic, and tried to read; but there was nothing visible upon the whirling page except "Punch! punch in the presence of the passenjare." By sunrise I was out of my mind, and everybody marveled and was distressed at the idiotic burden of my ravings—"Punch! oh, punch! punch in the presence of the passenjare!"

Two days later, on Saturday morning, I arose, a tottering wreck, and went forth to fulfil an engagement with a valued friend, the Rev. Mr.———, to walk to the Talcott Tower, ten miles distant. He stared at me, but asked no questions. We started. Mr.——— talked, talked, talked as is his wont. I said nothing; I heard nothing. At the end of a mile, Mr.——— said "Mark, are you sick? I never saw a man look so haggard and worn and absent-minded. Say something, do!"

Drearily, without enthusiasm, I said: "Punch brothers, punch with care! Punch in the presence of the passenjare!"

My friend eyed me blankly, looked perplexed, then said:

"I do not think I get your drift, Mark. There does not seem to be any relevancy in what you have said, certainly nothing sad; and yet—maybe it was the way you said the words—I never heard anything that sounded so pathetic.

What is—"

But I heard no more. I was already far away with my pitiless, heartbreaking "blue trip slip for an eight-cent fare, buff trip slip for a six-cent fare, pink trip slip for a three-cent fare; punch in the presence of the passenjare." I do not know what occurred during the other nine miles. However, all of a sudden Mr.——— laid his hand on my shoulder and shouted:—

"Oh, wake up! wake up! wake up! Don't sleep all day! Here we are at the Tower, man! I have talked myself deaf and dumb and blind, and never got a response. Just look at this magnificent autumn landscape! Look at it! look at it! Feast your eye on it! You have traveled; you have seen boasted landscapes elsewhere. Come, now, deliver an honest opinion. What do you say to this?"

I sighed wearily; and murmured:—

"A buff trip slip for a six-cent fare, a pink trip slip for a three-cent fare, punch in the presence of the passenjare."

Rev. Mr. ——— stood there, very grave, full of concern, apparently, and looked long at me; then he said:—

"Mark, there is something about this that I cannot understand. Those are about the same words you said before; there does not seem to be anything in them, and yet they nearly break my heart when you say them. Punch in the—how is it they go?"

I began at the beginning and repeated all the lines.

My friend's face lighted with interest. He said:—

"Why, what a captivating jingle it is! It is almost music. It flows along so nicely. I have nearly caught the rhymes myself. Say them over just once more, and then I'll have them, sure."

I said them over. Then Mr.——— said them. He made

one little mistake, which I corrected. The next time and the next he got them right. Now a great burden seemed to tumble from my shoulders. That torturing jingle departed out of my brain, and a grateful sense of rest and peace descended upon me. I was light-hearted enough to sing; and I did sing for half an hour, straight along, as we went jogging homeward. Then my freed tongue found blessed speech again, and the pent talk of many a weary hour began to gush and flow. It flowed on and on, joyously, jubilantly, until the fountain was empty and dry. As I wrung my friend's hand at parting, I said:—

"Haven't we had a royal good time! But now I remember, you haven't said a word for two hours. Come, come, out with something!"

The Rev. Mr.——— turned a lack-lustre eye upon me, drew a deep sigh, and said, without animation, without apparent consciousness:

"Punch, brothers, punch with care! Punch in the presence of the passenjare!"

A pang shot through me as I said to myself, "Poor fellow, poor fellow! he has got it, now."

I did not see Mr.——— for two or three days after that. Then, on Tuesday evening, he staggered into my presence and sank dejectedly into a seat. He was pale, worn; he was a wreck. He lifted his faded eyes to my face and said:—

"Ah, Mark, it was a ruinous investment that I made in those heartless rhymes. They have ridden me like a nightmare, day and night, hour after hour, to this very moment. Since I saw you I have suffered the torments of the lost. Saturday evening I had a sudden call, by telegraph, and took the night train for Boston. The occasion was the death of a valued old friend who had requested that I should preach his funeral sermon. I took my seat in the cars and set myself to framing the discourse. But I never got beyond the opening paragraph; for then the train started and the car-wheels began their 'clack, clack-clack-clack-clack! clack-clack!—clack-clack-clack!' and right away those odious rhymes fitted themselves to that accompaniment. For an hour I sat there and set a syllable of those rhymes to every separate and distinct clack the car-wheels made. Why, I was as fagged out, then, as if I had been chopping wood all day. My skull was splitting with headache. It seemed to me that I must go mad if I sat there any longer; so I undressed and went to bed. I stretched myself out in my berth, and—well, you know what the result was. The thing went right along, just the same. 'Clack-clack clack, a blue trip slip, clack-clack-clack, for an eight-cent fare; clack-clack-clack, a buff trip slip, clack clack-clack, for a six-cent fare, and so on, and so on, and so on punch in the presence of the passenjare!' Sleep? Not a single wink! I was almost a lunatic when I got to Boston. Don't ask me about the funeral. I did the best I could, but every solemn individual sentence was meshed and tangled and woven in and out with 'Punch, brothers, punch with care, punch in the presence of the passenjare.' And the most distressing thing was that my delivery dropped into the undulating rhythm of those pulsing rhymes, and I could actually catch absent-minded people nodding time to the swing of it with their stupid heads. And, Mark, you may believe it or not, but before I got through the entire assemblage were placidly bobbing their heads in solemn unison, mourners, undertaker, and all. The moment I had finished, I fled to the anteroom in a state bordering on frenzy. Of course it would be my luck to find a sorrowing and aged maiden aunt of the deceased there, who had arrived from Springfield too late to get into the church. She began to sob, and said:—

"'Oh, oh, he is gone, he is gone, and I didn't see him before he died!'

"'Yes!' I said, 'he is gone, he is gone, he is gone—oh, will this suffering never cease!'

"'You loved him, then! Oh, you too loved him!'

"'Loved him! Loved who?'

"'Why, my poor George! my poor nephew!'

"'Oh—him! Yes—oh, yes, yes. Certainly—certainly. Punch—punch—oh, this misery will kill me!'

"'Bless you! bless you, sir, for these sweet words! I, too, suffer in this dear loss. Were you present during his last moments?'

"'Yes. I—whose last moments?'

"'His. The dear departed's.'

"'Yes! Oh, yes—yes—yes! I suppose so, I think so, I don't know! Oh, certainly—I was there—I was there!'

"'Oh, what a privilege! what a precious privilege! And his last words—oh, tell me, tell me his last words! What did he say?'

"'He said—he said—oh, my head, my head, my head! He said—he said—he never said anything but Punch, punch, punch in the presence of the passenjare! Oh, leave me, madam! In the name of all that is generous, leave me to my madness, my misery, my despair!—a buff trip slip for a six-cent fare, a pink trip slip for a three-cent fare—endu—rance can no fur—ther go!—PUNCH in the presence of the passenjare!"

My friend's hopeless eyes rested upon mine a pregnant minute, and then he said impressively:—

"Mark, you do not say anything. You do not offer me

any hope. But, ah me, it is just as well—it is just as well. You could not do me any good. The time has long gone by when words could comfort me. Something tells me that my tongue is doomed to wag forever to the jigger of that remorseless jingle. There—there it is coming on me again: a blue trip slip for an eight-cent fare, a buff trip slip for a—"

Thus murmuring faint and fainter, my friend sank into a peaceful trance and forgot his sufferings in a blessed respite.

How did I finally save him from an asylum? I took him to a neighboring university and made him discharge the burden of his persecuting rhymes into the eager ears of the poor, unthinking students. How is it with them, now? The result is too sad to tell. Why did I write this article? It was for a worthy, even a noble, purpose. It was to warn you, reader, if you should came across those merciless rhymes, to avoid them—avoid them as you would a pestilence!

UNSEEN—UNFEARED

BY FRANCIS STEVENS
(GERTRUDE BARROWS
BENNETT)

INTRODUCTION

ELVIA WILK

In its dual fascination with ancient, invisible forces and their technological mediation, "Unseen—Unfeared" is both the media theorist's and the Lovecraft scholar's wet dream. Written by Gertrude Barrows Bennett and published under her male pseudonym, Francis Stevens, in February 1919, the story is equal parts detective tale, dark fantasy fiction, and diatribe on human nature — although its moral stance remains deeply ambivalent.

We first meet our narrator, known as Blaisdell, sharing an Italian dinner with his "ever-interesting" detective friend Mark Jenkins. Jenkins has been describing to Blaisdell one of his recent cases that's made the morning papers: the implication of a certain mad scientist named "Doc Holt" in the mysterious poisoning of a young man. After dining, the detective has to run out, ostensibly on urgent business related to the case at hand, but before leaving, he offers Blaisdell one of his "invariably good cigars". In this short introductory scene Bennett offers a rich setup against the backdrop setting of a foreign restaurant — whose "highly seasoned food and sour, thin, red wine" Blaisdell remarks upon heavily — and a smoking gun, or in this case, cigar.

Into the night Blaisdell wanders, puffing his cigar. He finds himself in a neighbourhood "so unlike the rest of the city, so foreign", where he is surprised at his own instinctive disgust at what he perceives as the cheap wares, foul-smelling air, and suspicious faces of passers-by. "The mixture of Italians, Jews, and a few negroes, mostly bareheaded, unkempt and generally unhygienic in appearance, struck me as merely revolting." It is Blaisdell's shock at his own revulsion here that is worth noting. He immediately self-reflects, wondering why his usual tendency to "sympathize with poverty" has been replaced by a physical reaction of horror and revulsion at the poor. Observing the strangers and his reactions, he admits that "They were all humans, and I, too, was human", but that, oddly, "Some way I did not like the idea."

Determined to overcome his fear and perhaps recover his humanist self-respect, Blaisdell decides to stick around until he can conquer his irrational repulsion. He is immediately attracted by a window sign for what appears to be a cheap attraction, perhaps a cabinet of curiosities, beckoning: "SEE THE GREAT UNSEEN! FREE TO ALL!" A little kitschy entertainment seems like a fine way to calm his nerves. Yet upon entering, he's greeted by a raving, demented white-haired man (your quintessential mad scientist) who, after much fanfare, beckons him into what turns out to be a scientific laboratory.

What happens in the laboratory is, in short, the revelation to Blaisdell of the unseen world parallel to our own — a world that can only be revealed via a complex photographic projection technology Doc Holt has invented, requiring a particular frequency of green light and a special "membrane" filter. That world, invisible to the naked eye, is populated by infinite, enormous, wormy, spidery, tentacled, loathsome creatures. In Doc Holt's opinion, these mind-boggling beings, some of which even have terrifying human faces, are in fact the *manifestations* of man's dirty and evil thoughts. Says Doc: they are "the shape and body of your FEAR!"

The existence of giant germ-like creatures is not the true subject of this tale. Its subject is fear and fear's embodiment. Or perhaps, given the media apparatus in the laboratory, fear and fear's *projection* onto certain bodies. The plot climaxes in Blaisdell's mental breakdown at the sight of that other world, followed by a coda in which "seen" and logical reality reasserts itself. By following a trail of clues, Detective Jenkins discovers a comatose Blaisdell in the laboratory, explaining that the whole hallucinatory experience was caused by the cigar — apparently poisoned.

Much hinges on this cigar. How much of Blaisdell's whole account can be chalked up to its influence? If it indeed caused Blaisdell's horror at the filthy immigrant neighbourhood, the Lovecraftian frightening Other (rising from the distant or ancient heart of darkness) becomes, in Bennett's world, a chimeric projection caused by a toxic substance. But does this mean Blaisdell's self-proclaimed typical empathy and humanism is a sham masking his true racism and xenophobia, which were revealed through chemical intervention? Or are we to think racism and xenophobia can only be the result of a deranged or poisoned mind?

The cigar is also the proposed logical "explanation" for the unseen world of creatures that embody man's fear, always living among us, unbeknownst to our senses. The obvious implication is that humanity generates its own monsters through fear and prejudice, realities that we choose to "unsee" unless forced to. But what forces us to see them? Here, technological novelty. Do we really want to "see" what technology can show us about human nature, or is it better to be kept in the dark?

"Doubt", Blaisdell summarises near the end, "is better

than certainty". Certainty about human nature, not to mention true knowledge about the *non*human world, might be too horrifying for us to bear. But certainty that there is nothing to fear, that the world is clean and safe, is equally dangerous. To be certain that we are clean and safe will always mean preserving an *us* versus a *them* — a them from whom we must be kept safe.

UNSEEN—UNFEARED

FRANCIS STEVENS
(GERTRUDE BARROWS BENNETT)

I.

I had been dining with my ever-interesting friend, Mark Jenkins, at a little Italian restaurant near South Street. It was a chance meeting. Jenkins is too busy, usually, to make dinner engagements. Over our highly seasoned food and sour, thin, red wine, he spoke of little odd incidents and adventures of his profession. Nothing very vital or important, of course. Jenkins is not the sort of detective who first detects and then pours the egotistical and revealing details of achievement in the ears of every acquaintance, however appreciative.

But when I spoke of something I had seen in the morning papers, he laughed. "Poor old 'Doc' Holt! Fascinating old codger, to anyone who really knows him. I've had his friendship for years — since I was first on the city force and saved a young assistant of his from jail on a false charge. And they had to drag him into the poisoning of this young sport, Ralph Peeler!"

"Why are you so sure he couldn't have been implicated?" I asked.

But Jenkins only shook his head, with a quiet smile. "I have reasons for believing otherwise," was all I could get out of him on that score, "But," he added, "the only reason he was suspected at all is the superstitious dread of these ignorant people around him. Can't see why he lives in such a place. I know for a fact he doesn't have to. Doc's got money of his own. He's an amateur chemist and dabbler in different sorts of research work, and I suspect he's been guilty of 'showing off.' Result, they all swear he has the evil eye and holds forbidden communion with invisible powers. Smoke?"

Jenkins offered me one of his invariably good cigars, which I accepted, saying thoughtfully: "A man has no right to trifle with the superstitions of ignorant people. Sooner or later, it spells trouble."

"Did in his case. They swore up and down that he sold love charms openly and poisons secretly, and that, together with his living so near to somebody else — got him temporarily suspected. But my tongue's running away with me, as usual!"

"As usual," I retorted impatiently, "you open up with all the frankness of a Chinese diplomat."

He beamed upon me engagingly and rose from the table, with a glance at his watch. "Sorry to leave you, Blaisdell, but I have to meet Jimmy Brennan in ten minutes."

He so clearly did not invite my further company that I remained seated for a little while after his departure; then took my own way homeward. Those streets always held for me a certain fascination, particularly at night. They are so unlike the rest of the city, so foreign in appearance, with their little shabby stores, always open until late evening, their unbelievably cheap goods, displayed as much outside the shops as in them, hung on the fronts and laid out on tables by the curb and in the street itself. Tonight, however, neither people nor stores in any sense appealed to me. The mixture of Italians, Jews and a few Negroes, mostly bareheaded, unkempt and generally unhygienic in appearance, struck me as merely revolting. They were all humans, and I, too, was human. Some way I did not like the idea.

Puzzled a trifle, for I am more inclined to sympathize with poverty than accuse it, I watched the faces that I passed. Never before had I observed how bestial, how brutal were the countenances of the dwellers in this region. I actually shuddered when an old-clothes man, a gray-bearded Hebrew, brushed me as he toiled past with his barrow.

There was a sense of evil in the air, a warning of things which it is wise for a clean man to shun and keep clear of. The impression became so strong that before I had walked two squares I began to feel physically ill. Then it occurred to me that the one glass of cheap Chianti I had drunk might have something to do with the feeling. Who knew how that stuff had been manufactured, or whether the juice of the grape entered at all into its ill-flavored composition? Yet I doubted if that were the real cause of my discomfort.

By nature I am rather a sensitive, impressionable sort of chap. In some way tonight this neighborhood, with its sordid sights and smells, had struck me wrong.

My sense of impending evil was merging into actual fear. This would never do. There is only one way to deal with an imaginative temperament like mine — conquer its vagaries. If I left South Street with this nameless dread upon me, I could never pass down it again without a recurrence of the feeling. I should simply have to stay here until I got the better of it — that was all.

I paused on a corner before a shabby but brightly lighted little drug store. Its gleaming windows and the luminous green of its conventional glass show jars made the brightest spot on the block. I realized that I was tired, but hardly wanted to go in there and rest. I knew what the company would be like at its shabby, sticky soda fountain. As I stood there, my eyes fell on a long white canvas sign across from me, and its black-and-red lettering caught my attention.

SEE THE GREAT UNSEEN!
COME IN! THIS MEANS YOU!
FREE TO ALL!

A museum of fakes, I thought, but also reflected that if it were a show of some kind I could sit down for a while, rest, and fight off this increasing obsession of nonexistent evil. That side of the street was almost deserted, and the place itself might well be nearly empty.

II.

I walked over, but with every step my sense of dread increased. Dread of I knew not what. Bodiless, inexplicable horror had me as in a net, whose strands, being intangible, without reason for existence, I could by no means throw off. It was not the people now. None of them were about me. There, in the open, lighted street, with no sight nor sound of terror to assail me, I was the shivering victim of such fear as I had never known was possible. Yet still I would not yield.

Setting my teeth, and fighting with myself as with some pet animal gone mad, I forced my steps to slowness and walked along the sidewalk, seeking entrance. Just here there were no shops, but several doors reached in each case by means of a few iron-railed stone steps. I chose the one in the middle beneath the sign. In that neighborhood there are museums, shops and other commercial enterprises conducted in many shabby old residences, such as were these. Behind the glazing of the door I had chosen I could see a dim, pinkish light, but on either side the windows were quite dark.

Trying the door, I found it unlocked. As I opened it a party of Italians passed on the pavement below and I looked back at them over my shoulder. They were gayly dressed, men, women and children, laughing and chattering to one another; probably on their way to some wedding or other festivity.

In passing, one of the men glanced up at me and involuntarily I shuddered back against the door. He was a young man, handsome after the swarthy manner of his race, but never in my life had I see a face so expressive of pure, malicious cruelty, naked and unashamed. Our eyes met and his seemed to light up with a vile gleaming, as if all the wickedness of his nature had come to a focus in the look of concentrated hate he gave me.

They went by, but for some distance I could see him watching me, chin on shoulder, till he and his party were swallowed up in the crowd of marketers farther down the street.

Sick and trembling from that encounter, merely of eyes though it had been, I threw aside my partly smoked cigar and entered. Within there was a small vestibule, whose ancient tesselated floor was grimy with the passing of many feet. I could feel the grit of dirt under my shoes, and it rasped on my rawly quivering nerves. The inner door stood partly open, and going on I found myself in a bare, dirty hallway, and was greeted by the sour, musty, poverty-stricken smell common to dwellings of the very ill-to-do. Beyond there was a stairway, carpeted with ragged grass matting. A gas jet, turned low inside a very dusty pink globe, was the light I had seen from without.

Listening, the house seemed entirely silent. Surely, this was no place of public amusement of any kind whatever. More likely it was a rooming house, and I had, after all, mistaken the entrance.

To my intense relief, since coming inside, the worst agony of my unreasonable terror had passed away. If I could only get in some place where I could sit down and be quiet, probably I should be rid of it for good. Determining to try another entrance, I was about to leave the bare hallway when one of several doors along the side of it suddenly opened and a man stepped out into the hall.

"Well?" he said, looking at me keenly, but with not the least show of surprise at my presence.

"I beg your pardon," I replied. "The door was unlocked and I came in here, thinking it was the entrance to the exhibit — what do they call it? the 'Great Unseen.' The one that is mentioned on that long white sign. Can you tell me which door is the right one?"

"I can."

With that brief answer he stopped and stared at me again. He was a tall, lean man, somewhat stooped, but possessing considerable dignity of bearing. For that neighborhood, he appeared uncommonly well dressed, and his long, smooth-shaven face was noticeable because, while his complexion was dark and his eyes coal-black, above them the heavy brows and his hair were almost silvery-white. His age might have been anything over the threescore mark.

I grew tired of being stared at. "If you can and — won't,

then never mind," I observed a trifle irritably, and turned to go. But his sharp exclamation halted me.

"No!" he said. "No — no! Forgive me for pausing — it was not hesitation, I assure you. To think that one — one, even, has come! All day they pass my sign up there — pass and fear to enter. But you are different. You are not of these timorous, ignorant foreign peasants. You ask me to tell you the right door? Here it is! Here!"

And he struck the panel of the door, which he had closed behind him, so that the sharp yet hollow sound of it echoed up through the silent house.

*

Now it may be thought that after all my senseless terror in the open street, so strange a welcome from so odd a showman would have brought the feeling back, full force. But there is an emotion stronger, to a certain point, than fear. This queer old fellow aroused my curiosity. What kind of museum could it be that he accused the passing public of fearing to enter? Nothing really terrible, surely, or it would have been closed by the police. And normally I am not an unduly timorous person. "So it's in there, is it?" I asked, coming toward him. "And I'm to be sole audience? Come, that will be an interesting experience." I was half laughing now.

"The most interesting in the world," said the old man, with a solemnity which rebuked my lightness.

With that he opened the door, passed inward and closed it again — in my very face. I stood staring at it blankly. The panels, I remember, had been originally painted white, but now the paint was flaked and blistered, gray with dirt and dirty finger marks. Suddenly it occurred to me that I had no wish to enter there. Whatever was behind it could be scarcely worth seeing, or he would not choose such a place for its exhibition. With the old man's vanishing my curiosity had cooled, but just as I again turned to leave, the door opened and this singular showman stuck his white-eyebrowed face through the aperture. He was frowning impatiently. "Come in — come in!" he snapped, and promptly withdrawing his head, once more closed the door.

"He has something there he doesn't want should get out," was the very natural conclusion which I drew. "Well, since it can hardly be anything dangerous, and he's so anxious I should see it — here goes!"

With that I turned the soiled white porcelain handle, and entered.

*

The room I came into was neither very large nor very brightly lighted. In no way did it resemble a museum or lecture room. On the contrary, it seemed to have been fitted up as a quite well-appointed laboratory. The floor was linoleum-covered, there were glass cases along the walls whose shelves were filled with bottles, specimen jars, graduates, and the like. A large table in one corner bore what looked like some odd sort of camera, and a larger one in the middle of the room was fitted with a long rack filled with bottles and test tubes, and was besides littered with papers, glass slides, and various paraphernalia which my ignorance failed to identify. There were several cases of books, a few plain wooden chairs, and in the corner a large iron sink with running water.

My host of the white hair and black eyes was awaiting me, standing near the larger table. He indicated one of the wooden chairs with a thin forefinger that shook a little, either from age or eagerness. "Sit down — sit down! Have no fear but that you will be interested, my friend. Have no fear at all — of anything!"

As he said it he fixed his dark eyes upon me and stared harder than ever. But the effect of his words was the opposite of their meaning. I did sit down, because my knees gave under me, but if in the outer hall I had lost my terror, it now returned twofold upon me. Out there the light had been faint, dingily roseate, indefinite. By it I had not perceived how this old man's face was a mask of living malice — of cruelty, hate and a certain masterful contempt. Now I knew the meaning of my fear, whose warning I would not heed. Now I knew that I had walked into the very trap from which my abnormal sensitiveness had striven in vain to save me.

III.

Again I struggled within me, bit at my lip till I tasted blood, and presently the blind paroxysm passed. It must have been longer in going than I thought, and the old man must have all that time been speaking, for when I could once more control my attention, hear and see him, he had taken up a position near the sink, about ten feet away, and was addressing me with a sort of "platform" manner, as if I had been the large audience whose absence he had deplored.

"And so," he was saying, "I was forced to make these plates very carefully, to truly represent the characteristic hues of each separate organism. Now, in color work of every kind the film is necessarily extremely sensitive. Doubtless you are familiar in a general way with the exquisite transparencies produced by color photography of the single-plate type."

He paused, and trying to act like a normal human being, I observed: "I saw some nice landscapes done in that way — last week at an illustrated lecture in Franklin Hall."

He scowled, and made an impatient gesture at me with his hand. "I can proceed better without interruptions," he said. "My pause was purely oratorical."

I meekly subsided, and he went on in his original loud, clear voice. He would have made an excellent lecturer before a much larger audience — if only his voice could have lost that eerie, ringing note. Thinking of that I must have missed some more, and when I caught it again he was saying:

"As I have indicated, the original plate is the final picture. Now, many of these organisms are extremely hard to photograph, and microphotography in color is particularly difficult. In consequence, to spoil a plate tries the patience of the photographer. They are so sensitive that the ordinary darkroom ruby lamp would instantly ruin them, and they must therefore be developed either in darkness or by a special light produced by interposing thin sheets of tissue of a particular shade of green and of yellow between lamp and plate, and even that will often cause ruinous fog. Now I, finding it hard to handle them so, made numerous experiments with a view of discovering some glass or fabric of a color which should add to the safety of the green, without robbing it of all efficiency. All proved equally useless, but intermittently I persevered — until last week."

His voice dropped to an almost confidential tone, and he

leaned slightly toward me. I was cold from my neck to my feet, though my head was burning, but I tried to force an appreciative smile.

"Last week," he continued impressively, "I had a prescription filled at the corner drug store. The bottle was sent home to me wrapped in a piece of what I first took to be whitish, slightly opalescent paper. Later I decided that it was some kind of membrane. When I questioned the druggist, seeking its source, he said it was a sheet of 'paper' that was around a bundle of herbs from South America. That he had no more, and doubted if I could trace it. He had wrapped my bottle so, because he was in haste and the sheet was handy.

"I can hardly tell you what first inspired me to try that membrane in my photographic work. It was merely dull white with a faint hint of opalescence, except when held against the light. Then it became quite translucent and quite brightly prismatic. For some reason it occurred to me that this refractive effect might help in breaking up the actinic rays — the rays which affect the sensitive emulsion. So that night I inserted it behind the sheets of green and yellow tissue, next the lamp prepared my trays and chemicals, laid my plate holders to hand, turned off the white light and — turned on the green!"

There was nothing in his words to inspire fear. It was a wearisomely detailed account of his struggles with photography. Yet, as he again paused impressively, I wished that he might never speak again. I was desperately, contemptibly in dread of the thing he might say next.

*

Suddenly, he drew himself erect, the stoop went out of his shoulders, he threw back his head and laughed. It was a hollow sound, as if he laughed into a trumpet. "I won't tell you what I saw! Why should I? Your own eyes shall bear witness. But this much I'll say, so that you may better understand — later. When our poor, faultily sensitive vision can perceive a thing, we say that it is visible. When the nerves of touch can feel it, we say that it is tangible. Yet I tell you there are beings intangible to our physical sense, yet whose presence is felt by the spirit, and invisible to our eyes merely because those organs are not attuned to the light as reflected from their bodies. But light passed through the screen, which we are about to use has a wave length novel to the scientific world, and by it you shall see with the eyes of the flesh that which has been invisible since life began. Have no fear!"

He stopped to laugh again, and his mirth was yellow-toothed — menacing.

"Have no fear!" he reiterated, and with that stretched his hand toward the wall, there came a click and we were in black, impenetrable darkness. I wanted to spring up, to seek the door by which I had entered and rush out of it, but the paralysis of unreasoning terror held me fast.

I could hear him moving about in the darkness, and a moment later a faint green glimmer sprang up in the room. Its source was over the large sink, where I suppose he developed his precious "color plates."

Every instant, as my eyes became accustomed to the dimness, I could see more clearly. Green light is peculiar. It may be far fainter than red, and at the same time far more illuminating. The old man was standing beneath it, and his face by that ghastly radiance had the exact look of a dead man's. Besides this, however, I could observe nothing appalling.

"That," continued the man, "is the simple developing light of which I have spoken — now watch, for what you are about to behold no mortal man but myself has ever seen before."

For a moment he fussed with the green lamp over the sink. It was so constructed that all the direct rays struck downward. He opened a flap at the side, for a moment there was a streak of comforting white luminance from within, then he inserted something, slid it slowly in — and closed the flap.

The thing he put in — that South American "membrane" it must have been — instead of decreasing the light increased it — amazingly. The hue was changed from green to greenish-gray, and the whole room sprang into view, a livid, ghastly chamber, filled with — overcrawled by — what?

My eyes fixed themselves, fascinated, on something that moved by the old man's feet. It writhed there on the floor like a huge, repulsive starfish, an immense, armed, legged thing, that twisted convulsively. It was smooth, as if made of rubber, was whitish-green in color; and presently raised its great round blob of a body on tottering tentacles, crept toward my host and writhed upward — yes, climbed up his legs, his body. And he stood there, erect, arms folded, and stared sternly down at the thing which climbed.

But the room — the whole room was alive with other creatures than that. Everywhere I looked they were — centipedish things, with yard-long bodies, detestable, furry spiders that lurked in shadows, and sausage-shaped translucent horrors that moved — and floated through the air. They dived — here and there between me and the light, and I could see its bright greenness through their greenish bodies.

Worse, though; far worse than these were the things with human faces. Mask-like, monstrous, huge gaping mouths and slitlike eyes — I find I cannot write of them. There was that about them which makes their memory even now intolerable.

The old man was speaking again, and every word echoed in my brain like the ringing of a gong. "Fear nothing! Among such as these do you move every hour of the day and night. Only you and I have seen, for God is merciful and has spared our race from sight. But I am not merciful! I loathe the race which gave these creatures birth — the race which might be so surrounded by invisible, unguessed but blessed beings — and chooses these for its companions! All the world shall see and know. One by one shall they come here, learn the truth, and perish. For who can survive the ultimate of terror? Then I, too, shall find peace, and leave the earth to its heritage of man-created horrors. Do you know what these are — whence they come?"

This voice boomed now like a cathedral bell. I could not answer, him, but he waited for no reply. "Out of the ether — out of the omnipresent ether from whose intangible substance the mind of God made the planets, all living things, and man — man has made these! By his evil thoughts, by his selfish panics, by his lusts and his interminable, never-ending hate he has made them, and they are everywhere! Fear nothing — but see where there comes to you, its creator, the shape and the body of your FEAR!"

And as he said it I perceived a great Thing coming toward

me — a Thing — but consciousness could endure no more. The ringing, threatening voice merged in a roar within my ears, there came a merciful dimming of the terrible, lurid vision, and blank nothingness succeeded upon horror too great for bearing.

IV.

There was a dull, heavy pain above my eyes. I knew that they were closed, that I was dreaming, and that the rack full of colored bottles which I seemed to see so clearly was no more than a part of the dream. There was some vague but imperative reason why I should rouse myself. I wanted to awaken, and thought that by staring very hard indeed I could dissolve this foolish vision of blue and yellow-brown bottles. But instead of dissolving they grew clearer, more solid and substantial of appearance, until suddenly the rest of my senses rushed to the support of sight, and I became aware that my eyes were open, the bottles were quite real, and that I was sitting in a chair, fallen sideways so that my cheek rested most uncomfortably on the table which held the rack.

I straightened up slowly and with difficulty, groping in my dulled brain for some clue to my presence in this unfamiliar place, this laboratory that was lighted only by the rays of an arc light in the street outside its three large windows. Here I sat, alone, and if the aching of cramped limbs meant anything, here I had sat for more than a little time.

Then, with the painful shock which accompanies awakening to the knowledge of some great catastrophe, came memory. It was this very room, shown by the street lamp's rays to be empty of life, which I had seen thronged with creatures too loathsome for description. I staggered to my feet, staring fearfully about. There were the glass-floored cases, the bookshelves, the two tables with their burdens, and the long iron sink above which, now only a dark blotch of shadow, hung the lamp from which had emanated that livid, terrifically revealing illumination. Then the experience had been no dream, but a frightful reality. I was alone here now. With callous indifference my strange host had allowed me to remain for hours unconscious, with not the least effort to aid or revive me. Perhaps, hating me so, he had hoped that I would die there.

At first I made no effort to leave the place. Its appearance filled me with reminiscent loathing. I longed to go, but as yet felt too weak and ill for the effort. Both mentally and physically my condition was deplorable, and for the first time I realized that a shock to the mind may react upon the body as vilely as any debauch of self-indulgence.

Quivering in every nerve and muscle, dizzy with headache and nausea, I dropped back into the chair, hoping that before the old man returned I might recover sufficient self-control to escape him. I knew that he hated me, and why. As I waited, sick, miserable, I understood the man. Shuddering, I recalled the loathsome horrors he had shown me. If the mere desires and emotions of mankind were daily carnified in such forms as those, no wonder that he viewed his fellow beings with detestation and longed only to destroy them.

I thought, too, of the cruel, sensuous faces I had seen in the streets outside — seen for the first time, as if a veil had been withdrawn from eyes hitherto blinded by self-delusion. Fatuously trustful as a month-old puppy, I had lived in a grim, evil world, where goodness is a word and crude selfishness the only actuality. Drearily my thoughts drifted back through my own life, its futile purposes, mistakes and activities. All of evil that I knew returned to overwhelm me. Our gropings toward divinity were a sham, a writhing sunward of slime-covered beasts who claimed sunlight as their heritage, but in their hearts preferred the foul and easy depths.

Even now, though I could neither see nor feel them, this room, the entire world, was acrawl with the beings created by our real natures. I recalled the cringing, contemptible fear to which my spirit had so readily yielded, and the faceless Thing to which the emotion had given birth.

Then abruptly, shockingly, I remembered that every moment I was adding to the horde. Since my mind could conceive only repulsive incubi, and since while I lived I must think, feel, and so continue to shape them, was there no way to check so abominable a succession? My eyes fell on the long shelves with their many-colored bottles. In the chemistry of photography there are deadly poisons — I knew that. Now was the time to end it — now! Let him return and find his desire accomplished. One good thing I could do, if one only. I could abolish my monster-creating self.

V.

My friend Mark Jenkins is an intelligent and usually a very careful man.

When he took from "Smiler" Callahan a cigar which had

every appearance of being excellent, innocent Havana, the act denoted both intelligence and caution. By very clever work he had traced the poisoning of young Ralph Peeler to Mr. Callahan's door, and he believed this particular cigar to be the mate of one smoked by Peeler just previous to his demise. And if, upon arresting Callahan, he had not confiscated this bit of evidence, it would have doubtless been destroyed by its regrettably unconscientious owner.

But when Jenkins shortly afterward gave me that cigar, as one of his own, he committed one of those almost inconceivable blunders which, I think, are occasionally forced upon clever men to keep them from overweening vanity. Discovering his slight mistake, my detective friend spent the night searching for his unintended victim, myself; and that his search was successful was due to Pietro Marini, a young Italian of Jenkins' acquaintance, whom he met about the hour of 2:00 a.m. returning from a dance.

Now, Marini had seen me standing on the steps of the house where Doctor Frederick Holt had his laboratory and living rooms, and he had stared at me, not with any ill intent, but because he thought I was the sickest-looking, most ghastly specimen of humanity that he had ever beheld. And, sharing the superstition of his South Street neighbors, he wondered if the worthy doctor had poisoned me as well as Peeler. This suspicion he imparted to Jenkins, who, however, had the best of reasons for believing otherwise. Moreover, as he informed Marini, Holt was dead, having drowned himself late the previous afternoon. An hour or so after our talk in the restaurant, news of his suicide reached Jenkins.

It seemed wise to search any place where a very sick-looking young man had been seen to enter, so Jenkins came straight to the laboratory. Across the fronts of those houses was the long sign with its mysterious inscription, "See the Great Unseen," not at all mysterious to the detective. He knew that next door to Doctor Holt's the second floor had been thrown together into a lecture room, where at certain hours a young man employed by settlement workers displayed upon a screen stereopticon views of various deadly bacilli, the germs of diseases appropriate to dirt and indifference. He knew, too, that Doctor Holt himself had helped the educational effort along by providing some really wonderful lantern slides, done by micro-color photography.

On the pavement outside, Jenkins found the two-thirds remnant of a cigar, which he gathered in and came up the steps, a very miserable and self-reproachful detective. Neither outer nor inner door was locked, and in the laboratory he found me, alive, but on the verge of death by another means that he had feared.

In the extreme physical depression following my awakening from drugged sleep, and knowing nothing of its cause, I believed my adventure fact in its entirety. My mentality was at too low an ebb to resist its dreadful suggestion. I was searching among Holt's various bottles when Jenkins burst in. At first I was merely annoyed at the interruption of my purpose, but before the anticlimax of his explanation the mists of obsession drifted away and left me still sick in body, but in spirit happy as any man may well be who has suffered a delusion that the world is wholly bad — and learned that its badness springs from his own poisoned brain.

The malice which I had observed in every face, including young Marini's, existed only in my drug-affected vision.

Last week's "popular-science" lecture had been recalled to my subconscious mind — the mind that rules dreams and delirium — by the photographic apparatus in Holt's workroom. "See the Great Unseen" assisted materially, and even the corner drug store before which I had paused, with its green-lit show vases, had doubtless played a part. But presently, following something Jenkins told me, I was driven to one protest. "If Holt was not here," I demanded, "if Holt is dead, as you say, how do you account for the fact that I, who have never seen the man, was able to give you an accurate description which you admit to be that of Doctor Frederick Holt?"

He pointed across the room. "See that?" It was a life-size bust portrait, in crayons, the picture of a white-haired man with bushy eyebrows and the most piercing black eyes I had ever seen — until the previous evening. It hung facing the door and near the windows, and the features stood out with a strangely lifelike appearance in the white rays of the arc lamp just outside. "Upon entering," continued Jenkins, "the first thing you saw was that portrait, and from it your delirium built a living, speaking man. So, there are your white-haired showman, your unnatural fear, your color photography and your pretty green golliwogs all nicely explained for you, Blaisdell, and thank God you're alive to hear the explanation. If you had smoked the whole of that cigar — well, never mind. You didn't. And now, my very dear friend, I think it's high time that you interviewed a real, flesh-and-blood doctor. I'll phone for a taxi."

"Don't," I said. "A walk in the fresh air will do me more good than fifty doctors."

"Fresh air! There's no fresh air on South Street in July," complained Jenkins, but reluctantly yielded.

I had a reason for my preference. I wished to see people, to meet face to face even such stray prowlers as might be about at this hour, nearer sunrise than midnight, and rejoice in the goodness and kindliness of the human countenance — particularly as found in the lower classes.

But even as we were leaving there occurred to me a curious inconsistency.

"Jenkins," I said, "you claim that the reason Holt, when I first met him in the hall, appeared to twice close the door in my face, was because the door never opened until I myself unlatched it."

"Yes," confirmed Jenkins, but he frowned, foreseeing my next question.

"Then why, if it was from that picture that I built so solid, so convincing a vision of the man, did I see Holt in the hall before the door was open?"

"You confuse your memories," retorted Jenkins rather shortly.

"Do I? Holt was dead at that hour, but — I tell you I saw Holt outside the door! And what was his reason for committing suicide?"

Before my friend could reply I was across the room, fumbling in the dusk there at the electric lamp above the sink. I got the tin flap open and pulled out the sliding screen, which consisted of two sheets of glass with fabric between, dark on one side, yellow on the other. With it came the very thing I dreaded —a sheet of whitish, parchmentlike, slightly opalescent stuff.

Jenkins was beside me as I held it at arm's length toward the windows. Through it the light of the arc lamp fell — divided into the most astonishingly brilliant rainbow hues. And instead of diminishing the light, it was perceptibly increased in the oddest way. Almost one thought that the sheet itself was luminous, and yet when held in shadow it gave off no light at all.

"Shall we — put it in the lamp again — and try it?" asked Jenkins slowly, and in his voice there was no hint of mockery.

I looked him straight in the eyes. "No," I said, "we won't. I was drugged. Perhaps in that condition I received a merciless revelation of the discovery that caused Holt's suicide, but I don't believe it. Ghost or no ghost, I refuse to ever again believe in the depravity of the human race. If the air and the earth are teeming with invisible horrors, they are not of our making, and — the study of demonology is better let alone. Shall we burn this thing, or tear it up?"

"We have no right to do either," returned Jenkins thoughtfully, "but you know, Blaisdell, there's a little too darn much realism about some parts of your 'dream.' I haven't been smoking any doped cigars; but when you held that up to the light, I'll swear I saw — well, never mind. Burn it — send it back to the place it came from."

"South America?" said I.

"A hotter place than that. Burn it."

So he struck a match and we did. It was gone in one great white flash.

A large place was given by morning papers to the suicide of Doctor Frederick Holt, caused, it was surmised, by mental derangement brought about by his unjust implication in the Peeler murder. It seemed an inadequate reason, since he had never been arrested, but no other was ever discovered.

Of course, our action in destroying that "membrane" was illegal and rather precipitate, but, though he won't talk about it, I know that Jenkins agrees with me — doubt is sometimes better than certainty, and there are marvels better left unproved. Those, for instance, which concern the Powers of Evil.

THE BLACK CAT

BY EDGAR ALLAN POE

INTRODUCTION

Christiana Spens

A man gets drunk and starts lashing out at his pets, first, and then, eventually, his wife. He confesses these transgressions not in the hope of swinging the verdict on his crimes, but to unburden himself, perhaps even to "make sense of" what seems to him, in many ways, unconscionable. He wasn't himself, he says. That behaviour was "not like him". One is reminded of the tabloid profiles of certain young, white men after they have committed atrocities — "like any other father" (about a man who murdered his daughter for going out), "a sweet child" (turned fascist mass-murderer), "a loving husband" (countless abusers). Although aggression and dominance are widely attributed to ideas of masculinity, to become an insane murderer is usually considered not only toxic but in some ways beyond masculinity. To lose one's sense of reality, to become reactive, emotional, and mad, is to swing too far into the realm of "feminine" characteristics.

And so instances of domestic violence, and alcoholism for that matter, present a problem for those who seek to firmly establish gender binaries; a man who has become so paranoid and delirious as to harm those in his domestic sphere, whether a wife, children or pets, has collapsed the gender binaries that established stability in the family home. His falling apart is a challenge to gender binaries and also the Enlightenment notions behind any equation of masculinity with rationality. This is why madness, possession, and rage are explained away as a fleeting thing

— the doing of a demon, somehow — not really the man himself. To admit otherwise would be to concede that his masculinity is fragile, a house of cards. And so the black cat, in this story, becomes the convenient scapegoat, the demon who explains the evil we cannot attribute easily to ourselves (or to men). In other stories, perhaps the wife would fill this role — or the "other woman" — but Poe, writing in the 1800s, made it more palatable than that.

The narrator in "The Black Cat" is, he insists, a rational man. While he blames "Fiend Intemperance" — the devil drink — for allowing his soul to become so weak as to be possessed by violent madness, the narrator's concern seems to be his own propensity to transform as he does so, and to be so different from that which he understands his identity to revolve around. The drink is a catalyst, but it cannot explain everything. He does not even blame it entirely. He blames a *cat*. He is convinced, even as he knows it makes no sense, that a cat has driven him to murder. Here we have the fiction and impossibility at the heart of Western thought: our rational selves require irrational "Others"; men project their insanity, chaos, and monstrosity so that they don't have to admit it in themselves. Their suppressed "feminine" characteristics transform into everything they fear of femininity — Madness! Sin! Submission! — only projected onto something else, whether a cat or another person.

Femininity here is entangled with Poe's notion of "instinct" and irrationality, and their relation to one another. In drawing us into all this confusion — should we believe that the narrator has been possessed by a cat? What of his story is "real"? — Poe enacts his own sort of "demonic" possession of the reader. For a moment, our own understanding of reality may be suspended, confused. Poe challenges, therefore, "the hegemony of human reason" simply through writing this story. Echoing the insights of his previous essay, "Instinct vs. Reason: A Black Cat", where he wrote that, "the boundary between instinct and reason is of a very shadowy nature", in this story he uses an account of a man's transformation from "rational" to "mad" to reveal the fragility of our own grasp of reason on a conceptual as well as personal level. He reveals that "instinct" and "reason" often collapse into one another, that instinct is a form of intelligence. Certainly, possessing a reasonable nature does not necessarily require a refutation of "instinct".

Related to this, accepting rather than expunging "the feminine" may prove the key to a more stable personality, one could argue (and perhaps Poe does). Although "The Black Cat" would seem to imply, on one level, that "when a man loses his mind, he is losing his manhood as well", in collapsing into feminine cliché of being submissive, weak, and delirious; this only happens because the narrator refuses to consider that his original actions could betray his own implicit, human weakness. By suppressing an awareness of his weakness (as a man), he becomes convinced something exterior to his own personality has caused "the insanity", and so he actually spirals into madness and confusion. The pressure to be "a man" — a rational man — knocks him into the strange logic that a cat must have provoked him, rather than his own volatility, his difficulty with the drink.

Without giving too much away to those about to read "The Black Cat" (I fear I may have already), there is a motif — eye-gouging — that struck me as resembling certain scenes from Shakespeare's *King Lear*. In this famous presentation of the old king's descent into insanity, but also truth, he only truly "sees" when his actual eyesight has been destroyed. His own daughter, Cordelia, must transform (effectively) into the loyal fool, or court jester, to be able to communicate anything honest. Likewise, perhaps, only when our narrator has blinded the cat — who is really a projection of himself — does he begin to see his own, now damned, truth. Sadly, as he seems to lose his mind, he comes to his senses in some way — gradually seeing the error of his ways, and admitting his violent alcoholism. When he destroys his wife, he becomes the (toxic) feminine — submissive (to the cat), weak, and crazy. "Superstitious", as he noted that she had been.

In so doing, this story encapsulated the fears of many men in Poe's time, and perhaps women, too. That accepting and following the rules of gender binaries — and the Enlightenment — would not prevent one's fall. This is a story of a collapse of the domestic sphere; it is a sort of "Adam and Eve" of Victorian times. The poison, the demonic animal... It is a familiar tale. Some would place this story alongside Poe's "temperance tales"— moralistic and anti-alcohol — and certainly there is a streak of the cautionary tale. But I would think that Poe only uses this familiar trope to tell another, more terrifying story — something that would torment his audience far more than the prospect of "the devil drink" alone. This is a story where the ultimate horror is that being "a real man" is a fiction. The narrator, or story, is our own "black cat" — it is the space onto which we may project our greatest fears about what we truly are. And it is not just a man or a woman; it is a sprawling confusion of sense and instinct, masculinity and femininity, learned behaviours and the unpredictable unconscious, the desires we don't understand, or even know.

In this vein, Poe took inspiration from Henry Fuseli's painting *The Nightmare* (1790–91), which created a scandal upon its initial reception, and which was well-known to Poe. Here, a woman lies rapturously and receptively on a bed, as an incubus sits on her chest, and a horse emerges from her bedroom curtains. Revealing an interior world of erotic obsession and infatuation, albeit ambiguous and "subconscious", this is a Romantic exploration of desire and dreams. Poe's narrator describes his drunkenness as if it is a sort of sleep — a delirium, anyway — and portrays the black cat similarly to Fuseli's incubus, complete with staring, domineering, reckoning eyes. The demon is the narrator's, perhaps also the artist's mirror, as is the submissive human they torment in both works.

In this split personality, and in this disturbing dream made public, we see a fight between Enlightenment and Romantic values, where Poe and Fuseli both ultimately reveal that we are made up of both, and cannot rid ourselves of either. Poe's narrator finds some sort of truth, some self-reckoning, in his delirium (as well as damnation); Fuseli's repressed desires, the unrequited infatuation that drove him to torment, became something beautiful and true in being articulated as they are in this painting. A sense of the sublime influences both gothic works, clearly. There is no enlightenment without the deep, instinctual reckoning of chaos, no perfection in beauty without the will to order life, if not necessarily the ability (or intention) to fully compose it. The desire to transform, morph, emerge — to affect awe-inspiring, terrifying change drives us across our movements and philosophies, and drips into these Gothic subjects, sustaining their cataclysmic personal revolutions. It is the potential horror of personal transformation that Poe captures here, and interrogates so that he may reveal how fluid, fleeting — indeed, mortal — we are. The death of masculinity, the fracturing of the self (by one's self), the cataclysmic triggering of violence by alcohol, domestic violence — Poe's horror-scape is so bizarrely existential, so modern, that it is hard not to become enthralled, and horrified — like a once-favourite cat, a reckoning shadow.

THE BLACK CAT

EDGAR ALLAN POE

For the most wild, yet most homely narrative which I am about to pen, I neither expect nor solicit belief. Mad indeed would I be to expect it, in a case where my very senses reject their own evidence. Yet, mad am I not — and very surely do I not dream. But to-morrow I die, and to-day I would unburthen my soul. My immediate purpose is to place before the world, plainly, succinctly, and without comment, a series of mere household events. In their consequences, these events have terrified — have tortured — have destroyed me. Yet I will not attempt to expound them. To me, they have presented little but Horror — to many they will seem less terrible than barroques. Hereafter, perhaps, some intellect may be found which will reduce my phantasm to the common-place — some intellect more calm, more logical, and far less excitable than my own, which will perceive, in the circumstances I detail with awe, nothing more than an ordinary succession of very natural causes and effects.

From my infancy I was noted for the docility and humanity of my disposition. My tenderness of heart was even so conspicuous as to make me the jest of my companions. I was especially fond of animals, and was indulged by my parents with a great variety of pets. With these I spent most of my time, and never was so happy as when feeding and caressing them. This peculiarity of character grew with my growth, and, in my manhood, I derived from it one of my principal sources of pleasure. To those who have cherished an affection for a faithful and sagacious dog, I need hardly be at the trouble of explaining the nature or the intensity of the gratification thus derivable. There is something in the unselfish and self-sacrificing love of a brute, which goes directly to the heart of him who has had frequent occasion to test the paltry friendship and gossamer fidelity of mere Man.

I married early, and was happy to find in my wife a disposition not uncongenial with my own. Observing my partiality for domestic pets, she lost no opportunity of procuring those of the most agreeable kind. We had birds, gold-fish, a fine dog, rabbits, a small monkey, and a cat.

This latter was a remarkably large and beautiful animal, entirely black, and sagacious to an astonishing degree. In speaking of his intelligence, my wife, who at heart was not a little tinctured with superstition, made frequent allusion to the ancient popular notion, which regarded all black cats as witches in disguise. Not that she was ever serious upon this point — and I mention the matter at all for no better reason than that it happens, just now, to be remembered.

Pluto — this was the cat's name — was my favorite pet and playmate. I alone fed him, and he attended me wherever I went about the house. It was even with difficulty that I could prevent him from following me through the streets.

Our friendship lasted, in this manner, for several years, during which my general temperament and character — through the instrumentality of the Fiend Intemperance — had (I blush to confess it) experienced a radical alteration for the worse. I grew, day by day, more moody, more irritable, more regardless of the feelings of others. I suffered myself to use intemperate language to my wife. At length,

I even offered her personal violence. My pets, of course, were made to feel the change in my disposition. I not only neglected, but ill-used them. For Pluto, however, I still retained sufficient regard to restrain me from maltreating him, as I made no scruple of maltreating the rabbits, the monkey, or even the dog, when by accident, or through affection, they came in my way. But my disease grew upon me — for what disease is like Alcohol! — and at length even Pluto, who was now becoming old, and consequently somewhat peevish — even Pluto began to experience the effects of my ill temper.

One night, returning home, much intoxicated, from one of my haunts about town, I fancied that the cat avoided my presence. I seized him; when, in his fright at my violence, he inflicted a slight wound upon my hand with his teeth. The fury of a demon instantly possessed me. I knew myself no longer. My original soul seemed, at once, to take its flight from my body; and a more than fiendish malevolence, gin-nurtured, thrilled every fibre of my frame. I took from my waistcoat-pocket a pen-knife, opened it, grasped the poor beast by the throat, and deliberately cut one of its eyes from the socket! I blush, I burn, I shudder, while I pen the damnable atrocity.

When reason returned with the morning — when I had slept off the fumes of the night's debauch — I experienced a sentiment half of horror, half of remorse, for the crime of which I had been guilty; but it was, at best, a feeble and equivocal feeling, and the soul remained untouched. I again plunged into excess, and soon drowned in wine all memory of the deed.

In the meantime the cat slowly recovered. The socket of the lost eye presented, it is true, a frightful appearance, but he no longer appeared to suffer any pain. He went about the house as usual, but, as might be expected, fled in extreme terror at my approach. I had so much of my old heart left, as to be at first grieved by this evident dislike on the part of a creature which had once so loved me. But this feeling soon gave place to irritation. And then came, as if to my final and irrevocable overthrow, the spirit of PERVERSENESS. Of this spirit philosophy takes no account. Yet I am not more sure that my soul lives, than I am that perverseness is one of the primitive impulses of the human heart — one of the indivisible primary faculties, or sentiments, which give direction to the character of Man. Who has not, a hundred times, found himself committing a vile or a silly action, for no other reason than because he knows he should *not*? Have we not a perpetual inclination, in the teeth of our best judgment, to violate that which is Law, merely because we understand it to be such? This spirit of perverseness, I say, came to my final overthrow. It was this unfathomable longing of the soul to vex itself — to offer violence to its own nature — to do wrong for the wrong's sake only — that urged me to continue and finally to consummate the injury I had inflicted upon the unoffending brute. One morning, in cool blood, I slipped a noose about its neck and hung it to the limb of a tree; — hung it with the tears streaming from my eyes, and with the bitterest remorse at my heart; — hung it *because* I knew that it had loved me, and because I felt it had given me no reason of offence; — hung it because I knew that in so doing I was committing a sin — a deadly sin that would so jeopardize my immortal soul as to place it — if such a thing were possible — even beyond the reach of the infinite mercy of the Most Merciful and Most Terrible God.

On the night of the day on which this cruel deed was done, I was aroused from sleep by the cry of fire. The curtains of my bed were in flames. The whole house was blazing. It was with great difficulty that my wife, a servant, and myself, made our escape from the conflagration. The destruction was complete. My entire worldly wealth was swallowed up, and I resigned myself thenceforward to despair.

I am above the weakness of seeking to establish a sequence of cause and effect, between the disaster and the atrocity. But I am detailing a chain of facts — and wish not to leave even a possible link imperfect. On the day succeeding the fire, I visited the ruins. The walls, with one exception, had fallen in. This exception was found in a compartment wall, not very thick, which stood about the middle of the house, and against which had rested the head of my bed. The plastering had here, in great measure, resisted the action of the fire — a fact which I attributed to its having been recently spread. About this wall a dense crowd were collected, and many persons seemed to be examining a particular portion of it with very minute and eager attention. The words "strange!" "singular!" and other similar expressions, excited my curiosity. I approached and saw, as if graven in *bas relief* upon the white surface, the figure of a gigantic *cat*. The impression was given with an accuracy truly marvellous. There was a rope about the animal's neck.

When I first beheld this apparition — for I could scarcely regard it as less — my wonder and my terror were extreme. But at length reflection came to my aid. The cat, I remembered, had been hung in a garden adjacent to the house. Upon the alarm of fire, this garden had been immediately filled by the crowd — by some one of whom the animal must have been cut from the tree and thrown, through an open window, into my chamber. This had probably been done with the view of arousing me from sleep. The falling of other walls had compressed the victim of my cruelty into the substance of the freshly-spread plaster; the lime of which, with the flames, and the ammonia from the carcass, had then accomplished the portraiture as I saw it.

Although I thus readily accounted to my reason, if not altogether to my conscience, for the startling fact just detailed, it did not the less fail to make a deep impression upon my fancy. For months I could not rid myself of the phantasm of the cat; and, during this period, there came back into my spirit a half-sentiment that seemed, but was not, remorse. I went so far as to regret the loss of the animal, and to look about me, among the vile haunts which I now habitually frequented, for another pet of the same species, and of somewhat similar appearance, with which to supply its place.

One night as I sat, half stupefied, in a den of more than infamy, my attention was suddenly drawn to some black object, reposing upon the head of one of the immense hogsheads of Gin, or of Rum, which constituted the chief furniture of the apartment. I had been looking steadily at the top of this hogshead for some minutes, and what now caused me surprise was the fact that I had not sooner perceived the object thereupon. I approached it, and touched it with my hand. It was a black cat — a very large one — fully as large as Pluto, and closely resembling him in every respect but one. Pluto had not a white hair upon any portion of his body; but this cat had a large, although indefinite splotch of white, covering nearly the whole region of the breast.

Upon my touching him, he immediately arose, purred loudly, rubbed against my hand, and appeared delighted with my notice. This, then, was the very creature of which I was in search. I at once offered to purchase it of the landlord; but this person made no claim to it — knew nothing of it — had never seen it before.

I continued my caresses, and, when I prepared to go home, the animal evinced a disposition to accompany me. I permitted it to do so; occasionally stooping and patting it as I proceeded. When it reached the house it domesticated itself at once, and became immediately a great favorite with my wife.

For my own part, I soon found a dislike to it arising within me. This was just the reverse of what I had anticipated; but — I know not how or why it was — its evident fondness for myself rather disgusted and annoyed. By slow degrees, these feelings of disgust and annoyance rose into the bitterness of hatred. I avoided the creature; a certain sense of shame, and the remembrance of my former deed of cruelty, preventing me from physically abusing it. I did not, for some weeks, strike, or otherwise violently ill use it; but gradually — very gradually — I came to look upon it with unutterable loathing, and to flee silently from its odious presence, as from the breath of a pestilence.

What added, no doubt, to my hatred of the beast, was the discovery, on the morning after I brought it home, that, like Pluto, it also had been deprived of one of its eyes. This circumstance, however, only endeared it to my wife, who, as I have already said, possessed, in a high degree, that humanity of feeling which had once been my distinguishing trait, and the source of many of my simplest and purest pleasures.

With my aversion to this cat, however, its partiality for myself seemed to increase. It followed my footsteps with a pertinacity which it would be difficult to make the reader comprehend. Whenever I sat, it would crouch beneath my chair, or spring upon my knees, covering me with its loathsome caresses. If I arose to walk it would get between my feet and thus nearly throw me down, or, fastening its long and sharp claws in my dress, clamber, in this manner, to my breast. At such times, although I longed to destroy it with a blow, I was yet withheld from so doing, partly by a memory of my former crime, but chiefly — let me confess it at once — by absolute *dread* of the beast.

This dread was not exactly a dread of physical evil — and yet I should be at a loss how otherwise to define it. I am almost ashamed to own — yes, even in this felon's cell, I am almost ashamed to own — that the terror and horror with which the animal inspired me, had been heightened by one of the merest chimæras it would be possible to conceive. My wife had called my attention, more than once, to the character of the mark of white hair, of which I have spoken, and which constituted the sole visible difference between the strange beast and the one I had destroyed. The reader will remember that this mark, although large, had been originally very indefinite; but, by slow degrees — degrees nearly imperceptible, and which for a long time my Reason struggled to reject as fanciful — it had, at length, assumed a rigorous distinctness of outline. It was now the representation of an object that I shudder to name — and for this, above all, I loathed, and dreaded, and would have rid myself of the monster had I dared — it was now, I say, the image of a hideous — of a ghastly thing — of the GALLOWS! — oh, mournful and terrible engine of Horror and of Crime — of Agony and of Death!

And now was I indeed wretched beyond the wretchedness of mere Humanity. And *a brute* beast — whose fellow I had contemptuously destroyed — *a brute beast* to work out for me — for me a man, fashioned in the image of the High God — so much of insufferable wo! Alas! neither by day nor by night knew I the blessing of Rest any more! During the former the creature left me no moment alone; and, in the latter, I started, hourly, from dreams of unutterable fear, to find the hot breath of the thing upon my face, and its vast weight — an incarnate Night-Mare that I had no power to shake off — incumbent eternally upon my heart!

Beneath the pressure of torments such as these, the feeble remnant of the good within me succumbed. Evil thoughts became my sole intimates — the darkest and most evil of thoughts. The moodiness of my usual temper increased to hatred of all things and of all mankind; while, from the sudden, frequent, and ungovernable outbursts of a fury to which I now blindly abandoned myself, my uncomplaining wife, alas! was the most usual and the most patient of sufferers.

One day she accompanied me, upon some household errand, into the cellar of the old building which our poverty compelled us to inhabit. The cat followed me down the steep stairs, and, nearly throwing me headlong, exasperated me to madness. Uplifting an axe, and forgetting, in my wrath, the childish dread which had hitherto stayed my hand, I aimed a blow at the animal which, of course, would have proved instantly fatal had it descended as I wished. But this blow was arrested by the hand of my wife. Goaded, by the interference, into a rage more than demoniacal, I withdrew my arm from her grasp and buried the axe in her brain. She fell dead upon the spot, without a groan.

This hideous murder accomplished, I set myself forthwith, and with entire deliberation, to the task of concealing the body. I knew that I could not remove it from the house, either by day or by night, without the risk of being observed by the neighbors. Many projects entered my mind. At one period I thought of cutting the corpse into minute fragments, and destroying them by fire. At another, I resolved to dig a grave for it in the floor of the cellar. Again, I deliberated about casting it in the well in the yard — about packing it in a box, as if merchandize, with the usual arrangements, and so getting a porter to take it from the house. Finally I hit upon what I considered a far better expedient than either of these. I determined to wall it up in the cellar — as the monks of the middle ages are recorded to have walled up their victims.

For a purpose such as this the cellar was well adapted. Its walls were loosely constructed, and had lately been plastered throughout with a rough plaster, which the dampness of the atmosphere had prevented from hardening. Moreover, in one of the walls was a projection, caused by a false chimney, or fireplace, that had been filled up, and made to resemble the rest of the cellar. I made no doubt that I could readily displace the bricks at this point, insert the corpse, and wall the whole up as before, so that no eye could detect any thing suspicious.

And in this calculation I was not deceived. By means of a crow-bar I easily dislodged the bricks, and, having carefully deposited the body against the inner wall, I propped it in that position, while, with little trouble, I re-laid the whole structure as it originally stood. Having procured mortar, sand, and hair, with every possible precaution, I prepared a plaster which could not be distinguished from the old, and with this I very carefully went over the new brick-work. When I had finished, I felt satisfied that all was right. The wall did not present the slightest appearance of having been disturbed. The rubbish on the floor was picked up with the minutest care. I looked around triumphantly, and said to myself — "Here at least, then, my labor has not been in vain."

My next step was to look for the beast which had been the cause of so much wretchedness; for I had, at length, firmly resolved to put it to death. Had I been able to meet with it, at the moment, there could have been no doubt of its fate; but it appeared that the crafty animal had been alarmed at the violence of my previous anger, and forebore to present itself in my present mood. It is impossible to describe, or to imagine, the deep, the blissful sense of relief which the absence of the detested creature occasioned in my bosom. It did not make its appearance during the night — and thus for one night at least, since its introduction into the house, I soundly and tranquilly slept; aye, slept even with the burden of murder upon my soul!

The second and the third day passed, and still my tormentor came not. Once again I breathed as a freeman. The monster, in terror, had fled the premises forever! I should behold it no more! My happiness was supreme! The guilt of my dark deed disturbed me but little. Some few inquiries had been made, but these had been readily answered. Even a search had been instituted — but of course nothing was to be discovered. I looked upon my future felicity as secured.

Upon the fourth day of the assassination, a party of the police came, very unexpectedly, into the house, and proceeded again to make rigorous investigation of the premises. Secure, however, in the inscrutability of my place of concealment, I felt no embarrassment whatever. The officers bade me accompany them in their search. They left no nook or corner unexplored. At length, for the third or fourth time, they descended into the cellar. I quivered not in a muscle. My heart beat calmly as that of one who slumbers in innocence. I walked the cellar from end to end. I folded my arms upon my bosom, and roamed easily to and fro. The police were thoroughly satisfied and prepared to depart. The glee at my heart was too strong to be restrained. I burned to say if but one word, by way of triumph, and to render doubly sure their assurance of my guiltlessness.

"Gentlemen," I said at last, as the party ascended the steps, "I delight to have allayed your suspicions. I wish you all health, and a little more courtesy. By the bye, gentlemen, this — this is a very well constructed house." (In the rabid desire to say something easily, I scarcely knew what I uttered at all.) — "I may say an *excellently* well constructed house. These walls — are you going, gentlemen? — these walls are solidly put together;" and here, through the mere phrenzy of bravado, I rapped heavily, with a cane which I held in my hand, upon that very portion of the brick-work behind which stood the corpse of the wife of my bosom.

But may God shield and deliver me from the fangs of the Arch-Fiend! No sooner had the reverberation of my blows sunk into silence, than I was answered by a voice from within the tomb! — by a cry, at first muffled and broken, like the sobbing of a child, and then quickly swelling into one long, loud, and continuous scream, utterly anomalous and inhuman — a howl — a wailing shriek, half of horror and half of triumph, such as might have arisen only out of hell, conjointly from the throats of the dammed in their agony and of the demons that exult in the damnation.

Of my own thoughts it is folly to speak. Swooning, I staggered to the opposite wall. For one instant the party upon the stairs remained motionless, through extremity of terror and of awe. In the next, a dozen stout arms were toiling at the wall. It fell bodily. The corpse, already greatly decayed and clotted with gore, stood erect before the eyes of the spectators. Upon its head, with red extended mouth and solitary eye of fire, sat the hideous beast whose craft had seduced me into murder, and whose informing voice had consigned me to the hangman. I had walled the monster up within the tomb!

THE WILLOWS

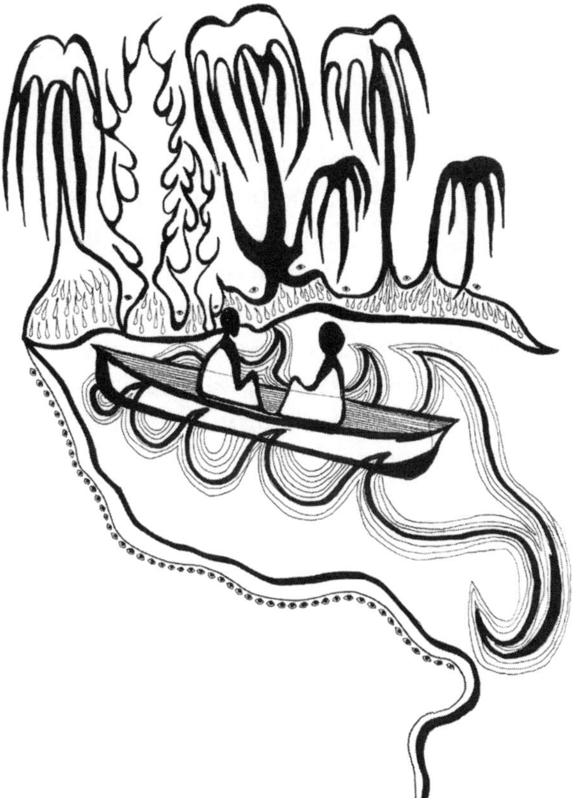

BY ALGERNON BLACKWOOD

INTRODUCTION

Eugene Thacker

In the summer of 1901, thirty-two-year-old Algernon Blackwood made two trips down the Danube River: the first with a friend and the second alone. Travelling by canoe and bringing with him only the sparsest of supplies, Blackwood's voyage began "not one hundred yards from the Black Forest" for a "journey of four and twenty hundred miles to the Black Sea". This was not the first such voyage Blackwood had taken, nor was it in any way unusual for him; though he was in many respects a modern, cosmopolitan figure — travelling widely, he worked as a farmer, bartender, hotel manager, business investor, radio presenter, and journalist — Blackwood, by his own account, was more apt to be found hiking in the mountains, camping in forests, or drifting down the isolate and languorous byways of winding rivers. But the Danube boat trip seemed to make a particular impact on Blackwood, so much so that he would later write about it in a two-part article, "Down the Danube in a Canadian Canoe", published in *Macmillan's Magazine* in the autumn of 1901. There Blackwood writes about those things we have come to expect in nature writing: the urge to flee the modern city, the peace of solitude in nature, encounters with rural village life along the way, and the many scenes of majestic natural landscapes. In one passage, savouring the solitude of the trip, he writes:

> Soon the water increased and the canoe sped onwards among the little waves and rapids like a winged thing. The

> mountains became higher, the valley narrower. Limestone cliffs, scooped and furrowed by the eddies of a far larger Danube thousands of years before, rose gleaming out of the pine-woods about their base… One moment we were in blazing sunlight, the next in deep shadow under the cliffs.

In the article, Blackwood shows himself to be an acute observer of nature, endlessly fascinated by the constant transformations of the landscape around him. But there was something about the Danube canoe trip that seemed to reveal to Blackwood another kind of nature. In certain passages he seems entranced by a kind of deep time, one of the indifference of the slowly swaying trees along the shore, of still waters and the stoppage of time, of landscapes shaping themselves according to an impersonal logic that evades even the shrewdest naturalist:

> When we went to bed at ten o'clock the full moon shone upon the white cliffs with a dazzling brilliance that seemed to turn them into ice, while the deep shadows over the river made the scene strangely impressive. Only the tumbling of the water and the chirping of the crickets broke the silence. In the night we woke and thought we heard people moving round the tent, but, on going out to see, the canoe was still safe, and the white moonshine revealed no figures. It was doubtless the river talking in its sleep, or the wind wandering lost among the bushes.

Already this is the stuff of Blackwood's many stories of supernatural horror. But what gives scenes like this their ambiance of otherworldliness is not that there are menacing monsters in the night, but rather that the entire environment — the mountains, sky, river, trees — are somehow alive, and alive in an impersonal but sublime way that far exceeds the taxonomies of the naturalist or the theories of the biologist. At one point in the journey, Blackwood makes note of a scene that, in itself, has nothing supernatural about it — circling crows, swaying trees, crepuscular sky — but it is precisely its naturalism that gives Blackwood the sense of "a something alive":

> Big grey hawks circled ever over head and grey crows by the thousand lined the shores. That evening, after crossing and re-crossing the river, we found a sheltered camp on a sandy island where pollards and willows roared in the wind. As if to show the loneliness of the spot an otter, rolling over and over among the eddies, swam past us as we landed. About sunset the clouds broke up momentarily and let out a flood of crimson light all over the wild country. Against the gorgeous red sky a stream of dark clouds, in all shapes and kinds, hurried over into the Carpathian mountains…

In short, a landscape without human beings — except, of course, for the enigma of the solitary observer Blackwood himself, bearing witness to the absence of all humanity. And the landscape, the river, the trees, the sky, all persist, doing what they do, almost as if nothing had happened. In a way, this enigma runs through nearly all of Blackwood's fiction, and, reading "Down the Danube…" one can easily trace the direct influence of this trip on tales like "The Willows", first published in Blackwood's 1907 collection *The Listener and Other Stories*.

However, this is only part of the story. Though Blackwood's life is a life of drifting, wandering, and seeking, there are arguably two abiding interests that run through his varied occupations and travels. The first we've already noted, which is his affinity for nature. The second is Blackwood's life-long interest in the occult, the paranormal, and alternative spiritualities. From an early age, he took an interest in Buddhism and Hinduism, would later delve into Kabbalah, Theosophy, and the varieties of mysticism, and would become a member of The Ghost Club as well as a member of the Hermetic Order of the Golden Dawn.

And yet, in spite of this life-long interest in the occult, Blackwood never threw in his lot with any one organisation or group; nor did he ever settle on any single theory, system, or hypothesis. In his intellectual interests, as in his life, he continued wandering. In "The Willows" — as in nearly all of Blackwood's tales of supernatural horror — one finds a highly syncretic array of references, ebbing and flowing throughout the story, but never settling: from ancient animism to philosophical pantheism to modern scientific hypotheses of other-dimensional space-time.

This openness to possibility (really, a possibility beyond the comprehension of what is possible), as well as the reticence to believe in any single explanation, are also what ground "The Willows" as a story. The narrator is continually fascinated by the increasing unreality of the natural world, the deeper and deeper their travels take them into the willows, and yet he seems even more uncertain of what "nature" is by the end of the story than at the beginning. Blackwood himself is also there in the refreshingly un-intellectual, pragmatic, down-to-earth character of "the Swede", whose reliance on empirical evidence only leads the pair to question their own senses, eventually unravelling into a swarm of half-formed superstitions and dimly-intuited, metaphysical conspiracies. As different as they are as types, both characters are perpetually uncertain about what they've experienced, or indeed if they've experienced anything at all.

Here, as in other Blackwood stories, there is a basic sense of a "something else" behind it all, a numinous, impersonal agency that eerily animates the undulating willows and that is even there in the equally eerie moments of total stillness on the river. Though a wide range of explanations for what the characters experience are attempted (and subsequently rejected), there is also an underlying suspicion that this "something else" resides in a cognitive blind spot for them as human beings, forever beyond the pale of comprehension. "Nature" is not some bounteous Eden of generosity, providentially gifting itself to the provenance of human beings for their benefit, enjoyment, and utility. Instead, nature in "The Willows" becomes occluded from human understanding, hiding in plain sight — nature becomes "occulted". A "something" makes its presence known, at the very same time that it recedes into a tenebrous blind spot that the limited range of human experience can only register in broken terms: a faltering of speech, a freezing of thought, a failure of reason, the inadequacy of faith.

The overall affect that results is a kind of negative epiphany: the awareness of the possibility of an impersonal — and ultimately cosmic — order, but an order beyond the horizon of intelligibility. If there is "nature" in a story like "The Willows" perhaps it is neither the nature of physics and its laws of nature, nor is it nature in the sense of forests, rivers, and mountains. Perhaps it is "nature" in the sense of the collapse of our human-bound categories of "natural" and "supernatural"; the point of frozen thought.

If we are to call Blackwood a naturalist, then we must do so with caution, for his sublime awe before the mysteries of nature is always coupled with an acute awareness of the indifference of what we dutifully tag as "nature". "The Willows" suggests something different: perhaps what we call the "supernatural" is simply the nature either we don't see or don't comprehend. It is the site of myth, religion, metaphysics — and perhaps of science as well. At one point the narrator suggests as much: the strangest or "weirdest" understanding of nature is given to us not from ancient superstitions but from modern science. Perhaps the natural is supernatural, and vice-versa.

Blackwood, like many authors of weird fiction, revels in this affect. But instead of eliciting mortal terror or gothic horrors, for Blackwood this moment of frozen thought is a moment of tranquillity. In his autobiography Blackwood repeatedly writes with startling honestly about his affinity for the natural world:

> By far the strongest influence in my life, however, was Nature... Bringing comfort, companionship, inspiration, joy, the spell of Nature has remained dominant, a truly magical spell... The early feeling that everything was alive, a dim sense that some kind of consciousness struggled through every form, even that a sort of inarticulate communication with this "other life" was possible, could I but discover the way — these moods coloured its opening wonder.

In this sense "The Willows" is a story that allows the mania for comprehension to flip into a kind of affective incomprehension — the human being confronting the horizon of its own intelligibility, producing not horror or terror but a strange sense of wonder.

It is difficult to write about Blackwood's stories without one's writing itself taking on the vast, zoomed-out perspective that those stories evoke. I am, admittedly, too biased to give "The Willows" the proper critical analysis it deserves. And while I've taught "The Willows" more times than I can count, I never tire of the way Blackwood uses language that is at once unadorned yet lyrical to articulate the ambivalent allure of the indifferent, the impersonal, and the unhuman. But there is also something very contemporary about "The Willows", especially in an era haunted by an emerging consciousness of planetary microbes, tectonic shifts, climate-engineered skies, and a dark suspicion concerning a rare earth. Blackwood's story raises deeply ambiguous questions concerning human-centric attitudes and the anthropomorphic world that has been arrayed around us, for us, by us.

"The Willows" is less a flight of fancy and more an attempt to articulate the ways in which what we dubiously still call "nature" is at once an object of human systems of knowledge and yet also something that undermines those same systems. Thus if "The Willows" is indeed a classic of "supernatural horror" (as H.P. Lovecraft would famously note), we might also be justified in calling it "natural horror" as well. In Blackwood's wonderfully slow, patiently constructed scenes of atmospheric suspense, there is the sense of an impersonal sublime, a lyricism of the unhuman that shores up the limitations of anthropocentric thinking, as well as evoking the attendant smallness of human beings against the backdrop of this deep time perspective.

THE WILLOWS

ALGERNON BLACKWOOD

After leaving Vienna, and long before you come to Budapest, the Danube enters a region of singular loneliness and desolation, where its waters spread away on all sides regardless of a main channel, and the country becomes a swamp for miles upon miles, covered by a vast sea of low willow-bushes. On the big maps this deserted area is painted in a fluffy blue, growing fainter in color as it leaves the banks, and across it may be seen in large straggling letters the word Sumpfe, meaning marshes.

In high flood this great acreage of sand, shingle-beds, and willow-grown islands is almost topped by the water, but in normal seasons the bushes bend and rustle in the free winds, showing their silver leaves to the sunshine in an ever-moving plain of bewildering beauty. These willows never attain to the dignity of trees; they have no rigid trunks; they remain humble bushes, with rounded tops and soft outline, swaying on slender stems that answer to the least pressure of the wind; supple as grasses, and so continually shifting that they somehow give the impression that the entire plain is moving and alive. For the wind sends waves rising and falling over the whole surface, waves of leaves instead of waves of water, green swells like the sea, too, until the branches turn and lift, and then silvery white as their underside turns to the sun.

Happy to slip beyond the control of the stern banks, the Danube here wanders about at will among the intricate network of channels intersecting the islands everywhere with broad avenues down which the waters pour with a shouting sound; making whirlpools, eddies, and foaming rapids; tearing at the sandy banks; carrying away masses of shore and willow-clumps; and forming new islands innumerably which shift daily in size and shape and possess at best an impermanent life, since the flood-time obliterates their very existence.

Properly speaking, this fascinating part of the river's life begins soon after leaving Pressburg, and we, in our Canadian canoe, with gipsy tent and frying-pan on board, reached it on the crest of a rising flood about mid-July. That very same morning, when the sky was reddening before sunrise, we had slipped swiftly through still-sleeping Vienna, leaving it a couple of hours later a mere patch of smoke against the blue hills of the Wienerwald on the horizon; we had breakfasted below Fischeramend under a grove of birch trees roaring in the wind; and had then swept on the tearing current past Orth, Hainburg, Petronell (the old Roman Carnuntum of Marcus Aurelius), and so under the frowning heights of Thelsen on a spur of the Carpathians, where the March steals in quietly from the left and the frontier is crossed between Austria and Hungary.

Racing along at twelve kilometers an hour soon took us well into Hungary, and the muddy waters—sure sign of flood—sent us aground on many a shingle-bed, and twisted us like a cork in many a sudden belching whirlpool before the towers of Pressburg (Hungarian, Poszony) showed against the sky; and then the canoe, leaping like a spirited horse, flew at top speed under the grey walls, negotiated safely the sunken chain of the Fliegende Brucke ferry, turned the corner sharply to the left, and plunged on yellow foam into the wilderness of islands, sandbanks, and swamp-land beyond—the land of the willows.

The change came suddenly, as when a series of bioscope pictures snaps down on the streets of a town and shifts without warning into the scenery of lake and forest. We entered the land of desolation on wings, and in less than half an hour there was neither boat nor fishing-hut nor red roof, nor any single sign of human habitation and civilization within sight. The sense of remoteness from the world of humankind, the utter isolation, the fascination of this singular world of willows, winds, and waters, instantly laid its spell upon us both, so that we allowed laughingly to one another that we ought by rights to have held some special kind of passport to admit us, and that we had, somewhat audaciously, come without asking leave into a separate little kingdom of wonder and magic—a kingdom that was reserved for the use of others who had a right to it, with everywhere unwritten warnings to trespassers for those who had the imagination to discover them.

Though still early in the afternoon, the ceaseless buffetings of a most tempestuous wind made us feel weary, and we at once began casting about for a suitable camping-ground for the night. But the bewildering character of the islands made landing difficult; the swirling flood carried us in shore and then swept us out again; the willow branches tore our hands as we seized them to stop the canoe, and we pulled many a yard of sandy bank into the water before at length we shot with a great sideways blow from the wind into a backwater and managed to beach the bows in a cloud of spray. Then we lay panting and laughing after our exertions on the hot yellow sand, sheltered from the wind, and in the full blaze of a scorching sun, a cloudless blue sky above, and an immense army of dancing, shouting willow bushes, closing in from all sides, shining with spray and clapping their thousand little hands as though to applaud the success of our efforts.

"What a river!" I said to my companion, thinking of all the way we had traveled from the source in the Black Forest, and how he had often been obliged to wade and push in the upper shallows at the beginning of June.

"Won't stand much nonsense now, will it?" he said, pulling the canoe a little farther into safety up the sand, and then composing himself for a nap.

I lay by his side, happy and peaceful in the bath of the elements—water, wind, sand, and the great fire of the sun—thinking of the long journey that lay behind us, and of the great stretch before us to the Black Sea, and how lucky I was to have such a delightful and charming traveling companion as my friend, the Swede.

We had made many similar journeys together, but the Danube, more than any other river I knew, impressed us from the very beginning with its aliveness. From its tiny bubbling entry into the world among the pinewood gardens of Donaueschingen, until this moment when it began to play the great river-game of losing itself among the deserted swamps, unobserved, unrestrained, it had seemed to us like following the growth of some living creature. Sleepy at first, but later developing violent desires as it became conscious of its deep soul, it rolled, like some huge fluid being, through all the countries we had passed, holding our little craft on its mighty shoulders, playing roughly with us sometimes, yet always friendly and well-meaning, till at length we had come inevitably to regard it as a Great Personage.

How, indeed, could it be otherwise, since it told us so much of its secret life? At night we heard it singing to the moon as we lay in our tent, uttering that odd sibilant note peculiar to itself and said to be caused by the rapid tearing of the pebbles along its bed, so great is its hurrying speed. We knew, too, the voice of its gurgling whirlpools, suddenly bubbling up on a surface previously quite calm; the roar of its shallows and swift rapids; its constant steady thundering below all mere surface sounds; and that ceaseless tearing of its icy waters at the banks. How it stood up and shouted when the rains fell flat upon its face! And how its laughter roared out when the wind blew up-stream and tried to stop its growing speed! We knew all its sounds and voices, its tumblings and foamings, its unnecessary splashing against the bridges; that self-conscious chatter when there were hills to look on; the affected dignity of its speech when it passed through the little towns, far too important to laugh; and all these faint, sweet whisperings when the sun caught it fairly in some slow curve and poured down upon it till the steam rose.

It was full of tricks, too, in its early life before the great world knew it. There were places in the upper reaches among the Swabian forests, when yet the first whispers of its destiny had not reached it, where it elected to disappear through holes in the ground, to appear again on the other side of the porous limestone hills and start a new river with another name; leaving, too, so little water in its own bed that we had to climb out and wade and push the canoe through miles of shallows.

And a chief pleasure, in those early days of its irresponsible youth, was to lie low, like Brer Fox, just before the little turbulent tributaries came to join it from the Alps, and to refuse to acknowledge them when in, but to run for miles side by side, the dividing line well marked, the very levels different, the Danube utterly declining to recognize the newcomer. Below Passau, however, it gave up this particular trick, for there the Inn comes in with a thundering power impossible to ignore, and so pushes and incommodes the parent river that there is hardly room for them in the long twisting gorge that follows, and the Danube is shoved this way and that against the cliffs, and forced to hurry itself with great waves and much dashing to and fro in order to get through in time. And during the fight our canoe slipped down from its shoulder to its breast, and had the time of its life among the struggling waves. But the Inn taught the old river a lesson, and after Passau it no longer pretended to ignore new arrivals.

This was many days back, of course, and since then we had come to know other aspects of the great creature, and across the Bavarian wheat plain of Straubing she wandered so slowly under the blazing June sun that we could well imagine only the surface inches were water, while below there moved, concealed as by a silken mantle, a whole army of Undines, passing silently and unseen down to the sea, and very leisurely too, lest they be discovered.

Much, too, we forgave her because of her friendliness to the birds and animals that haunted the shores. Cormorants lined the banks in lonely places in rows like short black palings; grey crows crowded the shingle-beds; storks stood fishing in the vistas of shallower water that opened up between the islands, and hawks, swans, and marsh birds of all sorts filled the air with glinting wings and singing, petulant cries. It was impossible to feel annoyed with the river's vagaries after seeing a deer leap with a splash into the water at sunrise and swim past the bows of the canoe; and often we saw fawns peering at us from the underbrush, or looked straight into the brown eyes of a stag as we charged full tilt round a corner and entered another reach of the river. Foxes, too, everywhere haunted the banks, tripping daintily among the driftwood and disappearing so suddenly that it was impossible to see how they managed it.

But now, after leaving Pressburg, everything changed a little, and the Danube became more serious. It ceased trifling. It was half-way to the Black Sea, within seeming distance almost of other, stranger countries where no tricks would be permitted or understood. It became suddenly grown-up, and claimed our respect and even our awe. It broke out into three arms, for one thing, that only met again a hundred kilometers farther down, and for a canoe there were no indications which one was intended to be followed.

"If you take a side channel," said the Hungarian officer we met in the Pressburg shop while buying provisions, "you may find yourselves, when the flood subsides, forty miles from anywhere, high and dry, and you may easily starve. There are no people, no farms, no fishermen. I warn you not to continue. The river, too, is still rising, and this wind will increase."

The rising river did not alarm us in the least, but the matter of being left high and dry by a sudden subsidence of the waters might be serious, and we had consequently laid in an extra stock of provisions. For the rest, the officer's prophecy held true, and the wind, blowing down a perfectly clear sky, increased steadily till it reached the dignity of a westerly gale.

It was earlier than usual when we camped, for the sun was a good hour or two from the horizon, and leaving my friend still asleep on the hot sand, I wandered about in desultory examination of our hotel. The island, I found, was less than an acre in extent, a mere sandy bank standing some two or three feet above the level of the river. The far end, pointing into the sunset, was covered with flying spray which the tremendous wind drove off the crests of the broken waves. It was triangular in shape, with the apex up stream.

I stood there for several minutes, watching the impetuous crimson flood bearing down with a shouting roar, dashing in waves against the bank as though to sweep it bodily away, and then swirling by in two foaming streams on either side. The ground seemed to shake with the shock and rush, while the furious movement of the willow bushes as the wind poured over them increased the curious illusion that the island itself actually moved. Above, for a mile or two, I could see the great river descending upon me; it was like looking up the slope of a sliding hill, white with foam, and leaping up everywhere to show itself to the sun.

The rest of the island was too thickly grown with willows to make walking pleasant, but I made the tour, nevertheless. From the lower end the light, of course, changed, and the river looked dark and angry. Only the backs of the flying waves were visible, streaked with foam, and pushed forcibly by the great puffs of wind that fell upon them from behind. For a short mile it was visible, pouring in and out among the islands, and then disappearing with a huge sweep into the willows, which closed about it like a herd of monstrous antediluvian creatures crowding down to drink. They made me think of gigantic sponge-like growths that sucked the river up into themselves. They caused it to vanish from sight. They herded there together in such overpowering numbers.

Altogether it was an impressive scene, with its utter loneliness, its bizarre suggestion; and as I gazed, long and curiously, a singular emotion began to stir somewhere in the depths of me. Midway in my delight of the wild beauty, there crept, unbidden and unexplained, a curious feeling of disquietude, almost of alarm.

A rising river, perhaps, always suggests something of the ominous; many of the little islands I saw before me would probably have been swept away by the morning; this resistless, thundering flood of water touched the sense of awe. Yet I was aware that my uneasiness lay deeper far than the emotions of awe and wonder. It was not that I felt. Nor had it directly to do with the power of the driving wind—this shouting hurricane that might almost carry up a few acres of willows into the air and scatter them like so much chaff over the landscape. The wind was simply enjoying itself, for nothing rose out of the flat landscape to stop it, and I was conscious of sharing its great game with a kind of pleasurable excitement. Yet this novel emotion had nothing to do with the wind. Indeed, so vague was the sense of distress I experienced, that it was impossible to trace it to its source and deal with it accordingly, though I was aware somehow that it had to do with my realization of our utter insignificance before this unrestrained power of the elements about me. The huge-grown river had something to do with it too—a vague, unpleasant idea that we had somehow trifled with these great elemental forces in whose power we lay helpless every hour of the day and night. For here, indeed, they were gigantically at play together, and the sight appealed to the imagination.

But my emotion, so far as I could understand it, seemed to attach itself more particularly to the willow bushes, to these acres and acres of willows, crowding, so thickly growing there, swarming everywhere the eye could reach, pressing upon the river as though to suffocate it, standing in dense array mile after mile beneath the sky, watching, waiting, listening. And, apart quite from the elements, the willows connected themselves subtly with my malaise, attacking the mind insidiously somehow by reason of their vast numbers, and contriving in some way or other to represent to the imagination a new and mighty power, a power, moreover, not altogether friendly to us.

Great revelations of nature, of course, never fail to impress in one way or another, and I was no stranger to moods of the kind. Mountains overawe and oceans terrify, while the mystery of great forests exercises a spell peculiarly its own. But all these, at one point or another, somewhere link on intimately with human life and human experience. They stir comprehensible, even if alarming, emotions. They tend on the whole to exalt.

With this multitude of willows, however, it was something far different, I felt. Some essence emanated from them that besieged the heart. A sense of awe awakened, true, but of awe touched somewhere by a vague terror. Their serried ranks, growing everywhere darker about me as the shadows deepened, moving furiously yet softly in the wind, woke in me the curious and unwelcome suggestion that we had trespassed here upon the borders of an alien world, a world where we were intruders, a world where we were not wanted or invited to remain—where we ran grave risks perhaps!

The feeling, however, though it refused to yield its meaning entirely to analysis, did not at the time trouble me by passing into menace. Yet it never left me quite, even during the very practical business of putting up the tent in a hurricane of wind and building a fire for the stew-pot. It remained, just enough to bother and perplex, and to rob a most delightful camping-ground of a good portion of its charm. To my companion, however, I said nothing, for he was a man I considered devoid of imagination. In the first place, I could never have explained to him what I meant, and in the second, he would have laughed stupidly at me if I had.

There was a slight depression in the center of the island, and here we pitched the tent. The surrounding willows broke the wind a bit.

"A poor camp," observed the imperturbable Swede when at last the tent stood upright, "no stones and precious little firewood. I'm for moving on early tomorrow—eh? This sand won't hold anything."

But the experience of a collapsing tent at midnight had taught us many devices, and we made the cozy gipsy house as safe as possible, and then set about collecting a store of wood to last till bed-time. Willow bushes drop no branches, and driftwood was our only source of supply. We hunted the shores pretty thoroughly. Everywhere the banks were crumbling as the rising flood tore at them and carried away great portions with a splash and a gurgle.

"The island's much smaller than when we landed," said the accurate Swede. "It won't last long at this rate. We'd better drag the canoe close to the tent, and be ready to start at a moment's notice. I shall sleep in my clothes."

He was a little distance off, climbing along the bank, and I heard his rather jolly laugh as he spoke.

"By Jove!" I heard him call, a moment later, and turned to see what had caused his exclamation. But for the moment he was hidden by the willows, and I could not find him.

"What in the world's this?" I heard him cry again, and this time his voice had become serious.

I ran up quickly and joined him on the bank. He was looking over the river, pointing at something in the water.

"Good heavens, it's a man's body!" he cried excitedly. "Look!"

A black thing, turning over and over in the foaming waves, swept rapidly past. It kept disappearing and coming up to the surface again. It was about twenty feet from the shore, and just as it was opposite to where we stood it lurched round and looked straight at us. We saw its eyes reflecting the sunset, and gleaming an odd yellow as the body turned over. Then it gave a swift, gulping plunge, and dived out of sight in a flash.

"An otter, by gad!" we exclaimed in the same breath, laughing. It was an otter, alive, and out on the hunt; yet it had looked exactly like the body of a drowned man turning helplessly in the current. Far below it came to the surface once again, and we saw its black skin, wet and shining in the sunlight.

Then, too, just as we turned back, our arms full of driftwood, another thing happened to recall us to the river bank. This time it really was a man, and what was more, a man in a boat. Now a small boat on the Danube was an unusual sight at any time, but here in this deserted region, and at flood time, it was so unexpected as to constitute a real event. We stood and stared.

Whether it was due to the slanting sunlight, or the refraction from the wonderfully illumined water, I cannot say, but, whatever the cause, I found it difficult to focus my sight properly upon the flying apparition. It seemed, however, to be a man standing upright in a sort of flat-bottomed boat, steering with a long oar, and being carried down the opposite shore at a tremendous pace. He apparently was looking across in our direction, but the distance was too great and the light too uncertain for us to make out very plainly what he was about. It seemed to me that he was gesticulating and making signs at us. His voice came across the water to us shouting something furiously, but the wind drowned it so that no single word was audible. There was something curious about the whole appearance—man, boat, signs, voice—that made an impression on me out of all proportion to its cause.

"He's crossing himself!" I cried. "Look, he's making the sign of the Cross!"

"I believe you're right," the Swede said, shading his eyes with his hand and watching the man out of sight. He seemed to be gone in a moment, melting away down there into the sea of willows where the sun caught them in the bend of the river and turned them into a great crimson wall of beauty. Mist, too, had begun to ruse, so that the air was hazy.

"But what in the world is he doing at nightfall on this flooded river?" I said, half to myself. "Where is he going at such a time, and what did he mean by his signs and shouting? D'you think he wished to warn us about something?"

"He saw our smoke, and thought we were spirits probably," laughed my companion. "These Hungarians believe in all sorts of rubbish; you remember the shopwoman at Pressburg warning us that no one ever landed here because it belonged to some sort of beings outside man's world! I suppose they believe in fairies and elementals, possibly demons, too. That peasant in the boat saw people on the islands for the first time in his life," he added, after a slight pause, "and it scared him, that's all."

The Swede's tone of voice was not convincing, and his manner lacked something that was usually there. I noted the change instantly while he talked, though without being able to label it precisely.

"If they had enough imagination," I laughed loudly—I remember trying to make as much noise as I could—"they might well people a place like this with the old gods of antiquity. The Romans must have haunted all this region more or less with their shrines and sacred groves and elemental deities."

The subject dropped and we returned to our stew-pot, for my friend was not given to imaginative conversation as a rule. Moreover, just then I remember feeling distinctly glad that he was not imaginative; his stolid, practical nature suddenly seemed to me welcome and comforting. It was an admirable temperament, I felt; he could steer down rapids like a red Indian, shoot dangerous bridges and whirlpools better than any white man I ever saw in a canoe. He was a grand fellow for an adventurous trip, a tower of strength when untoward things happened. I looked at his strong face and light curly hair as he staggered along under his pile of driftwood (twice the size of mine!), and I experienced a feeling of relief. Yes, I was distinctly glad just then that the Swede was—what he was, and that he never made remarks that suggested more than they said.

"The river's still rising, though," he added, as if following out some thoughts of his own, and dropping his load with a gasp. "This island will be under water in two days if it goes on."

"I wish the wind would go down," I said. "I don't care a fig for the river."

The flood, indeed, had no terrors for us; we could get off at ten minutes' notice, and the more water the better we liked it. It meant an increasing current and the obliteration of the treacherous shingle-beds that so often threatened to tear the bottom out of our canoe.

Contrary to our expectations, the wind did not go down with the sun. It seemed to increase with the darkness, howling overhead and shaking the willows round us like straws. Curious sounds accompanied it sometimes, like the explosion of heavy guns, and it fell upon the water and the island in great flat blows of immense power. It made me think of the sounds a planet must make, could we only hear it, driving along through space.

But the sky kept wholly clear of clouds, and soon after supper the full moon rose up in the east and covered the river and the plain of shouting willows with a light like the day.

We lay on the sandy patch beside the fire, smoking, listening to the noises of the night round us, and talking happily of the journey we had already made, and of our plans ahead. The map lay spread in the door of the tent, but the high wind made it hard to study, and presently we lowered the curtain and extinguished the lantern. The firelight was enough to smoke and see each other's faces by, and the sparks flew about overhead like fireworks. A few yards beyond, the river gurgled and hissed, and from time to time a heavy splash announced the falling away of further portions of the bank.

Our talk, I noticed, had to do with the faraway scenes and incidents of our first camps in the Black Forest, or of other subjects altogether remote from the present setting, for neither of us spoke of the actual moment more than was necessary—almost as though we had agreed tacitly to avoid discussion of the camp and its incidents. Neither the otter nor the boatman, for instance, received the honor of a single mention, though ordinarily these would have furnished discussion for the greater part of the evening. They were, of course, distinct events in such a place.

The scarcity of wood made it a business to keep the fire going, for the wind, that drove the smoke in our faces wherever we sat, helped at the same time to make a forced draught. We took it in turn to make some foraging expeditions into the darkness, and the quantity the Swede brought back always made me feel that he took an absurdly long time finding it; for the fact was I did not care much about being left alone, and yet it always seemed to be my turn to grub about among the bushes or scramble along the slippery banks in the moonlight. The long day's battle with wind and water—such wind and such water!—had tired us both, and an early bed was the obvious program. Yet neither of us made the move for the tent. We lay there, tending the fire, talking in desultory fashion, peering about us into the dense willow bushes, and listening to the thunder of wind and river. The loneliness of the place had entered our very bones, and silence seemed natural, for after a bit the sound of our voices became a trifle unreal and forced; whispering would have been the fitting mode of communication, I felt, and the human voice, always rather absurd amid the roar of the elements, now carried with it something almost illegitimate. It was like talking out loud in church, or in some place where it was not lawful, perhaps not quite safe, to be overheard.

The eeriness of this lonely island, set among a million willows, swept by a hurricane, and surrounded by hurrying deep waters, touched us both, I fancy. Untrodden by man, almost unknown to man, it lay there beneath the moon, remote from human influence, on the frontier of another world, an alien world, a world tenanted by willows only and the souls of willows. And we, in our rashness, had dared to invade it, even to make use of it! Something more than the power of its mystery stirred in me as I lay on the sand, feet to fire, and peered up through the leaves at the stars. For the last time I rose to get firewood.

"When this has burnt up," I said firmly, "I shall turn in," and my companion watched me lazily as I moved off into the surrounding shadows.

For an unimaginative man I thought he seemed unusually receptive that night, unusually open to suggestion of things other than sensory. He too was touched by the beauty and loneliness of the place. I was not altogether pleased, I remember, to recognize this slight change in him, and instead of immediately collecting sticks, I made my way to the far point of the island where the moonlight on plain and river could be seen to better advantage. The desire to be alone had come suddenly upon me; my former dread returned in force; there was a vague feeling in me I wished to face and probe to the bottom.

When I reached the point of sand jutting out among the waves, the spell of the place descended upon me with a positive shock. No mere "scenery" could have produced such an effect. There was something more here, something to alarm.

I gazed across the waste of wild waters; I watched the whispering willows; I heard the ceaseless beating of the tireless wind; and, one and all, each in its own way, stirred in me this sensation of a strange distress. But the willows especially; for ever they went on chattering and talking among themselves, laughing a little, shrilly crying out, sometimes sighing—but what it was they made so much to-do about belonged to the secret life of the great plain they inhabited. And it was utterly alien to the world I knew, or to that of the wild yet kindly elements. They made me think of a host of beings from another plane of life, another evolution altogether, perhaps, all discussing a mystery known only to themselves. I watched them moving busily together, oddly shaking their big bushy heads, twirling their myriad leaves even when there was no wind. They moved of their own will as though alive, and they touched, by some incalculable method, my own keen sense of the horrible.

There they stood in the moonlight, like a vast army surrounding our camp, shaking their innumerable silver spears defiantly, formed all ready for an attack.

The psychology of places, for some imaginations at least, is very vivid; for the wanderer, especially, camps have their "note" either of welcome or rejection. At first it may not always be apparent, because the busy preparations of tent and cooking prevent, but with the first pause—after supper usually—it comes and announces itself. And the note of this willow-camp now became unmistakably plain to me; we were interlopers, trespassers; we were not welcomed. The sense of unfamiliarity grew upon me as I stood there watching. We touched the frontier of a region where our presence was resented. For a night's lodging we might perhaps be tolerated; but for a prolonged and inquisitive stay—No! by all the gods of the trees and wilderness, no! We were the first human influences upon this island, and we were not wanted. The willows were against us.

Strange thoughts like these, bizarre fancies, borne I know not whence, found lodgment in my mind as I stood listening. What, I thought, if, after all, these crouching willows proved to be alive; if suddenly they should rise up, like a swarm of living creatures, marshaled by the gods whose territory we had invaded, sweep towards us off the vast swamps, booming overhead in the night—and then settle down! As I looked it was so easy to imagine they actually moved, crept nearer, retreated a little, huddled together in masses, hostile, waiting for the great wind that should finally start them a-running. I could have sworn their aspect changed a little, and their ranks deepened and pressed more closely together.

The melancholy shrill cry of a night-bird sounded overhead, and suddenly I nearly lost my balance as the piece of bank I stood upon fell with a great splash into the river, undermined by the flood. I stepped back just in time, and went on hunting for firewood again, half laughing at the odd fancies that crowded so thickly into my mind and cast their spell upon me. I recalled the Swede's remark about moving on next day, and I was just thinking that I fully agreed with him, when I turned with a start and saw the subject of my thoughts standing immediately in front of me. He was quite close. The roar of the elements had covered his approach.

II

"You've been gone so long," he shouted above the wind, "I thought something must have happened to you."

But there was that in his tone, and a certain look in his face as well, that conveyed to me more than his usual words, and in a flash I understood the real reason for his coming. It was because the spell of the place had entered his soul too, and he did not like being alone.

"River still rising," he cried, pointing to the flood in the moonlight, "and the wind's simply awful."

He always said the same things, but it was the cry for companionship that gave the real importance to his words.

"Lucky," I cried back, "our tent's in the hollow. I think it'll hold all right." I added something about the difficulty of finding wood, in order to explain my absence, but the wind caught my words and flung them across the river, so that he did not hear, but just looked at me through the branches, nodding his head.

"Lucky if we get away without disaster!" he shouted, or words to that effect; and I remember feeling half angry with him for putting the thought into words, for it was exactly what I felt myself. There was disaster impending somewhere, and the sense of presentiment lay unpleasantly upon me.

We went back to the fire and made a final blaze, poking it up with our feet. We took a last look round. But for the wind the heat would have been unpleasant. I put this thought into words, and I remember my friend's reply struck me oddly: that he would rather have the heat, the ordinary July weather, than this "diabolical wind."

Everything was snug for the night; the canoe lying turned over beside the tent, with both yellow paddles beneath her; the provision sack hanging from a willow-stem, and the washed-up dishes removed to a safe distance from the fire, all ready for the morning meal. We smothered the embers of the fire with sand, and then turned in. The flap of the tent door was up, and I saw the branches and the stars and the white moonlight. The shaking willows and the heavy buffetings of the wind against our taut little house were the last things I remembered as sleep came down and covered all with its soft and delicious forgetfulness.

Suddenly I found myself lying awake, peering from my sandy mattress through the door of the tent. I looked at my watch pinned against the canvas, and saw by the bright moonlight that it was past twelve o'clock—the threshold of a new day—and I had therefore slept a couple of hours. The Swede was asleep still beside me; the wind howled as before; something plucked at my heart and made me feel afraid. There was a sense of disturbance in my immediate neighborhood.

I sat up quickly and looked out. The trees were swaying violently to and fro as the gusts smote them, but our little bit of green canvas lay snugly safe in the hollow, for the wind passed over it without meeting enough resistance to make it vicious. The feeling of disquietude did not pass, however, and I crawled quietly out of the tent to see if our belongings were safe. I moved carefully so as not to waken my companion. A curious excitement was on me.

I was half-way out, kneeling on all fours, when my eye first took in that the tops of the bushes opposite, with their moving tracery of leaves, made shapes against the sky. I sat back on my haunches and stared. It was incredible, surely, but there, opposite and slightly above me, were shapes of some indeterminate sort among the willows, and as the branches swayed in the wind they seemed to group themselves about these shapes, forming a series of monstrous outlines that shifted rapidly beneath the moon.

Close, about fifty feet in front of me, I saw these things.

My first instinct was to waken my companion, that he too might see them, but something made me hesitate—the sudden realization, probably, that I should not welcome corroboration; and meanwhile I crouched there staring in amazement with smarting eyes. I was wide awake. I remember saying to myself that I was not dreaming.

They first became properly visible, these huge figures, just within the tops of the bushes—immense, bronze-colored, moving, and wholly independent of the swaying of the branches. I saw them plainly and noted, now I came to examine them more calmly, that they were very much larger than human, and indeed that something in their appearance proclaimed them to be not human at all. Certainly they were not merely the moving tracery of the branches against the moonlight. They shifted independently. They rose upwards in a continuous stream from earth to sky, vanishing utterly as soon as they reached the dark of the sky. They were interlaced one with another, making a great column, and I saw their limbs and huge bodies melting in and out of each other, forming this serpentine line that bent and swayed and twisted spirally with the contortions of the wind-tossed trees. They were nude, fluid shapes, passing up the bushes, within the leaves almost—rising up in a living column into the heavens. Their faces I never could see. Unceasingly they poured upwards, swaying in great bending curves, with a hue of dull bronze upon their skins.

I stared, trying to force every atom of vision from my eyes. For a long time I thought they must every moment disappear and resolve themselves into the movements of the branches and prove to be an optical illusion. I searched everywhere for a proof of reality, when all the while I understood quite well that the standard of reality had changed. For the longer I looked the more certain I became that these figures were real and living, though perhaps not according to the standards that the camera and the biologist would insist upon.

Far from feeling fear, I was possessed with a sense of awe and wonder such as I have never known. I seemed to be gazing at the personified elemental forces of this haunted and primeval region. Our intrusion had stirred the powers of the place into activity. It was we who were the cause of the disturbance, and my brain filled to bursting with stories and legends of the spirits and deities of places that have been acknowledged and worshipped by men in all ages of the world's history. But, before I could arrive at any possible explanation, something impelled me to go farther out, and I crept forward on the sand and stood upright. I felt the ground still warm under my bare feet; the wind tore at my hair and face; and the sound of the river burst upon my ears with a sudden roar. These things, I knew, were real, and proved that my senses were acting normally. Yet the figures still rose from earth to heaven, silent, majestically, in a great spiral of grace and strength that overwhelmed me at length with a genuine deep emotion of worship. I felt that I must fall down and worship—absolutely worship.

Perhaps in another minute I might have done so, when a gust of wind swept against me with such force that it blew me sideways, and I nearly stumbled and fell. It seemed to shake the dream violently out of me. At least it gave me another point of view somehow. The figures still remained, still ascended into heaven from the heart of the night, but my reason at last began to assert itself. It must be a subjective experience, I argued—none the less real for that, but still subjective. The moonlight and the branches combined to work out these pictures upon the mirror of my imagination, and for some reason I projected them outwards and made them appear objective. I knew this must be the case, of course. I took courage, and began to move forward across the open patches of sand. By Jove, though, was it all hallucination? Was it merely subjective? Did not my reason argue in the old futile way from the little standard of the known?

I only know that great column of figures ascended darkly into the sky for what seemed a very long period of time, and with a very complete measure of reality as most men are accustomed to gauge reality. Then suddenly they were gone!

And, once they were gone and the immediate wonder of their great presence had passed, fear came down upon me with a cold rush. The esoteric meaning of this lonely and haunted region suddenly flamed up within me, and I began to tremble dreadfully. I took a quick look round—a look of horror that came near to panic—calculating vainly ways of escape; and then, realizing how helpless I was to achieve anything really effective, I crept back silently into the tent and lay down again upon my sandy mattress, first lowering the door-curtain to shut out the sight of the willows in the moonlight, and then burying my head as deeply as possible beneath the blankets to deaden the sound of the terrifying wind.

As though further to convince me that I had not been dreaming, I remember that it was a long time before I fell again into a troubled and restless sleep; and even then only the upper crust of me slept, and underneath there was something that never quite lost consciousness, but lay alert and on the watch.

But this second time I jumped up with a genuine start of terror. It was neither the wind nor the river that woke me, but the slow approach of something that caused the sleeping portion of me to grow smaller and smaller till at last it vanished altogether, and I found myself sitting bolt upright—listening.

Outside there was a sound of multitudinous little patterings. They had been coming, I was aware, for a long time, and in my sleep they had first become audible. I sat there nervously wide awake as though I had not slept at all. It seemed to me that my breathing came with difficulty, and that there was a great weight upon the surface of my body. In spite of the hot night, I felt clammy with cold and shivered. Something surely was pressing steadily against the sides of the tent and weighing down upon it from above. Was it the body of the wind? Was this the pattering rain, the dripping of the leaves? The spray blown from the river by the wind and gathering in big drops? I thought quickly of a dozen things.

Then suddenly the explanation leaped into my mind: a bough from the poplar, the only large tree on the island, had fallen with the wind. Still half caught by the other branches, it would fall with the next gust and crush us, and meanwhile its leaves brushed and tapped upon the tight canvas surface of the tent. I raised a loose flap and rushed out, calling to the Swede to follow.

But when I got out and stood upright I saw that the tent was free. There was no hanging bough; there was no rain or spray; nothing approached.

A cold, grey light filtered down through the bushes and

lay on the faintly gleaming sand. Stars still crowded the sky directly overhead, and the wind howled magnificently, but the fire no longer gave out any glow, and I saw the east reddening in streaks through the trees. Several hours must have passed since I stood there before watching the ascending figures, and the memory of it now came back to me horribly, like an evil dream. Oh, how tired it made me feel, that ceaseless raging wind! Yet, though the deep lassitude of a sleepless night was on me, my nerves were tingling with the activity of an equally tireless apprehension, and all idea of repose was out of the question. The river I saw had risen further. Its thunder filled the air, and a fine spray made itself felt through my thin sleeping shirt.

Yet nowhere did I discover the slightest evidence of anything to cause alarm. This deep, prolonged disturbance in my heart remained wholly unaccounted for.

My companion had not stirred when I called him, and there was no need to waken him now. I looked about me carefully, noting everything; the turned-over canoe; the yellow paddles—two of them, I'm certain; the provision sack and the extra lantern hanging together from the tree; and, crowding everywhere about me, enveloping all, the willows, those endless, shaking willows. A bird uttered its morning cry, and a string of duck passed with whirring flight overhead in the twilight. The sand whirled, dry and stinging, about my bare feet in the wind.

I walked round the tent and then went out a little way into the bush, so that I could see across the river to the farther landscape, and the same profound yet indefinable emotion of distress seized upon me again as I saw the interminable sea of bushes stretching to the horizon, looking ghostly and unreal in the wan light of dawn. I walked softly here and there, still puzzling over that odd sound of infinite pattering, and of that pressure upon the tent that had wakened me. It must have been the wind, I reflected—the wind bearing upon the loose, hot sand, driving the dry particles smartly against the taut canvas—the wind dropping heavily upon our fragile roof.

Yet all the time my nervousness and malaise increased appreciably.

I crossed over to the farther shore and noted how the coast-line had altered in the night, and what masses of sand the river had torn away. I dipped my hands and feet into the cool current, and bathed my forehead. Already there was a glow of sunrise in the sky and the exquisite freshness of coming day. On my way back I passed purposely beneath the very bushes where I had seen the column of figures rising into the air, and midway among the clumps I suddenly found myself overtaken by a sense of vast terror. From the shadows a large figure went swiftly by. Someone passed me, as sure as ever man did....

It was a great staggering blow from the wind that helped me forward again, and once out in the more open space, the sense of terror diminished strangely. The winds were about and walking, I remember saying to myself, for the winds often move like great presences under the trees. And altogether the fear that hovered about me was such an unknown and immense kind of fear, so unlike anything I had ever felt before, that it woke a sense of awe and wonder in me that did much to counteract its worst effects; and when I reached a high point in the middle of the island from which I could see the wide stretch of river, crimson in the sunrise, the whole magical beauty of it all was so overpowering that a sort of wild yearning woke in me and almost brought a cry up into the throat.

But this cry found no expression, for as my eyes wandered from the plain beyond to the island round me and noted our little tent half hidden among the willows, a dreadful discovery leaped out at me, compared to which my terror of the walking winds seemed as nothing at all.

For a change, I thought, had somehow come about in the arrangement of the landscape. It was not that my point of vantage gave me a different view, but that an alteration had apparently been effected in the relation of the tent to the willows, and of the willows to the tent. Surely the bushes now crowded much closer—unnecessarily, unpleasantly close. They had moved nearer.

Creeping with silent feet over the shifting sands, drawing imperceptibly nearer by soft, unhurried movements, the willows had come closer during the night. But had the wind moved them, or had they moved of themselves? I recalled the sound of infinite small patterings and the pressure upon the tent and upon my own heart that caused me to wake in terror. I swayed for a moment in the wind like a tree, finding it hard to keep my upright position on the sandy hillock. There was a suggestion here of personal agency, of deliberate intention, of aggressive hostility, and it terrified me into a sort of rigidity.

Then the reaction followed quickly. The idea was so bizarre, so absurd, that I felt inclined to laugh. But the laughter came no more readily than the cry, for the knowledge that my mind was so receptive to such dangerous imaginings brought the additional terror that it was through our minds and not through our physical bodies that the attack would come, and was coming.

The wind buffeted me about, and, very quickly it seemed, the sun came up over the horizon, for it was after four o'clock, and I must have stood on that little pinnacle of sand longer than I knew, afraid to come down to close quarters with the willows. I returned quietly, creepily, to the tent, first taking another exhaustive look round and—yes, I confess it—making a few measurements. I paced out on the warm sand the distances between the willows and the tent, making a note of the shortest distance particularly.

I crawled stealthily into my blankets. My companion, to all appearances, still slept soundly, and I was glad that this was so. Provided my experiences were not corroborated, I could find strength somehow to deny them, perhaps. With the daylight I could persuade myself that it was all a subjective hallucination, a fantasy of the night, a projection of the excited imagination.

Nothing further came in to disturb me, and I fell asleep almost at once, utterly exhausted, yet still in dread of hearing again that weird sound of multitudinous pattering, or of feeling the pressure upon my heart that had made it difficult to breathe.

The sun was high in the heavens when my companion woke me from a heavy sleep and announced that the porridge was cooked and there was just time to bathe. The grateful smell of frizzling bacon entered the tent door.

"River still rising," he said, "and several islands out in mid-stream have disappeared altogether. Our own island's much smaller."

"Any wood left?" I asked sleepily.

"The wood and the island will finish tomorrow in a dead heat," he laughed, "but there's enough to last us till then."

I plunged in from the point of the island, which had

indeed altered a lot in size and shape during the night, and was swept down in a moment to the landing-place opposite the tent. The water was icy, and the banks flew by like the country from an express train. Bathing under such conditions was an exhilarating operation, and the terror of the night seemed cleansed out of me by a process of evaporation in the brain. The sun was blazing hot; not a cloud showed itself anywhere; the wind, however, had not abated one little jot.

Quite suddenly then the implied meaning of the Swede's words flashed across me, showing that he no longer wished to leave post-haste, and had changed his mind. "Enough to last till tomorrow"—he assumed we should stay on the island another night. It struck me as odd. The night before he was so positive the other way. How had the change come about?

Great crumblings of the banks occurred at breakfast, with heavy splashings and clouds of spray which the wind brought into our frying-pan, and my fellow-traveler talked incessantly about the difficulty the Vienna-Pesth steamers must have to find the channel in flood. But the state of his mind interested and impressed me far more than the state of the river or the difficulties of the steamers. He had changed somehow since the evening before. His manner was different—a trifle excited, a trifle shy, with a sort of suspicion about his voice and gestures. I hardly know how to describe it now in cold blood, but at the time I remember being quite certain of one thing—that he had become frightened?

He ate very little breakfast, and for once omitted to smoke his pipe. He had the map spread open beside him, and kept studying its markings.

"We'd better get off sharp in an hour," I said presently, feeling for an opening that must bring him indirectly to a partial confession at any rate. And his answer puzzled me uncomfortably: "Rather! If they'll let us."

"Who'll let us? The elements?" I asked quickly, with affected indifference.

"The powers of this awful place, whoever they are," he replied, keeping his eyes on the map. "The gods are here, if they are anywhere at all in the world."

"The elements are always the true immortals," I replied, laughing as naturally as I could manage, yet knowing quite well that my face reflected my true feelings when he looked up gravely at me and spoke across the smoke:

"We shall be fortunate if we get away without further disaster."

This was exactly what I had dreaded, and I screwed myself up to the point of the direct question. It was like agreeing to allow the dentist to extract the tooth; it had to come anyhow in the long run, and the rest was all pretence.

"Further disaster! Why, what's happened?"

"For one thing—the steering paddle's gone," he said quietly.

"The steering paddle gone!" I repeated, greatly excited, for this was our rudder, and the Danube in flood without a rudder was suicide.

"But what—"

"And there's a tear in the bottom of the canoe," he added, with a genuine little tremor in his voice.

I continued staring at him, able only to repeat the words in his face somewhat foolishly. There, in the heat of the sun, and on this burning sand, I was aware of a freezing atmosphere descending round us. I got up to follow him, for he merely nodded his head gravely and led the way towards the tent a few yards on the other side of the fireplace. The canoe still lay there as I had last seen her in the night, ribs uppermost, the paddles, or rather, the paddle, on the sand beside her.

"There's only one," he said, stooping to pick it up. "And here's the rent in the base-board."

It was on the tip of my tongue to tell him that I had clearly noticed two paddles a few hours before, but a second impulse made me think better of it, and I said nothing. I approached to see.

There was a long, finely made tear in the bottom of the canoe where a little slither of wood had been neatly taken clean out; it looked as if the tooth of a sharp rock or snag had eaten down her length, and investigation showed that the hole went through. Had we launched out in her without observing it we must inevitably have foundered. At first the water would have made the wood swell so as to close the hole, but once out in mid-stream the water must have poured in, and the canoe, never more than two inches above the surface, would have filled and sunk very rapidly.

"There, you see an attempt to prepare a victim for the sacrifice," I heard him saying, more to himself than to me, "two victims rather," he added as he bent over and ran his fingers along the slit.

I began to whistle—a thing I always do unconsciously when utterly nonplussed—and purposely paid no attention to his words. I was determined to consider them foolish.

"It wasn't there last night," he said presently, straightening up from his examination and looking anywhere but at me.

"We must have scratched her in landing, of course," I stopped whistling to say. "The stones are very sharp."

I stopped abruptly, for at that moment he turned round and met my eye squarely. I knew just as well as he did how impossible my explanation was. There were no stones, to begin with.

"And then there's this to explain too," he added quietly, handing me the paddle and pointing to the blade.

A new and curious emotion spread freezingly over me as I took and examined it. The blade was scraped down all over, beautifully scraped, as though someone had sand-papered it with care, making it so thin that the first vigorous stroke must have snapped it off at the elbow.

"One of us walked in his sleep and did this thing," I said feebly, "or—or it has been filed by the constant stream of sand particles blown against it by the wind, perhaps."

"Ah," said the Swede, turning away, laughing a little, "you can explain everything."

"The same wind that caught the steering paddle and flung it so near the bank that it fell in with the next lump that crumbled," I called out after him, absolutely determined to find an explanation for everything he showed me.

"I see," he shouted back, turning his head to look at me before disappearing among the willow bushes.

Once alone with these perplexing evidences of personal agency, I think my first thoughts took the form of "One of us must have done this thing, and it certainly was not I." But my second thought decided how impossible it was to suppose, under all the circumstances, that either of us had done it. That my companion, the trusted friend of a dozen similar expeditions, could have knowingly had a hand in it, was a suggestion not to be entertained for a moment. Equally absurd seemed the explanation that this imperturbable and densely practical nature had suddenly become insane and was busied with insane purposes.

Yet the fact remained that what disturbed me most, and kept my fear actively alive even in this blaze of sunshine and wild beauty, was the clear certainty that some curious alteration had come about in his mind—that he was nervous, timid, suspicious, aware of goings on he did not speak about, watching a series of secret and hitherto unmentionable events—waiting, in a word, for a climax that he expected, and, I thought, expected very soon. This grew up in my mind intuitively—I hardly knew how.

I made a hurried examination of the tent and its surroundings, but the measurements of the night remained the same. There were deep hollows formed in the sand I now noticed for the first time, basin-shaped and of various depths and sizes, varying from that of a tea-cup to a large bowl. The wind, no doubt, was responsible for these miniature craters, just as it was for lifting the paddle and tossing it towards the water. The rent in the canoe was the only thing that seemed quite inexplicable; and, after all, it was conceivable that a sharp point had caught it when we landed. The examination I made of the shore did not assist this theory, but all the same I clung to it with that diminishing portion of my intelligence which I called my "reason." An explanation of some kind was an absolute necessity, just as some working explanation of the universe is necessary—however absurd—to the happiness of every individual who seeks to do his duty in the world and face the problems of life. The simile seemed to me at the time an exact parallel.

I at once set the pitch melting, and presently the Swede joined me at the work, though under the best conditions in the world the canoe could not be safe for traveling till the following day. I drew his attention casually to the hollows in the sand.

"Yes," he said, "I know. They're all over the island. But you can explain them, no doubt!"

"Wind, of course," I answered without hesitation. "Have you never watched those little whirlwinds in the street that twist and twirl everything into a circle? This sand's loose enough to yield, that's all."

He made no reply, and we worked on in silence for a bit. I watched him surreptitiously all the time, and I had an idea he was watching me. He seemed, too, to be always listening attentively to something I could not hear, or perhaps for something that he expected to hear, for he kept turning about and staring into the bushes, and up into the sky, and out across the water where it was visible through the openings among the willows. Sometimes he even put his hand to his ear and held it there for several minutes. He said nothing to me, however, about it, and I asked no questions. And meanwhile, as he mended that torn canoe with the skill and address of a red Indian, I was glad to notice his absorption in the work, for there was a vague dread in my heart that he would speak of the changed aspect of the willows. And, if he had noticed that, my imagination could no longer be held a sufficient explanation of it.

III

At length, after a long pause, he began to talk.

"Queer thing," he added in a hurried sort of voice, as though he wanted to say something and get it over. "Queer thing. I mean, about that otter last night."

I had expected something so totally different that he caught me with surprise, and I looked up sharply.

"Shows how lonely this place is. Otters are awfully shy things—"

"I don't mean that, of course," he interrupted. "I mean—do you think—did you think it really was an otter?"

"What else, in the name of Heaven, what else?"

"You know, I saw it before you did, and at first it seemed—so much bigger than an otter."

"The sunset as you looked up-stream magnified it, or something," I replied.

He looked at me absently a moment, as though his mind were busy with other thoughts.

"It had such extraordinary yellow eyes," he went on half to himself.

"That was the sun too," I laughed, a trifle boisterously. "I suppose you'll wonder next if that fellow in the boat—"

I suddenly decided not to finish the sentence. He was in the act again of listening, turning his head to the wind, and something in the expression of his face made me halt. The subject dropped, and we went on with our caulking. Apparently he had not noticed my unfinished sentence. Five minutes later, however, he looked at me across the canoe, the smoking pitch in his hand, his face exceedingly grave.

"I did rather wonder, if you want to know," he said slowly, "what that thing in the boat was. I remember thinking at the time it was not a man. The whole business seemed to rise quite suddenly out of the water."

I laughed again boisterously in his face, but this time there was impatience, and a strain of anger too, in my feeling.

"Look here now," I cried, "this place is quite queer

enough without going out of our way to imagine things! That boat was an ordinary boat, and the man in it was an ordinary man, and they were both going down-stream as fast as they could lick. And that otter was an otter, so don't let's play the fool about it!"

He looked steadily at me with the same grave expression. He was not in the least annoyed. I took courage from his silence.

"And, for Heaven's sake," I went on, "don't keep pretending you hear things, because it only gives me the jumps, and there's nothing to hear but the river and this cursed old thundering wind."

"You fool!" he answered in a low, shocked voice, "you utter fool. That's just the way all victims talk. As if you didn't understand just as well as I do!" he sneered with scorn in his voice, and a sort of resignation. "The best thing you can do is to keep quiet and try to hold your mind as firm as possible. This feeble attempt at self-deception only makes the truth harder when you're forced to meet it."

My little effort was over, and I found nothing more to say, for I knew quite well his words were true, and that I was the fool, not he. Up to a certain stage in the adventure he kept ahead of me easily, and I think I felt annoyed to be out of it, to be thus proved less psychic, less sensitive than himself to these extraordinary happenings, and half ignorant all the time of what was going on under my very nose. He knew from the very beginning, apparently. But at the moment I wholly missed the point of his words about the necessity of there being a victim, and that we ourselves were destined to satisfy the want. I dropped all pretence thenceforward, but thenceforward likewise my fear increased steadily to the climax.

"But you're quite right about one thing," he added, before the subject passed, "and that is that we're wiser not to talk about it, or even to think about it, because what one thinks finds expression in words, and what one says, happens."

That afternoon, while the canoe dried and hardened, we spent trying to fish, testing the leak, collecting wood, and watching the enormous flood of rising water. Masses of driftwood swept near our shores sometimes, and we fished for them with long willow branches. The island grew perceptibly smaller as the banks were torn away with great gulps and splashes. The weather kept brilliantly fine till about four o'clock, and then for the first time for three days the wind showed signs of abating. Clouds began to gather in the south-west, spreading thence slowly over the sky.

This lessening of the wind came as a great relief, for the incessant roaring, banging, and thundering had irritated our nerves. Yet the silence that came about five o'clock with its sudden cessation was in a manner quite as oppressive. The booming of the river had everything in its own way then; it filled the air with deep murmurs, more musical than the wind noises, but infinitely more monotonous. The wind held many notes, rising, falling always beating out some sort of great elemental tune; whereas the river's song lay between three notes at most—dull pedal notes, that held a lugubrious quality foreign to the wind, and somehow seemed to me, in my then nervous state, to sound wonderfully well the music of doom.

It was extraordinary, too, how the withdrawal suddenly of bright sunlight took everything out of the landscape that made for cheerfulness; and since this particular landscape had already managed to convey the suggestion of something sinister, the change of course was all the more unwelcome and noticeable. For me, I know, the darkening outlook became distinctly more alarming, and I found myself more than once calculating how soon after sunset the full moon would get up in the east, and whether the gathering clouds would greatly interfere with her lighting of the little island.

With this general hush of the wind—though it still indulged in occasional brief gusts—the river seemed to me to grow blacker, the willows to stand more densely together. The latter, too, kept up a sort of independent movement of their own, rustling among themselves when no wind stirred, and shaking oddly from the roots upwards. When common objects in this way become charged with the suggestion of horror, they stimulate the imagination far more than things of unusual appearance; and these bushes, crowding huddled about us, assumed for me in the darkness a bizarre grotesquerie of appearance that lent to them somehow the aspect of purposeful and living creatures. Their very ordinariness, I felt, masked what was malignant and hostile to us. The forces of the region drew nearer with the coming of night. They were focusing upon our island, and more particularly upon ourselves. For thus, somehow, in the terms of the imagination, did my really indescribable sensations in this extraordinary place present themselves.

I had slept a good deal in the early afternoon, and had thus recovered somewhat from the exhaustion of a disturbed night, but this only served apparently to render me more susceptible than before to the obsessing spell of the haunting. I fought against it, laughing at my feelings as absurd and childish, with very obvious physiological explanations, yet, in spite of every effort, they gained in strength upon me so that I dreaded the night as a child lost in a forest must dread the approach of darkness.

The canoe we had carefully covered with a waterproof sheet during the day, and the one remaining paddle had been securely tied by the Swede to the base of a tree, lest the wind should rob us of that too. From five o'clock onwards I busied myself with the stew-pot and preparations for dinner, it being my turn to cook that night. We had potatoes, onions, bits of bacon fat to add flavor, and a general thick residue from former stews at the bottom of the pot; with black bread broken up into it the result was most excellent, and it was followed by a stew of plums with sugar and a brew of strong tea with dried milk. A good pile of wood lay close at hand, and the absence of wind made my duties easy. My companion sat lazily watching me, dividing his attentions between cleaning his pipe and giving useless advice—an admitted privilege of the off-duty man. He had been very quiet all the afternoon, engaged in re-caulking the canoe, strengthening the tent ropes, and fishing for driftwood while I slept. No more talk about undesirable things had passed between us, and I think his only remarks had to do with the gradual destruction of the island, which he declared was not fully a third smaller than when we first landed.

The pot had just begun to bubble when I heard his voice calling to me from the bank, where he had wandered away without my noticing. I ran up.

"Come and listen," he said, "and see what you make of it." He held his hand cupwise to his ear, as so often before.

"Now do you hear anything?" he asked, watching me curiously.

We stood there, listening attentively together. At first

I heard only the deep note of the water and the hissings rising from its turbulent surface. The willows, for once, were motionless and silent. Then a sound began to reach my ears faintly, a peculiar sound—something like the humming of a distant gong. It seemed to come across to us in the darkness from the waste of swamps and willows opposite. It was repeated at regular intervals, but it was certainly neither the sound of a bell nor the hooting of a distant steamer. I can liken it to nothing so much as to the sound of an immense gong, suspended far up in the sky, repeating incessantly its muffled metallic note, soft and musical, as it was repeatedly struck. My heart quickened as I listened.

"I've heard it all day," said my companion. "While you slept this afternoon it came all round the island. I hunted it down, but could never get near enough to see—to localize it correctly. Sometimes it was overhead, and sometimes it seemed under the water. Once or twice, too, I could have sworn it was not outside at all, but within myself—you know—the way a sound in the fourth dimension is supposed to come."

I was too much puzzled to pay much attention to his words. I listened carefully, striving to associate it with any known familiar sound I could think of, but without success. It changed in the direction, too, coming nearer, and then sinking utterly away into remote distance. I cannot say that it was ominous in quality, because to me it seemed distinctly musical, yet I must admit it set going a distressing feeling that made me wish I had never heard it.

"The wind blowing in those sand-funnels," I said determined to find an explanation, "or the bushes rubbing together after the storm perhaps."

"It comes off the whole swamp," my friend answered. "It comes from everywhere at once." He ignored my explanations. "It comes from the willow bushes somehow—"

"But now the wind has dropped," I objected. "The willows can hardly make a noise by themselves, can they?"

His answer frightened me, first because I had dreaded it, and secondly, because I knew intuitively it was true.

"It is because the wind has dropped we now hear it. It was drowned before.

It is the cry, I believe, of the—"

I dashed back to my fire, warned by the sound of bubbling that the stew was in danger, but determined at the same time to escape further conversation. I was resolute, if possible, to avoid the exchanging of views. I dreaded, too, that he would begin about the gods, or the elemental forces, or something else disquieting, and I wanted to keep myself well in hand for what might happen later. There was another night to be faced before we escaped from this distressing place, and there was no knowing yet what it might bring forth.

"Come and cut up bread for the pot," I called to him, vigorously stirring the appetizing mixture. That stew-pot held sanity for us both, and the thought made me laugh.

He came over slowly and took the provision sack from the tree, fumbling in its mysterious depths, and then emptying the entire contents upon the ground-sheet at his feet.

"Hurry up!" I cried; "it's boiling."

The Swede burst out into a roar of laughter that startled me. It was forced laughter, not artificial exactly, but mirthless.

"There's nothing here!" he shouted, holding his sides.

"Bread, I mean."

"It's gone. There is no bread. They've taken it!"

I dropped the long spoon and ran up. Everything the sack had contained lay upon the ground-sheet, but there was no loaf.

The whole dead weight of my growing fear fell upon me and shook me. Then I burst out laughing too. It was the only thing to do: and the sound of my laughter also made me understand his. The stain of psychical pressure caused it—this explosion of unnatural laughter in both of us; it was an effort of repressed forces to seek relief; it was a temporary safety-valve. And with both of us it ceased quite suddenly.

"How criminally stupid of me!" I cried, still determined to be consistent and find an explanation. "I clean forgot to buy a loaf at Pressburg. That chattering woman put everything out of my head, and I must have left it lying on the counter or—"

"The oatmeal, too, is much less than it was this morning," the Swede interrupted.

Why in the world need he draw attention to it? I thought angrily.

"There's enough for tomorrow," I said, stirring vigorously, "and we can get lots more at Komorn or Gran. In twenty-four hours we shall be miles from here."

"I hope so—to God," he muttered, putting the things back into the sack, "unless we're claimed first as victims for the sacrifice," he added with a foolish laugh. He dragged the sack into the tent, for safety's sake, I suppose, and I heard him mumbling to himself, but so indistinctly that it seemed quite natural for me to ignore his words.

Our meal was beyond question a gloomy one, and we ate it almost in silence, avoiding one another's eyes, and keeping the fire bright. Then we washed up and prepared for the night, and, once smoking, our minds unoccupied with any definite duties, the apprehension I had felt all day long became more and more acute. It was not then active fear, I think, but the very vagueness of its origin distressed me far more than if I had been able to ticket and face it squarely. The curious sound I have likened to the note of a gong became now almost incessant, and filled the stillness of the night with a faint, continuous ringing rather than a series of distinct notes. At one time it was behind and at another time in front of us. Sometimes I fancied it came from the bushes on our left, and then again from the clumps on our right. More often it hovered directly overhead like the whirring of wings. It was really everywhere at once, behind, in front, at our sides and over our heads, completely surrounding us. The sound really defies description. But nothing within my knowledge is like that ceaseless muffled humming rising off the deserted world of swamps and willows.

We sat smoking in comparative silence, the strain growing every minute greater. The worst feature of the situation seemed to me that we did not know what to expect, and could therefore make no sort of preparation by way of defense. We could anticipate nothing. My explanations made in the sunshine, moreover, now came to haunt me with their foolish and wholly unsatisfactory nature, and it was more and more clear to us that some kind of plain talk with my companion was inevitable, whether I liked it or not. After all, we had to spend the night together, and to sleep in the same tent side by side. I saw that I could not get along much longer without the support of his mind, and for that, of course, plain talk was imperative. As long as possible, however, I postponed this little climax, and tried to ignore or laugh at the occasional sentences he flung into the emptiness.

Some of these sentences, moreover, were confoundedly disquieting to me, coming as they did to corroborate much that I felt myself; corroboration, too—which made it so much more convincing—from a totally different point of view. He composed such curious sentences, and hurled them at me in such an inconsequential sort of way, as though his main line of thought was secret to himself, and these fragments were mere bits he found it impossible to digest. He got rid of them by uttering them. Speech relieved him. It was like being sick.

"There are things about us, I'm sure, that make for disorder, disintegration, destruction, our destruction," he said once, while the fire blazed between us. "We've strayed out of a safe line somewhere."

And, another time, when the gong sounds had come nearer, ringing much louder than before, and directly over our heads, he said as though talking to himself:

"I don't think a gramophone would show any record of that. The sound doesn't come to me by the ears at all. The vibrations reach me in another manner altogether, and seem to be within me, which is precisely how a fourth dimensional sound might be supposed to make itself heard."

I purposely made no reply to this, but I sat up a little closer to the fire and peered about me into the darkness. The clouds were massed all over the sky, and no trace of moonlight came through. Very still, too, everything was, so that the river and the frogs had things all their own way.

"It has that about it," he went on, "which is utterly out

of common experience. It is unknown. Only one thing describes it really; it is a non-human sound; I mean a sound outside humanity."

Having rid himself of this indigestible morsel, he lay quiet for a time, but he had so admirably expressed my own feeling that it was a relief to have the thought out, and to have confined it by the limitation of words from dangerous wandering to and fro in the mind.

The solitude of that Danube camping-place, can I ever forget it? The feeling of being utterly alone on an empty planet! My thoughts ran incessantly upon cities and the haunts of men. I would have given my soul, as the saying is, for the "feel" of those Bavarian villages we had passed through by the score; for the normal, human commonplaces; peasants drinking beer, tables beneath the trees, hot sunshine, and a ruined castle on the rocks behind the red-roofed church. Even the tourists would have been welcome.

Yet what I felt of dread was no ordinary ghostly fear. It was infinitely greater, stranger, and seemed to arise from some dim ancestral sense of terror more profoundly disturbing than anything I had known or dreamed of. We had "strayed," as the Swede put it, into some region or some set of conditions where the risks were great, yet unintelligible to us; where the frontiers of some unknown world lay close about us. It was a spot held by the dwellers in some outer space, a sort of peep-hole whence they could spy upon the earth, themselves unseen, a point where the veil between had worn a little thin. As the final result of too long a sojourn here, we should be carried over the border and deprived of what we called "our lives," yet by mental, not physical, processes. In that sense, as he said, we should be the victims of our adventure—a sacrifice.

It took us in different fashion, each according to the measure of his sensitiveness and powers of resistance. I translated it vaguely into a personification of the mightily disturbed elements, investing them with the horror of a deliberate and malefic purpose, resentful of our audacious intrusion into their breeding-place; whereas my friend threw it into the unoriginal form at first of a trespass on some ancient shrine, some place where the old gods still held sway, where the emotional forces of former worshippers still clung, and the ancestral portion of him yielded to the old pagan spell.

At any rate, here was a place unpolluted by men, kept clean by the winds from coarsening human influences, a place where spiritual agencies were within reach and aggressive. Never, before or since, have I been so attacked by indescribable suggestions of a "beyond region," of another scheme of life, another revolution not parallel to the human. And in the end our minds would succumb under the weight of the awful spell, and we should be drawn across the frontier into their world.

Small things testified to the amazing influence of the place, and now in the silence round the fire they allowed themselves to be noted by the mind. The very atmosphere had proved itself a magnifying medium to distort every indication: the otter rolling in the current, the hurrying boatman making signs, the shifting willows, one and all had been robbed of its natural character, and revealed in something of its other aspect—as it existed across the border to that other region. And this changed aspect I felt was now not merely to me, but to the race. The whole experience whose verge we touched was unknown to humanity at all.

It was a new order of experience, and in the true sense of the word unearthly.

"It's the deliberate, calculating purpose that reduces one's courage to zero," the Swede said suddenly, as if he had been actually following my thoughts. "Otherwise imagination might count for much. But the paddle, the canoe, the lessening food—"

"Haven't I explained all that once?" I interrupted viciously.

"You have," he answered dryly; "you have indeed."

He made other remarks too, as usual, about what he called the "plain determination to provide a victim"; but, having now arranged my thoughts better, I recognized that this was simply the cry of his frightened soul against the knowledge that he was being attacked in a vital part, and that he would be somehow taken or destroyed. The situation called for a courage and calmness of reasoning that neither of us could compass, and I have never before been so clearly conscious of two persons in me—the one that explained everything, and the other that laughed at such foolish explanations, yet was horribly afraid.

Meanwhile, in the pitchy night the fire died down and the wood pile grew small. Neither of us moved to replenish the stock, and the darkness consequently came up very close to our faces. A few feet beyond the circle of firelight it was inky black. Occasionally a stray puff of wind set the willows shivering about us, but apart from this not very welcome sound a deep and depressing silence reigned, broken only by the gurgling of the river and the humming in the air overhead.

We both missed, I think, the shouting company of the winds.

At length, at a moment when a stray puff prolonged itself as though the wind were about to rise again, I reached the point for me of saturation, the point where it was absolutely necessary to find relief in plain speech, or else to betray myself by some hysterical extravagance that must have been far worse in its effect upon both of us. I kicked the fire into a blaze, and turned to my companion abruptly. He looked up with a start.

"I can't disguise it any longer," I said; "I don't like this place, and the darkness, and the noises, and the awful feelings I get. There's something here that beats me utterly. I'm in a blue funk, and that's the plain truth. If the other shore was—different, I swear I'd be inclined to swim for it!"

The Swede's face turned very white beneath the deep tan of sun and wind. He stared straight at me and answered quietly, but his voice betrayed his huge excitement by its unnatural calmness. For the moment, at any rate, he was the strong man of the two. He was more phlegmatic, for one thing.

"It's not a physical condition we can escape from by running away," he replied, in the tone of a doctor diagnosing some grave disease; "we must sit tight and wait. There are forces close here that could kill a herd of elephants in a second as easily as you or I could squash a fly. Our only chance is to keep perfectly still. Our insignificance perhaps may save us."

I put a dozen questions into my expression of face, but found no words. It was precisely like listening to an accurate description of a disease whose symptoms had puzzled me.

"I mean that so far, although aware of our disturbing presence, they have not found us—not 'located' us, as the

Americans say," he went on. "They're blundering about like men hunting for a leak of gas. The paddle and canoe and provisions prove that. I think they feel us, but cannot actually see us. We must keep our minds quiet—it's our minds they feel. We must control our thoughts, or it's all up with us."

"Death, you mean?" I stammered, icy with the horror of his suggestion.

"Worse—by far," he said. "Death, according to one's belief, means either annihilation or release from the limitations of the senses, but it involves no change of character. You don't suddenly alter just because the body's gone. But this means a radical alteration, a complete change, a horrible loss of oneself by substitution—far worse than death, and not even annihilation. We happen to have camped in a spot where their region touches ours, where the veil between has worn thin"—horrors! he was using my very own phrase, my actual words—"so that they are aware of our being in their neighborhood."

"But who are aware?" I asked.

I forgot the shaking of the willows in the windless calm, the humming overhead, everything except that I was waiting for an answer that I dreaded more than I can possibly explain.

He lowered his voice at once to reply, leaning forward a little over the fire, an indefinable change in his face that made me avoid his eyes and look down upon the ground.

"All my life," he said, "I have been strangely, vividly conscious of another region—not far removed from our own world in one sense, yet wholly different in kind—where great things go on unceasingly, where immense and terrible personalities hurry by, intent on vast purposes compared to which earthly affairs, the rise and fall of nations, the destinies of empires, the fate of armies and continents, are all as dust in the balance; vast purposes, I mean, that deal directly with the soul, and not indirectly with more expressions of the soul—"

"I suggest just now—" I began, seeking to stop him, feeling as though I was face to face with a madman. But he instantly overbore me with his torrent that had to come.

"You think," he said, "it is the spirit of the elements, and I thought perhaps it was the old gods. But I tell you now it is—neither. These would be comprehensible entities, for they have relations with men, depending upon them for worship or sacrifice, whereas these beings who are now about us have absolutely nothing to do with mankind, and it is mere chance that their space happens just at this spot to touch our own."

The mere conception, which his words somehow made so convincing, as I listened to them there in the dark stillness of that lonely island, set me shaking a little all over. I found it impossible to control my movements.

"And what do you propose?" I began again.

"A sacrifice, a victim, might save us by distracting them until we could get away," he went on, "just as the wolves stop to devour the dogs and give the sleigh another start. But—I see no chance of any other victim now."

I stared blankly at him. The gleam in his eye was dreadful. Presently he continued.

IV

"It's the willows, of course. The willows mask the others, but the others are feeling about for us. If we let our minds betray our fear, we're lost, lost utterly." He looked at me with an expression so calm, so determined, so sincere, that I no longer had any doubts as to his sanity. He was as sane as any man ever was. "If we can hold out through the night," he added, "we may get off in the daylight unnoticed, or rather, undiscovered."

"But you really think a sacrifice would—"

That gong-like humming came down very close over our heads as I spoke, but it was my friend's scared face that really stopped my mouth.

"Hush!" he whispered, holding up his hand. "Do not mention them more than you can help. Do not refer to them by name. To name is to reveal; it is the inevitable clue, and our only hope lies in ignoring them, in order that they may ignore us."

"Even in thought?" He was extraordinarily agitated.

"Especially in thought. Our thoughts make spirals in their world. We must keep them out of our minds at all costs if possible."

I raked the fire together to prevent the darkness having everything its own way. I never longed for the sun as I longed for it then in the awful blackness of that summer night.

"Were you awake all last night?" he went on suddenly.

"I slept badly a little after dawn," I replied evasively, trying to follow his instructions, which I knew instinctively were true, "but the wind, of course—"

"I know. But the wind won't account for all the noises."

"Then you heard it too?"

"The multiplying countless little footsteps I heard," he said, adding, after a moment's hesitation, "and that other sound—"

"You mean above the tent, and the pressing down upon

us of something tremendous, gigantic?"

He nodded significantly.

"It was like the beginning of a sort of inner suffocation?" I said.

"Partly, yes. It seemed to me that the weight of the atmosphere had been altered—had increased enormously, so that we should have been crushed."

"And that," I went on, determined to have it all out, pointing upwards where the gong-like note hummed ceaselessly, rising and falling like wind. "What do you make of that?"

"It's their sound," he whispered gravely. "It's the sound of their world, the humming in their region. The division here is so thin that it leaks through somehow. But, if you listen carefully, you'll find it's not above so much as around us. It's in the willows. It's the willows themselves humming, because here the willows have been made symbols of the forces that are against us."

I could not follow exactly what he meant by this, yet the thought and idea in my mind were beyond question the thought and idea in his. I realized what he realized, only with less power of analysis than his. It was on the tip of my tongue to tell him at last about my hallucination of the ascending figures and the moving bushes, when he suddenly thrust his face again close into mine across the firelight and began to speak in a very earnest whisper. He amazed me by his calmness and pluck, his apparent control of the situation. This man I had for years deemed unimaginative, stolid!

"Now listen," he said. "The only thing for us to do is to go on as though nothing had happened, follow our usual habits, go to bed, and so forth; pretend we feel nothing and notice nothing. It is a question wholly of the mind, and the less we think about them the better our chance of escape. Above all, don't think, for what you think happens!"

"All right," I managed to reply, simply breathless with his words and the strangeness of it all; "all right, I'll try, but tell me one more thing first. Tell me what you make of those hollows in the ground all about us, those sand-funnels?"

"No!" he cried, forgetting to whisper in his excitement. "I dare not, simply dare not, put the thought into words. If you have not guessed I am glad. Don't try to. They have put it into my mind; try your hardest to prevent their putting it into yours."

He sank his voice again to a whisper before he finished, and I did not press him to explain. There was already just about as much horror in me as I could hold. The conversation came to an end, and we smoked our pipes busily in silence.

Then something happened, something unimportant apparently, as the way is when the nerves are in a very great state of tension, and this small thing for a brief space gave me an entirely different point of view. I chanced to look down at my sand-shoe—the sort we used for the canoe—and something to do with the hole at the toe suddenly recalled to me the London shop where I had bought them, the difficulty the man had in fitting me, and other details of the uninteresting but practical operation. At once, in its train, followed a wholesome view of the modern skeptical world I was accustomed to move in at home. I thought of roast beef, and ale, motor-cars, policemen, brass bands, and a dozen other things that proclaimed the soul of ordinariness or utility. The effect was immediate and astonishing even to myself. Psychologically, I suppose, it was simply a sudden and violent reaction after the strain of living in an atmosphere of things that to the normal consciousness must seem impossible and incredible. But, whatever the cause, it momentarily lifted the spell from my heart, and left me for the short space of a minute feeling free and utterly unafraid. I looked up at my friend opposite.

"You damned old pagan!" I cried, laughing aloud in his face. "You imaginative idiot! You superstitious idolater! You—"

I stopped in the middle, seized anew by the old horror. I tried to smother the sound of my voice as something sacrilegious. The Swede, of course, heard it too—the strange cry overhead in the darkness—and that sudden drop in the air as though something had come nearer.

He had turned ashen white under the tan. He stood bolt upright in front of the fire, stiff as a rod, staring at me.

"After that," he said in a sort of helpless, frantic way, "we must go! We can't stay now; we must strike camp this very instant and go on—down the river."

He was talking, I saw, quite wildly, his words dictated by abject terror—the terror he had resisted so long, but which had caught him at last.

"In the dark?" I exclaimed, shaking with fear after my hysterical outburst, but still realizing our position better than he did. "Sheer madness! The river's in flood, and we've only got a single paddle. Besides, we only go deeper into their country! There's nothing ahead for fifty miles but willows, willows, willows!"

He sat down again in a state of semi-collapse. The positions, by one of those kaleidoscopic changes nature loves, were suddenly reversed, and the control of our forces passed over into my hands. His mind at last had reached the point where it was beginning to weaken.

"What on earth possessed you to do such a thing?" he whispered with the awe of genuine terror in his voice and face.

I crossed round to his side of the fire. I took both his hands in mine, kneeling down beside him and looking straight into his frightened eyes.

"We'll make one more blaze," I said firmly, "and then turn in for the night. At sunrise we'll be off full speed for Komorn. Now, pull yourself together a bit, and remember your own advice about not thinking fear!"

He said no more, and I saw that he would agree and obey. In some measure, too, it was a sort of relief to get up and make an excursion into the darkness for more wood. We kept close together, almost touching, groping among the bushes and along the bank. The humming overhead never ceased, but seemed to me to grow louder as we increased our distance from the fire. It was shivery work!

We were grubbing away in the middle of a thickish clump of willows where some driftwood from a former flood had caught high among the branches, when my body was seized in a grip that made me half drop upon the sand. It was the Swede. He had fallen against me, and was clutching me for support. I heard his breath coming and going in short gasps.

"Look! By my soul!" he whispered, and for the first time in my experience I knew what it was to hear tears of terror in a human voice. He was pointing to the fire, some fifty feet away. I followed the direction of his finger, and I swear my heart missed a beat.

There, in front of the dim glow, something was moving.

I saw it through a veil that hung before my eyes like the

gauze drop-curtain used at the back of a theater—hazily a little. It was neither a human figure nor an animal. To me it gave the strange impression of being as large as several animals grouped together, like horses, two or three, moving slowly. The Swede, too, got a similar result, though expressing it differently, for he thought it was shaped and sized like a clump of willow bushes, rounded at the top, and moving all over upon its surface—"coiling upon itself like smoke," he said afterwards.

"I watched it settle downwards through the bushes," he sobbed at me. "Look, by God! It's coming this way! Oh, oh!"—he gave a kind of whistling cry. "They've found us."

I gave one terrified glance, which just enabled me to see that the shadowy form was swinging towards us through the bushes, and then I collapsed backwards with a crash into the branches. These failed, of course, to support my weight, so that with the Swede on top of me we fell in a struggling heap upon the sand. I really hardly knew what was happening. I was conscious only of a sort of enveloping sensation of icy fear that plucked the nerves out of their fleshly covering, twisted them this way and that, and replaced them quivering. My eyes were tightly shut; something in my throat choked me; a feeling that my consciousness was expanding, extending out into space, swiftly gave way to another feeling that I was losing it altogether, and about to die.

An acute spasm of pain passed through me, and I was aware that the Swede had hold of me in such a way that he hurt me abominably. It was the way he caught at me in falling.

But it was the pain, he declared afterwards, that saved me; it caused me to forget them and think of something else at the very instant when they were about to find me. It concealed my mind from them at the moment of discovery, yet just in time to evade their terrible seizing of me. He himself, he says, actually swooned at the same moment, and that was what saved him.

I only know that at a later date, how long or short is impossible to say, I found myself scrambling up out of the slippery network of willow branches, and saw my companion standing in front of me holding out a hand to assist me. I stared at him in a dazed way, rubbing the arm he had twisted for me. Nothing came to me to say, somehow.

"I lost consciousness for a moment or two," I heard him say. "That's what saved me. It made me stop thinking about them."

"You nearly broke my arm in two," I said, uttering my only connected thought at the moment. A numbness came over me.

"That's what saved you!" he replied. "Between us, we've managed to set them off on a false tack somewhere. The humming has ceased. It's gone—for the moment at any rate!"

A wave of hysterical laughter seized me again, and this time spread to my friend too—great healing gusts of shaking laughter that brought a tremendous sense of relief in their train. We made our way back to the fire and put the wood on so that it blazed at once. Then we saw that the tent had fallen over and lay in a tangled heap upon the ground.

We picked it up, and during the process tripped more than once and caught our feet in sand.

"It's those sand-funnels," exclaimed the Swede, when the tent was up again and the firelight lit up the ground for several yards about us. "And look at the size of them!"

All round the tent and about the fireplace where we had seen the moving shadows there were deep funnel-shaped hollows in the sand, exactly similar to the ones we had already found over the island, only far bigger and deeper, beautifully formed, and wide enough in some instances to admit the whole of my foot and leg.

Neither of us said a word. We both knew that sleep was the safest thing we could do, and to bed we went accordingly without further delay, having first thrown sand on the fire and taken the provision sack and the paddle inside the tent with us. The canoe, too, we propped in such a way at the end of the tent that our feet touched it, and the least motion would disturb and wake us.

In case of emergency, too, we again went to bed in our clothes, ready for a sudden start.

It was my firm intention to lie awake all night and watch, but the exhaustion of nerves and body decreed otherwise, and sleep after a while came over me with a welcome blanket of oblivion. The fact that my companion also slept quickened its approach. At first he fidgeted and constantly sat up, asking me if I "heard this" or "heard that." He tossed about on his cork mattress, and said the tent was moving and the river had risen over the point of the island, but each time I went out to look I returned with the report that all was well, and finally he grew calmer and lay still. Then at length his breathing became regular and I heard unmistakable sounds of snoring—the first and only time in my life when snoring has been a welcome and calming influence.

This, I remember, was the last thought in my mind before dozing off.

A difficulty in breathing woke me, and I found the blanket over my face. But something else besides the blanket was pressing upon me, and my first thought was that my companion had rolled off his mattress on to my own in his sleep. I called to him and sat up, and at the same moment it came to me that the tent was surrounded. That sound of multitudinous soft pattering was again audible outside, filling the night with horror.

I called again to him, louder than before. He did not answer, but I missed the sound of his snoring, and also noticed that the flap of the tent was down. This was the unpardonable sin. I crawled out in the darkness to hook it back securely, and it was then for the first time I realized positively that the Swede was not here. He had gone.

I dashed out in a mad run, seized by a dreadful agitation, and the moment I was out I plunged into a sort of torrent of humming that surrounded me completely and came out of every quarter of the heavens at once. It was that same familiar humming—gone mad! A swarm of great invisible bees might have been about me in the air. The sound seemed to thicken the very atmosphere, and I felt that my lungs worked with difficulty.

But my friend was in danger, and I could not hesitate.

The dawn was just about to break, and a faint whitish light spread upwards over the clouds from a thin strip of clear horizon. No wind stirred. I could just make out the bushes and river beyond, and the pale sandy patches. In my excitement I ran frantically to and fro about the island, calling him by name, shouting at the top of my voice the first words that came into my head. But the willows smothered my voice, and the humming muffled it, so that the sound only traveled a few feet round me. I plunged among the bushes, tripping headlong, tumbling over roots, and scraping my face as I tore this way and that among the preventing branches.

Then, quite unexpectedly, I came out upon the island's point and saw a dark figure outlined between the water and the sky. It was the Swede. And already he had one foot in the river! A moment more and he would have taken the plunge.

I threw myself upon him, flinging my arms about his waist and dragging him shorewards with all my strength. Of course he struggled furiously, making a noise all the time just like that cursed humming, and using the most outlandish phrases in his anger about "going inside to Them," and "taking the way of the water and the wind," and God only knows what more besides, that I tried in vain to recall afterwards, but which turned me sick with horror and amazement as I listened. But in the end I managed to get him into the comparative safety of the tent, and flung him breathless and cursing upon the mattress where I held him until the fit had passed.

I think the suddenness with which it all went and he grew calm, coinciding as it did with the equally abrupt cessation of the humming and pattering outside—I think this was almost the strangest part of the whole business perhaps. For he had just opened his eyes and turned his tired face up to me so that the dawn threw a pale light upon it through the doorway, and said, for all the world just like a frightened child:

"My life, old man—it's my life I owe you. But it's all over now anyhow.

They've found a victim in our place!"

Then he dropped back upon his blankets and went to

sleep literally under my eyes. He simply collapsed, and began to snore again as healthily as though nothing had happened and he had never tried to offer his own life as a sacrifice by drowning. And when the sunlight woke him three hours later—hours of ceaseless vigil for me—it became so clear to me that he remembered absolutely nothing of what he had attempted to do, that I deemed it wise to hold my peace and ask no dangerous questions.

He woke naturally and easily, as I have said, when the sun was already high in a windless hot sky, and he at once got up and set about the preparation of the fire for breakfast. I followed him anxiously at bathing, but he did not attempt to plunge in, merely dipping his head and making some remark about the extra coldness of the water.

"River's falling at last," he said, "and I'm glad of it."

"The humming has stopped too," I said.

He looked up at me quietly with his normal expression. Evidently he remembered everything except his own attempt at suicide.

"Everything has stopped," he said, "because—"

He hesitated. But I knew some reference to that remark he had made just before he fainted was in his mind, and I was determined to know it.

"Because 'They've found another victim'?" I said, forcing a little laugh.

"Exactly," he answered, "exactly! I feel as positive of it as though—as though—I feel quite safe again, I mean," he finished.

He began to look curiously about him. The sunlight lay in hot patches on the sand. There was no wind. The willows were motionless. He slowly rose to feet.

"Come," he said; "I think if we look, we shall find it."

He started off on a run, and I followed him. He kept to the banks, poking with a stick among the sandy bays and caves and little back-waters, myself always close on his heels.

"Ah!" he exclaimed presently, "ah!"

The tone of his voice somehow brought back to me a vivid sense of the horror of the last twenty-four hours, and I hurried up to join him. He was pointing with his stick at a large black object that lay half in the water and half on the sand. It appeared to be caught by some twisted willow roots so that the river could not sweep it away. A few hours before the spot must have been under water.

"See," he said quietly, "the victim that made our escape possible!"

And when I peered across his shoulder I saw that his stick rested on the body of a man. He turned it over. It was the corpse of a peasant, and the face was hidden in the sand. Clearly the man had been drowned, but a few hours before, and his body must have been swept down upon our island somewhere about the hour of the dawn—at the very time the fit had passed.

"We must give it a decent burial, you know."

"I suppose so," I replied. I shuddered a little in spite of myself, for there was something about the appearance of that poor drowned man that turned me cold.

The Swede glanced up sharply at me, an undecipherable expression on his face, and began clambering down the bank. I followed him more leisurely. The current, I noticed, had torn away much of the clothing from the body, so that the neck and part of the chest lay bare.

Halfway down the bank my companion suddenly stopped and held up his hand in warning; but either my foot slipped, or I had gained too much momentum to bring myself quickly to a halt, for I bumped into him and sent him forward with a sort of leap to save himself. We tumbled together on to the hard sand so that our feet splashed into the water. And, before anything could be done, we had collided a little heavily against the corpse.

The Swede uttered a sharp cry. And I sprang back as if I had been shot.

At the moment we touched the body there rose from its surface the loud sound of humming—the sound of several hummings—which passed with a vast commotion as of winged things in the air about us and disappeared upwards into the sky, growing fainter and fainter till they finally ceased in the distance. It was exactly as though we had disturbed some living yet invisible creatures at work.

My companion clutched me, and I think I clutched him, but before either of us had time properly to recover from the unexpected shock, we saw that a movement of the current was turning the corpse round so that it became released from the grip of the willow roots. A moment later it had turned completely over, the dead face uppermost, staring at the sky. It lay on the edge of the main stream. In another moment it would be swept away.

The Swede started to save it, shouting again something I did not catch about a "proper burial"—and then abruptly dropped upon his knees on the sand and covered his eyes with his hands. I was beside him in an instant.

I saw what he had seen.

For just as the body swung round to the current the face and the exposed chest turned full towards us, and showed plainly how the skin and flesh were indented with small hollows, beautifully formed, and exactly similar in shape and kind to the sand-funnels that we had found all over the island.

"Their mark!" I heard my companion mutter under his breath. "Their awful mark!"

And when I turned my eyes again from his ghastly face to the river, the current had done its work, and the body had been swept away into mid-stream and was already beyond our reach and almost out of sight, turning over and over on the waves like an otter.

CONTRIBUTORS

Tristam Adams is a theorist and writer. His first book, *The Psychopath Factory: How Capitalism Organises Empathy*, was published by Repeater Books in 2016.

Grace Augur is a journalist and independent scholar living in a commune in Esher, Surrey, on the outskirts of London. They have written on the history of spiritualism, fringe science, neo-paganism, and the wellness industry. Their auto-fictional novel *The Transvaluation of All Values: Memoirs of a Failed Medium* is forthcoming from Repeater Books.

Siouxzi Connor is an Australian-born writer, filmmaker, and researcher based in Berlin. She is the author of *Little Houses, Big Forests (desire is no light thing)* (Repeater Books, 2017) and a researcher at the Department of Gender and Cultural Studies at the University of Sydney.

Claire Cronin is a writer and musician currently based in California. She is the author of the nonfiction book *Blue Light of the Screen: On Horror, Ghosts, and God* (Repeater Books, 2020) and two poetry chapbooks.

Tariq Goddard is the publisher of Repeater Books and the author of *The Picture of Contented New Wealth*, Gold Medal Winner for Horror in the Independent Publisher Book Awards, 2010.

Rhian E. Jones writes on history, politics, popular culture, and the places where they intersect. She is co-editor of *Red Pepper* and writes for *Tribune* magazine, and is the author of several books, including *Under My Thumb* (Repeater Books, 2017) and *Clampdown: Pop-Cultural Wars on Class and Gender* (Zero Books, 2013).

Carl Neville is a novelist and critic based in London. His interests range from speculative science fiction, to new models of community ownership, to the films of Danny Dyer. He has most recently published the second half of the two-part utopian/dystopian novel sequence *Resolution Way/Eminent Domain* with Repeater Books.

Christiana Spens is a writer and artist based in London. She has written and illustrated several books in the past, including the graphic novel *The Socialite Manifesto* (Beautiful Books, 2009), and *Shooting Hipsters* (Repeater Books, 2016) and she writes regularly for publications such as *Studio International*, *The Irish Times*, *Prospect*, and *Art Quarterly* on culture and politics.

Leila Taylor, author of *Darkly: Black History and America's Gothic Soul* (Repeater Books, 2019), is a writer and designer whose work is focused on the Gothic in Black culture, horror, and the aesthetics of melancholy. She lives in Brooklyn where she is Creative Director for Brooklyn Public Library and hangs out in cemeteries for fun.

Eugene Thacker is the author of several books, including *In the Dust of This Planet* (Zero Books, 2011) and *Infinite Resignation* (Repeater Books, 2018). He teaches at The New School in New York City.

Elvia Wilk lives in New York. She is author of the novel *Oval* (Soft Skull, 2019) and her writing has appeared in publications such as *Frieze*, *Artforum*, *Bookforum*, *Granta*, *n+1*, *The White Review*, *BOMB*, *Mousse*, *Flash Art*, and *Art Agenda*. She is currently a contributing editor at *e-flux Journal* and is a 2020 fellow at the Berggruen Institute.

REPEATER BOOKS

is dedicated to the creation of a new reality. The landscape of twenty-first-century arts and letters is faded and inert, riven by fashionable cynicism, egotistical self-reference and a nostalgia for the recent past. Repeater intends to add its voice to those movements that wish to enter history and assert control over its currents, gathering together scattered and isolated voices with those who have already called for an escape from Capitalist Realism. Our desire is to publish in every sphere and genre, combining vigorous dissent and a pragmatic willingness to succeed where messianic abstraction and quiescent co-option have stalled: abstention is not an option: we are alive and we don't agree.

Repeater

Also Available from Repeater Books

The Psychopath Factory: How Capitalism Organises Empathy
by Tristam Adams

The Transvaluation of All Values: Memoirs of a Failed Medium
by Grace Augur (forthcoming)

Little Houses, Big Forests: Desire Is No Light Thing
by Siouxzi Connor

Blue Light of the Screen: On Horror, Ghosts, and God
by Claire Cronin

Under My Thumb: The Songs that Hate Women and the Women Who Love Them
by Rhian E. Jones

Eminent Domain
by Carl Neville

Shooting Hipsters: Rethinking Dissent in the Age of PR
by Christiana Spens

Darkly: Black History and America's Gothic Soul
by Leila Taylor